Advance Praise for Lee Houck and *Yield*

"In this deft debut, Lee Houck gives us Simon, a young man seeking direction and connection in a minefield of violence and exploitation. Witty and wrenching, *Yield* is required reading for anyone who wants to know what it means to be young, gay and without a roadmap in today's world."
—Vestal McIntyre, author of *Lake Overturn*

"*Yield* is a subtle novel which creeps into your soul. The characters are realistic and Lee Houck's writing is refreshing and provocative. It is a story of unexpectedly finding your place in the world by appreciating what it has to offer."
—Emanuel Xavier, poet and author of *Christ Like*

"Lee Houck's *Yield* is a rich mixture: a hustler's conflicted psyche, the emotional after-effects of a gay-bashing, a hot love interest, a romantic sojourn in the Vermont woods, and the nourishing powers of gay friendship. This is a complex, evocative, and unforgettable book."
—Jeff Mann, author of *A History of Barbed Wire* and *Loving Mountains, Loving Men*

"With perfect emotional pitch, Lee Houck has crafted an exuberant, often witty, always smart story about 20-something queers scrambling to make their way in contemporary Manhattan as they negotiate friendship, yearn for love, and—gotta pay the rent—sell sex. Brisk and buoyant, this engaging debut captures big-city hustle with small-town heart."
—Richard Labonte, Book Marks, Q Syndicate and series editor, *Best Gay Erotica*

"Lee Houck's writing is a portal, a crystal ball projecting the scapes of his mind and soul—where everything from ironic beauty to rebellious desire dances with abandon. His words construct vivid "stage sets" in your imagination, where his characters encounter disappointment, ecstasy, deception. *Yield* is a bold and shock~~~ story concerned with humanism—it's a dazzl~~~ dangerous foray into post-queer realis~~~
—Charlie Vázquez, author, blogger a~~~ reading series host

YIELD

LEE HOUCK

KENSINGTON BOOKS

KENSINGTON BOOKS are published by

Kensington Publishing Corp.
119 West 40th Street
New York, NY 10018

ISBN-13: 978-0-7582-4265-5

For Meg

Acknowledgments

This story was sometimes a lonely one to write. But during the years that it took shape, I was lucky to be surrounded by family and friends who brought me out of the apartment for rooftop phone calls to all corners of the earth, waxy paper cups of Italian ice, sour cream biscuits, swing sets in evening playgrounds, and endless (maybe they felt that way to *you*) hours of creative discourse:

To Clark and Tisa Houck for a whole lifetime of encouragement and support. To Stella Duffy, Becky Beahm, Laura Helton, Chris Lueck, and Andrea Maddox. To the initial readers: Amanda Baltazar, Manuel Muñoz, Alessandra Nichols, and especially John Summerour for his early and invaluable criticism.

To: Peter Senftleben, Jim McCarthy, Alexander Chee, Richard Labonte, Emanuel Xavier, James Lear, and Charlie Vázquez.

And to Kip Rathke, Mario Roman, Foster Corbin, Chris Cochrane, Witold Fitz-Simon, Sean Frankino, Cory Davis, and Sean Quinn.

We are amazed how hurt we are.
We would give anything for what we have.
—Tony Hoagland

Part One

Part One

Chapter One

My high school chemistry teacher was also a forensics investigator. He specialized in arson, burned bodies, and flammable chemicals, and he entertained us with some-times-gruesome stories from more than twenty-five years of duty. There was the skeleton of a woman, average height—which is to say five-foot-four—somewhere around thirty years old, reduced to blackened bones and cinders in a house fire. He gave us two clues: "For example, the middle finger on her right hand has a large calcification on the top section, like you might have if you wrote heavily with a pencil, for example." He said "for example" at the beginning and end of everything. "For example, she also has a tiny indentation, a notch, in her front tooth, also the right one, for example." It was our job as eager students, wound up by the grisly details, to figure out her occupation.

Work changes you. It shows itself on your body. In the same way that a carpenter's hands are tuned to the nuances of hammer and nail, the way wood can talk to you through your arms, my hands listen to numbers on files, to injection records and saturation levels, to painful and courageous histories. I filter through the hundreds of thousands (could be millions) of dead medical records at St. Vincent's Hospital, and line them up in ascending order by year of admittance.

The files begin with a complaint. Something like "My back hurts and I don't know why," or "My leg is broken," or worse things—usually only one sentence, typed up by someone in Admitting. Then a social and family history, which is dictated to the nurse by the patient, and handwritten. This is where the nurses fill in what's really happening, the stuff that doesn't show up in the complaint: "Woman claims to have walked into door," or "Child has bruises on back and legs, father says they are from falling off the bed." Then a medical history, a list of procedures performed, if any, and finally billing information. Sometimes there are X-rays, sometimes there are sonograms. Sometimes there's hardly anything—a blurry carbon copy and illegible signature. The files are stored vertically on shelves in thirty-two rows. They're accented by six different color-coded stickers (green for first-time emergency visit, orange for same-day dismissal, red for DOA, yellow, brown, and light blue for what I haven't been able to figure out yet).

My fingertips are tough, callused by the constant shuffling and reshuffling of paperwork and paper clips, removing the tiny staples, and my cuticles are often rubbed red and raw from jamming my hands in between two folders, cut open on the sharp edges of the files.

I work alone. I don't talk to anyone, don't see anyone. I don't know who deposits the manila folders into the wire in-box. I only know that when I arrive, the box is full, and the files are sometimes spilling over into two or even three stacks on the carpet. I work when I want to, so long as I've made a hefty dent at the end of the week. I don't make enough money to get by on this job alone, so I hustle. Truthfully, I was hustling before I took this job, and if you ever see a documentary film about strippers, or prostitutes, or hustlers, they always say something like: "I couldn't make enough money waiting tables, so I started turning tricks and here I am."

With me it was the opposite.

The fact that I work alone also means that, in some ways, I have no proof of the work at all. I have no product. Other than my fingers, I have nothing to show for it, no physical manifestation of time passing. Hustling is the same. If I flatten myself out enough (in my head, I mean) then it's easily forgettable. And because it's a secret, an almost invisible transaction between strangers, it doesn't really exist. But I will—reluctantly—say this: all the anonymous numbers, all those forgotten histories, the injuries and surgeries and remarkable recoveries, they hide in my fingers. Where the sex work goes, I don't know.

The burned woman? She held a pair of scissors that pressed on that knuckle, and she tucked bobby pins in that tooth, where over the years they carved out a little nick in the enamel. She was a hairdresser.

Right now I'm sucking this guy's cock in his rented BMW, and as he starts to fuck my face his balls tighten up like he's going to explode, and it's shoved too far down my throat for me to practice my practiced technique.

When I look over at my hand holding the armrest of the door, my fist is clenched tight around the brown leather and the dust starts to settle over my eyes. I reach down and start rubbing my finger across his asshole, then pushing it up until I can't get in any farther. He squirms, then moans. Not pleasure or pain. It's a moan of not knowing, of losing control. There is no before and there is no after, there is only now, like the queasy instant just before you sneeze.

He shakes, stops thrusting, grabs my ears, presses my head down. His cum squirts in three short bursts into the back of my throat and it's sour and acrid and awful.

I swallow.

Tomorrow, I think, it won't be so bitter.

Chapter Two

When I get back to my apartment my friend Louis is playing Nintendo and he offers me the second controller. "I challenge you to an all-night tournament of endurance," he says.

I make a joke about whether he means playing Mario Kart or having sex. His eyebrows rumple into a dark V, and he pushes the controller into my open hand. I kick off my shoes and take off my shirt. "One game," I say. Without looking at each other, only watching the screen, we start talking. "How long have you been here?"

"Most of the day," he says. "I thought you would be home. I played Nintendo mostly."

"You're at a disadvantage then, already worn out."

"Nope. I'm in the zone. Plus, I got past the Water Fortress. You steal the flute, play the Song of the Wind, and then the door explodes."

"Cool," I say. "I could never figure it out."

"A fairy in the Dark Lands tells you how to do it."

"Which level should we play?"

"Surprise me."

"I think there's something wrong with the Flower Cup. It gets fuzzy and blinking somewhere around the fourth heat. But I've been playing all day, so I don't know."

"Star Cup it is."

"Let's not argue over who gets to be the Princess."

"You're always the Princess."

"She has the best acceleration of all the cars in her class."

"Her cornering sucks."

The little cartoon carts line up on the screen, the balloons fly, the crowd roars, and the little Nintendo traffic light begins its countdown to go. "Louis, my dear, prepare to die."

We tear through the mud, slinging banana peels and turtle shells at each other, sliding off the track, through tunnels and over secret ramps. I eat a mushroom, which hits me with a burst of speed, and I dash across the screen. Sound effects explode into the room.

"I found a box of Jell-O in your cabinet, so I made that," Louis says. "And then I thought what if they could engineer Jell-O to include all the necessary vitamins and minerals. So that a person could live solely on Jell-O. Forever and ever."

I met Louis five years ago when a basically good-looking white-collar guy from Cleveland hired us to fuck while he watched. We cabbed up to the W Hotel and waited in the blue-haloed lobby, talking about whatever—the weather, a new restaurant, other small talk I've forgotten. Mr. Cleveland arrived only a few minutes late (not uncommon) and we fucked and he got off and it was very vanilla, only what he asked for. Then he paid us an extra hundred bucks to sit around with him and talk about ourselves.

Mostly when they pay you to sit around and talk what they really want is for you to sit around and pretend to be interested in their boring-as-shit lives while they fondle your nipple or smell your hair over and over. Pretty icky.

Louis and I exchanged numbers, figuring if we ever have to fuck while somebody watches, we'd be glad to fuck each other. And it happened a few more times, but not too many. And then, almost invisibly, instantaneously, Louis graduated to legit model status, signed an exclusive contract with Calvin Klein, and started to get paid buckets of money for doing what he used to do for a lot less—stand around in his underwear. All of a sudden, he was plastered all over bus stations and subway cars. He stopped hustling and moved into a loft in Tribeca.

Louis zaps me with a lightning bolt and I shrink to the size of a pea, puttering across the grass where I've skidded off the road.

"Take that, Princess!" he shouts, and zooms across the finish line.

Chapter Three

We're sitting in Central Park listening to the Metropolitan Opera do *Tosca* for the Fall Festival. The grass in all directions is covered with quilts, sheets, blankets, people sitting on flattened out garbage bags. The music is blaring and families are sitting all around us, eating picnic dinners and talking to each other.

"Doesn't she throw herself off the parapet?" I say.

"Not tonight. It's *in concert only*," Farmer says, rustling in the blue zippered bag that he always carries with him. I have never seen him without it.

"Well, that's a disappointment. There should still be a big jumping scene."

"Quit complaining. I think there are fireworks later." The grass brushes against my legs and forearms. It smells fresh and moist. I like it. "Hey, Simon," he says. "There're some red balloons floating away."

"Where?" I bend my neck around.

"Over there." He points. "Let's watch them until we can't see them anymore."

Farmer's lips tighten into a tiny grin. Wispy clouds and birds crowd the violet sky, which is framed on all sides by the skyscrapers, Central Park South and Central Park West and the Fifth Avenue penthouses. I squint, refocusing, as the balloons shrink and drift away. They get lost in my eyes, and I lie back down, frustrated.

"I can't watch anymore," I say.

Farmer's side is pressed against mine. He takes a breath and I know what's about to come out of his mouth is going to be something honest and sweet, and whatever it is, I probably won't understand. Farmer is everything good about humanity rolled into a squat, wrestlerlike package. He has read every one of the one hundred greatest books according to the Modern Library Association, even the boring ones, and he must read the entire *New York Times* every day—the print edition. His glasses are broken, not in the middle, but at the hinge, and he's repaired them, flawlessly, almost invisibly, with a piece of curved paper clip.

Also, Farmer has the smoothest chest in all of Manhattan.

Farmer speaks: "Did you ever tie a note to a balloon with your name and your address and a little postcard that says something like 'whoever finds this please mail this postcard and tell us where you found the balloon' or something like that? Then you wait and wait until you finally give up and you think that you'll never see that postcard again. Then months later you get your postcard back and it's from a little blond girl somewhere in Maine."

I am lost in the sounds of mothers telling their children what not to do. "No, I never did that."

"It's amazing," he says, his voice quiet and young.

"Let's do it. Let's tie a postcard to a balloon and let it go floating away."

I don't really answer, just touch his elbow, thinking he'll let it go. He waits a moment, and then says in this other voice, this collegiate voice, this voice that comes out of nowhere, "I'm so afraid for these families. I wonder if they know that their biology is programmed to work differently. All this talk of marriage and morality, and I'm not even sure that marriage is the correct organizational structure to begin with."

Farmer's apartment is covered in books—huge cabinets of books, their shelves sagging in the center. It looks like they are stacked here and there, wherever things might fit, in no particular arrangement, but I know that Farmer's books are delicately sorted in a kind of invented Dewey Decimal System. I know that he has tiny, emotionally draining dramas about why a book might remain on a certain shelf—at eye level or not, on the end or in the middle. Farmer loves not just the stories but the books themselves, as objects. He even loves the ones in other languages—the languages he can't even read.

I notice the grass against my ankles again and sit up. Jaron, a good friend of ours, an undereater, emerges from the chaos.

"Hello, boys," he says, drawing out the words for as long as his breath will let him. Jaron is fond of appearing when you least expect it—and always from the opposite direction. Wherever you're going, Jaron has just been there and, bored of it already, has decided to leave.

"What are you two doing out here among the people?" he says. Even in the dim light of dusk, Jaron has brought sunglasses. He pulls them off; his eyelids look wrinkled.

"It's good to see you," Farmer says.

"There never was a more lovely sight. Simon and Farmer sitting together on the grass listening to the happy music."

"Want something to eat?" I say.

"You know, I'm so hungry I could eat the ass out of a rag doll."

On any given day, Jaron might ingest five to ten no-salt crackers, a banana, a gazillion pills of various sorts, and a gallon of water. Perhaps some days he eats less. Your typical binge and starve. Once I caught him at my refrigerator with a soup spoon in the grape jelly, the purplish goop smeared across his lips and snaking down his chin. He smiled back at me, embarrassed, his mouth full of glossy indigo teeth. If we go out to dinner, which is historically rare, Jaron has a salad, removes the tomatoes ("The acid is bad for my stomach," he says), and proceeds to slowly, methodically, clean his plate. I wonder how he stays alive.

Jaron also cuts himself—a self-mutilator, they call it. Knives, razors, nail files, thumbtacks, whatever he can find that will make a mark. His arms and hands are scarred from the constant nicking. We mostly ignore it. He's made it clear that we're not to ask. And the times when he ends up in the hospital, from a combination of cutting and not eating, we never ask, "What was it this time?"

Sometimes I read the files after he's been discharged. It occasionally takes years for files to make it to my stack, so by the time they get to me, they're practically ancient. But once or twice I have reached into the bin to find a folder with his patient number—433.533.3—this thing that makes you what you are in these endless rows of bureaucracy. And I know that this means that Jaron was in the hospital long before I knew him. The nurses often mistake the cuts for a suicide attempt, and sometimes they try to send him to the psychiatric unit—which is a pink sticker. Sometimes I take the files home with me and bury them under the mattress. It feels like spying, in a way. Or lying, because I never mention it.

"What did I interrupt?" Jaron says.

"I was just telling Simon how sad I am for these families," Farmer says. "I don't know why the system hasn't failed. Or failed in a more obvious way."

"Television," Jaron says, "has taught the American family a spiraling pack of lies. If you want something to blame, blame that. But I'm tired of people acting like the television is an invasion. It merely lies there. You're the one who has to sit in front of it and pay attention. People only do what they want."

Farmer and I lie back in the grass. The arias ebb and swell, like water.

"And furthermore, these people out here, these sad families, they aren't here because they are fans of Puccini, or they want to spend time with one another. They're out here because it was on the news, or they saw their neighbors going. Herd mentality, you know. It's disturbing."

Jaron situates his sunglasses on his face again, like a final fantastic stage exit. I've turned off. Farmer is tossing little stones into the air above his head and catching them. He's startled and sits up fast. "More balloons, look."

Jaron turns his head slowly, as if it were filled to the crown with lead. "Don't tell me he tired you with that postcard from the blond girl in Maine mumbo jumbo." Farmer keeps staring into the cooling air.

I say, "No, not really."

Jaron looks around at the stage, at the happy people. "Here we are, all of us staring up at the sky, searching for these balloons, and he's the only one who isn't bored to tears. Do you ever wish that you didn't know some of the things you do?" Jaron says. "Do you ever wish you could let go, quiet your brain? All the silly voices in your head telling you truths about reality. Yapping all day, blah blah blah. I wish I could turn them off."

I rub my hands together, noticing for the first time how itchy my skin is. Farmer nudges me with his elbow. "Simon," he says. "The balloons."

"What about them?" I say.

"They're gone."

Chapter Four

I get called to do this S&M party and although I don't really want to go, I do anyway. I could use the money. At the last one someone paddled my nuts for like a thousand hours, and the next day it hurt to wear underwear. This guy's basement is filled with all kinds of slings and sex appliances, even a mechanical chair that fucks you while you sit in it. (No thanks.) When I get there everyone is already in their chaps and harnesses. "Fantasies are completely unoriginal these days," one of them is saying, "handed to us by Scandinavian illustrators and fake porn narratives from the seventies."

Still, I think, here we are.

My clothes come off. I feel a mouth on my asshole and then a tongue reaching inside. One guy sucks on my nipple while I bite down on his fingers. Eventually, I come in somebody's mouth.

Then I stand by the door while the host counts out my money, watching the faded green bills flip over in his hand, trying to count them as he's counting them—one hundred, two hundred, two-fifty—without being obvious about it.

That's my favorite part—the gathering up of clothes afterward. Everyone is more relaxed, the nervousness dissipates, and you can have interesting conversation sometimes. Boundaries are less important, and people tell you what they do for a living, or they complain about their boyfriends and how they never have sex anymore. They swear they're good husbands and fathers, despite our transaction—I think most of them are. Sometimes you still sound like strangers afterward, which of course you are, even though you've shared something personal. Or deeply impersonal, which itself is a certain kind of intimacy— what it says about the person who requests it. And all that can't make you completely unfamiliar. Can it?

After the party I went straight to work. From work to work, as I say. The hospital is basically calm today, nothing of note to relay—except a new brand of potato chips went into the snack machine in the waiting room. There seemed to be some ruckus in the emergency wing, but I didn't hang around long enough to see what it was.

I did seventeen files immediately, all outpatient visits that I could hold in one hand without much effort. Then I started on two stacks of thicker files from surgical, which were mostly in the same area of the filing room, meaning not a lot of walking, and one even ended up on the bottom shelf, which isn't all that common, because those files are older. The rest of the day was spent dealing with six cartons of files from the early '80s—five hours and I didn't even finish. It never ends. Last year's numbers for the entire hospital system, which includes several facilities throughout the city, when touted around by the PR department went something like: 625,000 home care visits, 90,000 inpatient discharges, and more than 1,000,000 outpatient visits. The emergency rooms alone saw 255,000 people.

It's not boring, what I do. It can be infuriating—when a particular file doesn't know where it belongs, and so I have to pore through the paper innards looking for the right detail. Anything that looks like a patient number will do in some cases. And it can be numbingly mechanical. Sometimes I get four hundred incidents in a single day, none of them admitted, just treated and released. Those files lack any sort of tangible personality, and often you can file several of them at a time because they're sequential, so there's no detective work. But I never find it boring, exactly.

Boredom indicates that although you are mentally fixed on a single task—waiting, reading, listening to a stranger's conversation—what you would rather be doing is something else. And I find that often what I would rather be doing is filing. Meaning, I never say to myself, "Wow, I'd rather be getting fucked right now by a dude on his lunch break." I like the motion of this work, the back and forth between the aisles, the quietness of the room. The immediate gratification—when I'm finished, I'm finished, and I get to go home.

There is a peace to the bureaucracy. Among the crowds of humanity I feel infinitely small. Inconsequential. These files were here long before I was, and they'll be here for years after I'm gone. I only intersect them briefly, passing into their lives and then out, invisibly. Someone once told me that the job sounded like horrific humdrum torture—stacks of befuddling paperwork and bloody, hapless fingertips—but I disagree. I take the opposite point of view. Didn't Camus say that we have to imagine Sisyphus happy?

Mr. Bartlett is in the kitchen when I open the door.

"Come in, Simon. It's so nice to see you again. I was wondering if you would show up today." Our meetings are weekly and scheduled. He likes me to pretend that I happen to be stopping by; it creates the illusion of a genuine friendship. "Would you like a glass of water?" A blur of lavender and baby powder introduces him to the foyer. A blue wash pauses in the air, the nebula around him congeals. I wonder if he's taken a bath.

He stands against the doorjamb, waiting for me to decide if I want a glass of water, which means he's hoping that I'll piss on him, or sometimes I piss in the ice cube trays so he can save it for later.

"Fine," I say. Mr. Bartlett keeps my money in a purple envelope. He has a strange sense of morality—he would never actually hand me the cash—and so he leaves it on a desk near the front door. "So you won't accidentally forget it," he says. Does he remember that this is what I do for a living?

The first time I fucked him at this house I went into the kitchen after he offered me a glass of water and looked into the looming china cabinet, probably antique, only to see that there was one plate, one glass, and one set of utensils. "Why do you only have one plate?" I asked. "Oh, you know," he said. "All the others must have broken."

Mr. Bartlett continues his monologue. "I thought about cooking a little dinner for the two of us and then I said to myself, 'You don't even know what that dear young thing likes to eat, or if he even prefers to eat dinner at this hour. Instead, simply offer a glass of water. Something to fill his stomach.' That's what I said to myself. And do you know what? I think I was exactly right in thinking those thoughts, don't you?"

"Water is fine," I say.

"Perfect." He smells my shoulder as he slides past me. "I've had the Brita in the cooler all day, because I knew you would say that yes, you would like a glass of water." He fills a glass and hands it to me. I take a big gulp.

Today he looks like a sagging version of himself, like his skin is two sizes too large, and the real Mr. Bartlett must be shrunken, perhaps captive, inside. His feet are like props from a horror film, pale and rubbery. Sometimes he smells like medicine, like an old person. And I don't tell him that, in some circles, there are plenty of men out there, some boys even, who would gladly do for free what I do for a measly hundred bucks. I wouldn't even know where to start guessing his age. Seventy?

"Oh dear, your hands," he says.

"Yes," I say. "I know."

"You've cut your fingers worse than ever."

No, not worse than ever. I remember worse.

"What do you want to do today?" I say. The sooner we're done the sooner I can get the hell out of here.

"Oh, honey, drink your water before rushing into the details of our evening. The last thing I want to do is to have my life planned out like prime-time television. Let's do things at random. Do you know what I mean? Let our hair down?"

"Okay." I finish the water and he offers to refill it. I decline. I had three glasses of iced tea an hour ago, figuring this would happen.

"Now, don't call me cloddish, but I seem to have left the latex in the bedroom. Would you mind following me in to retrieve it?" He runs his finger along a moth-eaten hole in his sweater.

"Sure." I follow Mr. Bartlett up the stairs and to the bedroom. He's pulled the sheets off the bed so that I have to fuck him on the bare mattress, which is okay. We've done that before.

After, while I'm putting my pants back on, he bothers me about another glass of water, and when I tell him that he forgot to stick the pitcher back into the "cooler" his face sinks. His posture slacks.

"At least have a glass of milk. It's still in the cooler, I'm sure." He sounds confused, lost like a victim of horrible temporary amnesia.

"No thanks," I tell him.

I take the envelope off the desk, open it, fold the bills and shove them into my pocket. He walks over and lays his hand on my shoulder. I try to move out of the way so he can't touch me, because he just had his hands all over me. And the money is in my pocket, which means that we're done, and if I don't want him to touch me, I don't have to let him.

"We could watch the television. I don't have cable, who needs all those hundreds of channels? But I'm sure we could find something worthy of our attention. Come on, sit down over here on the couch and I'll find something on the networks. Now, let me see." Mr. Bartlett moves quickly, brushing past me with the remote. He motions me with it and pushes some clothes off the cushion next to him. "Want to watch the networks?" he says. The screen flashes talk-show hosts, soap operas, an advertisement for a seafood restaurant with a crab leg snapping at the joint. "They're so different these days than they were when I was younger." He tucks a strand of hair behind his ear. I turn back to face the door. "Maybe I can find a new situation comedy. There're so many of them these days. Practically everyone watches different shows now. Oh, Simon, this electronic box used to bring whole neighborhoods together. Well, all that's gone now. New shows each season. No one to root for, really."

I don't turn around to look at him. I don't want to see him staring down at his feet, glaring at the loose skin, the old bones.

I do have a menu. And everything is negotiable. Blow job active, blow job passive, fuck top, fuck bottom, piss top, piss bottom. Jerk off and come, jerk off without coming, eat my own, come on my face, on my ass, come before, come during, come after. Pain, bad pain, *really* bad pain. Soldier, Motorcycle Guy, Surfer Dude, Captain of the Football Team, House Painter, Plumber, Farmboy, Airman, Marine, Cowboy, or Convict. Some people like Nazi stuff—I don't have the clothes, but I can borrow them. Chaps or jeans or jocks. Boots can be short, tall, dull, polished, oiled, clean, scruffy, lace up, or spurs. Rubber or denim or gloves. Spread-eagle or upside down. Spanking, whipping, flogging, strapping, sometimes punching. Weights on balls, cock, nipples. Menthol, ice, wax. Blindfold, gag, mask, chains, plastic wrap, adhesive tape, chastity belt, rope, restraints, cuffs, harness, hood, straitjacket. Enema, catheter, suppository. Shaving. Psychodrama!

I leave the apartment building and hold the door in the hallway for a man carrying too many groceries. Carrot tops and French bread stick out of the top of the bags, like an advertisement for groceries, not just plain old food. He thanks me and I wait for the door to close and click behind him. I pause for a moment between the doors, standing quietly in the airlock, staring into the gold inlay art deco mirror above the no-longer-functional fireplace. In the mirror, a river flows out from between two giant mountains with a bare, rocky summit that looms over the empty valley. The river curves in a few places, moving toward you with each turn. In the widest part, where my face is reflected, two cranes walk around among the lily pads, fishing for breakfast, their twiggy legs and knobby knees all polished and antique. I stare at myself in the river.

After, I take the subway down to the hospital. I slide my card through and listen for the high-pitched ring of the machine. The little window lights up a faded green GO and the turnstile cranks me through.

The guy playing guitar on the opposite platform sounds a lot like Woody Guthrie. About two dozen people pass by while he's playing but no one drops anything into the hat. He's not good, not terrible, just average—which is worse than good or bad. The only lyrics I can make out are "unravel threads of sanity" and something about "sinuous," which sort of destroys the Woody semblance. He's wearing a limp T-shirt, dingy around the collar, to go along with the image of "I'm a starving whatever."

Someone has drawn DIE FAGS in thick black marker along part of the tile. Then someone else, with another urgent agenda, has sprayed a big lavender smudge through it. Wow, I think, gay graffiti. The ceiling drips near the bench where I'm sitting, slick and greenish, seeping slowly into round drop-shaped mirrors. The guitar player looks over at me and sings some stupid line about "lace and cyanide," and I wonder for a second about whether I could take him home. But like I said, there isn't any money in the case—and I don't do freebies for strangers.

Plastered on the wall behind him is a movie poster, Hollywood starlets interlocking arms, perfect white teeth and eyes the color of ocean water in Barbados, like Icelandic glacial runoff. The train's headlights flash a muscular glare across my face and there's the enormous rattle and squeal of metal on metal. I look back at the guitar player. The train barrels down the track, hiding us from each other, separating us with glass and steel, heavy wheels, and magnificent advertising. The doors open and I take a seat near the end of the car. The conductor complains to us about using all the available doors, blah blah blah, haven't we all heard this before? Somebody with a baby stroller holds the door open for a man in a wheelchair and the people around me start to look annoyed. *Stand clear of the closing doors,* and the guitar guy is suddenly history. We pull away from the station, moving into the tunnel that runs under the river, and I sit back in the orange seat, watching the flashing lights go by, the knots of dirty plumbing.

I see my body reflected in the safety glass separating the steel-bright light of the train car from the dark of the tunnels. I shiver and pull my sweatshirt around me tighter until, when I grip my sides, I can only feel the soft bulky fabric and hardly any of my own skin. I look down at my legs and they look much larger than before. I feel embarrassed. I struggle, like in puberty, with my awkwardness, with what is suddenly—*me*.

Chapter Five

Sometimes I can tell what sort of files are going to find their way into my hands, and into my life, before I'm even in the room with them. First I get a feeling, an ominous weight to the morning, perhaps. A drizzle of rain which turns to fog and back to rain again all before I get out of bed. Weather as foreshadowing. And then my MetroCard won't read properly, and I swipe it ten times before the technology does what it is supposed to do, and I finally get on the train. Sometimes I say a quiet prayer—to nobody really, I don't actually believe in that stuff—that the day will behave as planned and whatever turbulence arises won't shake me right out of the sky.

For example, on my way to the basement a janitor accidentally dropped a tray full of silverware on the floor in front of me, forks skewing in every direction, the sound ringing down the corridors, halting movement in every direction. People in the waiting room covered their ears.

I knew right then that something in the files today would be a little too familiar. And now I've found it. It's a gay bashing from a few months ago. I find more and more of them every day—maybe twenty in the last year alone, spreading like a rash. In this case, a fag walking home from the gym decided to take a shortcut through the park and—zap—they got him with a stun gun. For approximately twelve minutes, they got him. So says the police report, which is strangely included, along with other documents and written statements—some of the forms I've never come across before. Signatures everywhere.

He was treated for bruises and swelling in his face where they punched him, two broken fingers (left third and fourth), marks on his throat where they strangled him. One of the doctors suspects it was a telephone cord, or something similar. "Shoelace?" says one of the papers. Plus a mysteriously dislocated kneecap. And the place where the stun gun shot him through with electricity was burned and bleeding.

I'm thinking about that spot—the two tiny holes in his side, halfway up his rib cage, the only place where they managed to enter his body. I'm thinking about how that feels, to have your flesh opened up like that, your aura burst like a soap bubble. But he survived.

One of the most difficult parts of my job is not knowing the rest of the story. I process the incidents without having all the details—I only know the beginning and end of the story. I don't know if a lover came to take him home, if family members rushed to the bedside. If they caught the jerks. There is an old custom of hiring mourners at a funeral, to be sure that the deceased are properly lamented. And that's sometimes what I feel like: a grief vessel.

I swallow the pain, shove the folder into the rows with all the others, and walk back to the in-box, where I pick up ten or twelve more. And just like that, the day continues.

* * *

First thunder. Then the hot metal crack of lightning in the distance. The vein-crackled sky opens, flashing blue-yellow light across Louis's face. He brushes the hair out of his eyes and stares up into the wind. His cigarette glows brighter as he inhales, and for the haze I can hardly see anything else.

The drops start to fall one at a time on my head; the air turns from moist to wet. The puddles that appear beneath us reflect Louis's yellow raincoat, my red vinyl. The arms of the storm reach from one end of the city to the other. The night brightens as light from the sky, from the neon, from the blinking *walk / don't walk* refracts and throws itself back up at us.

At the opposite end of the street several men are walking toward us in a pack. The smaller ones in front; the heavy strong ones in the middle; the fastest, most agile in the back. It occurs to me that what has been happening all over New York City in the past six, ten, twelve months is about to happen to us. I want to scream out. I want to punch my fists into the sidewalk.

I want to be responsible for my own bruises.

I feel a weight in my stomach and, seeing the world through a fish-eye focus, I move closer to Louis.

Drag queens can tell you what kind of lipstick covers best. They know which earrings hide scars. I thought at the time—you know, that shirt doesn't look half bad with bloodstains. If only they would run down a little more to the left.

I hear the ribs cracking, caving in. Blood tastes different when it comes up from your guts and not from a pricked finger—when it comes in buckets from the inside out. There's no sweet tang. It's bitter and thick, like motor oil.

They hold his head down in a puddle and he gasps for air. Two of them are watching me, threatening to make me next. So I just stand there, turning away, facing the brick wall like they tell me to, waiting for it to end.

Thirty, forty seconds it must have been. It happens so fast that it hardly registers in my mind as a single moment. It's a string of slow-motion movement, one thing morphing into another. Everything blurs.

A siren wails and the assholes run off.

Then we're in the hospital and he's hunched over my lap. He pukes onto the floor and I clean it up. The nurses see how much blood he throws up, but we still have to wait. We have to wait because some Greenwich Village landowner cut his finger on a vegetable peeler and requires six stitches. They give Louis something to stop, or at least calm, the vomiting. They bring a needle full of pinkish liquid and it goes down clean into his arm. I hold the cotton ball onto the drop of blood.

Later they wrap Louis's body in wide flesh-colored bandages. Broken ribs. Nothing has punctured his lungs and therefore it is not "too serious." We should simply go home and keep him in bed for several days. He should have lots of liquids. He should not walk or move around much. Yet, he should try to take deep breaths to stretch the muscles in his torso, which in turn will help strengthen his body. The doctors give us a bottle of aspirin and a bottle of ibuprofen. In case either upset his stomach.

Another patient, a sickly guy with white hair and blue tinted glasses, covered his mouth with his hand. "Why on earth would anyone do something like this?" he said.

But I know why they did it. They told us over and over again. They told us every time they shoved his body onto the concrete. They told us each time he vomited. They told us exactly what we had done to deserve this.

At home, he falls asleep. For a few minutes I sit watching him, the sheets lifting up and down with his breathing.

I turn on the shower. The steam billows around the poster tacked up on the ceiling—a Calvin Klein ad from a Manhattan bus stop. It's Louis in some briefs and a white pocket T. Farmer stole it from somewhere in the South Bronx. When I asked him how he got it out from behind the glass, he said, "I had some tools in my bag."

I step onto the tile, facing away from the spray. Slowly, I step back, centimeters at a time, until I feel the water rise up my neck and loosen the matted hair on my head. When I'm back far enough so that the water begins to fall over my eyes and across my lips I feel myself getting heavier. The water runs faster and faster, taking away parts of me. I start to slide down the tile and I feel my body weighing hundreds of pounds, thousands of tons, perched in a short, tight stack on my shaking heels. My hand clutches my genitals and the water takes more and more of me away, peeling back the layers, melting the muscle. Dissolving the bone.

I feel buoyant and numb.

Chapter Six

I sleep about four hours. I try to sleep some when I do these middle-of-the-night appointments—if I know beforehand that they'll be awful. I'll sleep, do the deal, then come home and sleep some more. This way, I can slip the sex into an indiscernible time slot between drifting and consciousness. In other words, I won't remember it as clearly. The whole mess will be blurred. The stupid shit will forget itself.

I think this guy lives in Florida, or at least I gather that from his talking about it nonstop over the phone. Gainesville? Tampa? One of those cities you forget exists. Coral-colored suburbs, alligator farms, and lime-green monkey grass. Shrimp on ice and suntan oil.

He stays in an apartment out in Jackson Heights. There's a whole clan of thirty-something closet cases living down there who collectively rent this apartment, vacationing in it every so often, like a time-share. I've fucked there about a million times. I wonder if they sit around clambakes in St. Petersburg comparing notes. There was a bald man from Orlando who only licked my nuts over and over. He was there to paint the place as well—turquoise latex drips all over his arms and chest. The doorbell is broken, so there is a little plastic loop connected to a long cord that goes to the top of the stairs, and when you pull on it, the string tugs on a tiny brass bell. Of course, if the radio happens to be on, or the television, forget it. The first time I went there, Louis and I were doing it together. Louis thought it was real cute and smart, and he rang it a few times on our way out.

Mr. Orlando stopped calling after Louis refused to come with me to a fourth appointment. We'd done him together for a couple of nights in a row, and then Louis decided he'd had enough of his ball licking. Mr. Orlando was furious when I showed up without him. He got all Looney Tunes and bug-eyed, spouting things about ethics in business.

So I ring the damn bell, diddling the loop and watching the thin string jiggle all the way up into the building. I figure it's near three, close enough to whenever I'm supposed to be here. He tells me to show up in the middle of the night. Says something about "Come when it's no longer today, and not yet tomorrow." And then he giggles.

I considered canceling this one, not wanting to leave Louis alone right away, but this guy didn't answer his phone, and not showing at all could mean the end of the Florida Fuckers requesting some time spent with me, and I can't afford to do that.

The guy comes down to let me in and I can tell right away that he's off. His eyes are glossy and look like all different colors at once, like he's rubbed them with Vaseline, like an oily parking lot slick with rain. And he looks sweaty, plastic, saccharine. He immediately starts kissing my neck and rubbing his hands in my crotch. Fucking door isn't even closed yet.

He's all misty and glistening, holding up a bag of little pills. Green triangle ones, blue capsules, yellow and white tablets. There's a brown glass bottle with a dropper cap, something else wrapped in foil. Red dot pills that look like candy. He holds the bag out to me, pooches it open, and shakes the contents around. "Pick what you like," he says. And, of course, I don't. So he helps himself, and I mean really helps himself. Not even picking through them, swallowing a handful.

He's rubbing his face all over my chest and stomach and he should be kissing me the way he's moving his mouth up and down, but instead he's dragging his limp mouth across my skin. Leaving slime wherever he stops. And he coughs and coughs and coughs. This goes on for about half an hour. Maybe more.

I start lowering myself into the flat place, where the only sound is a cavernous hush of wind, and everywhere it smells like burning sugar, teasing my nose. I count to four, focusing on the noise, on the distant horizon, which grows no closer no matter how far you walk, and I sink into the grayness.

Then this guy gets sick. Pukes all over the floor.

He collects himself, breathing hard, and wipes his face with a towel. He sits back, resting on his heels. "Why are your fingers so cut up?" he says.

Louis is sitting in the chair, which he moved to be near the window (and the TV), with his lap full of magazines. He set a floor lamp next to him too, and the whole thing makes for a little private space that looks quite calming.

The sun hurls light down at the hardwood floor, and it feels good against my bare feet.

"I'm home," I say.

"Like it?" He doesn't look up.

"*Architectural Digest,* here we come."

"*Good Housekeeping,*" I say, walking into the bathroom. I lift the toilet lid and unzip. I piss hard, emptying out my insides. My body shakes, that weird pee-shiver thing.

"Careful, I just cleaned that."

"You shouldn't be cleaning anything. Or moving furniture." He has been staying here since he was attacked. He came here because he needed help doing little things, and he has yet to leave.

"I'm feeling okay today, actually. I won't overdo it. Remember, it's good for me to move around a bit." He's breathing heavily, conscious of the air moving in and out of his chest. "You know what," he says, "the worst part of this whole ordeal is that I can't work out. I haven't been to the gym in over a week. Everything has atrophied."

His side is painted in all shades of blue, brown, even green, and the whole thing is shiny from the greasy white cream he keeps rubbing on it. He lifts his arm to examine the soft, bruised skin, wincing slightly, squeezing his eyes shut. "Make me a salad, will you? I had some groceries delivered."

In the fridge I find some red leaf lettuce, two plum tomatoes, and two-thirds of a carrot, which at first I think is a hunk of orange plastic wrapped in cellophane.

I say, "Do I have a salad spinner?"

"You do not," Louis says. He flips through the pages of the autumn Williams-Sonoma catalog, dog-earing pages, tearing out the recipes. I toss all the stuff in a bowl, the torn lettuce pieces, wedges of bleeding tomato, and thin, almost transparent carrot slices. Looking at it all mucked up together, I'm thinking that salad is such a stupid food.

"Why do I know your kitchen better than you do?" he says.

"Because I don't use it. And you buy all this stuff for me."

"Oh, yeah."

"I don't even know what half of this stuff is." I open a drawer and rifle through the clunky metal tools inside. "What is this?"

Louis eyes the gadget in my hand. He turns back to the magazine and, ripping out a page near the front, reaches for his cigarettes. "It's a nutmeg grater."

"I don't have any nutmeg."

"And this is my problem?"

"Louis, you can't smoke in my house."

"Since when?"

"Since always. And what's the deal with all these cigarettes? Why are there cartons all over the house?" On the kitchen table alone there are seven cartons; more wait in stacks in the bathroom, some on the bedside table.

"What's your problem?"

"Are you planning on going home?" He turns to look at me and his eyebrows become a dark V. "I don't mind if you stay here for a while. But I need to go out, or sometimes people will want to come over here. I need to make appointments. What will Mr. Bartlett do if I don't show up?"

"Does he think he's the only faggot in Manhattan that you pee on?"

"Yes, I'm sure he does."

"He's a freak. All that glass-of-water business."

"What can I say, I have precious piss."

"You should bottle that shit. You could be a million-aire." The word lifts out of his mouth like a crystal balloon. "Anyway," he says, "I can't go home now. Farmer called. I invited him and Jaron over for lunch."

"Today?"

"Around one."

"Was this your idea?"

"No, actually, it was Jaron's. He said he couldn't remember the last time all of us were in the same room together. Especially you."

"What are you cooking?"

"I am cooking a quiche," he says.

"Since when do you cook quiche?"

Chapter Seven

Louis can't decide whether to serve the quiche at room temperature or steaming hot. So it waits on the counter, having been in and out of the oven a few times already. "You're going to dry it out," I say. "Make up your mind."

"Leave me alone," he says, reaching up into the cabinets. He pauses to touch his hip, grimacing for a second with the pain that I'm sure is spiking up and down his side. I watch him take the next few movements more slowly.

"Take it easy," I say.

"I'm fine. I just forget sometimes."

My head feels slogged with mud, and my nipple is pink and tender around the ring. I can only half remember why that is. Only half remember which guy was tugging on it.

My feet crack as I move toward the table, ligament pulling dryly over bone. There are blue cloth napkins that I've never seen before folded in triangles on the plates. Shiny new silverware on top of that. The caramel smell of onions wanders through the room, bumping into me as I walk, savory but mostly sweet. Louis hops around, tidying, touching up. He holds two different color pillows, each out at arm's length, one green, one blue, seeing which belongs where. A cigarette hangs from his mouth, unlit.

"Why are you making such a fuss?" He decides on the green pillow, setting it on its side, laying it warmly on the couch. "We're not expecting the queen." He pulls the curtains shut, opens them again, then pushes them behind the chair so they stay out of the way.

My apartment is three rooms. One room serves as the kitchen and the dining room and the living room. The kitchen itself is along the wall, all the parts in a line—countertop, sink, stove. Unmatching cabinets, randomly placed here and there, above the stove, between the fridge and the heating pipes that snake into the ceiling. A table sits left of center, then a few places to sit opposite the television and the Nintendo setup—a tangle of cords and controllers. A skinny bathroom separates the first room and the bedroom. The faucet fills in the center of the tub, which, from endless repairs to the tiled floor, is slanted more than a few degrees, and drips. The drain gurgles in the middle of the night. The bedroom is only the bed scooted into one corner and a chest of drawers. Overall the place looks kind of empty, as if I'm not finished moving in, only there're more accessories than actual furniture: candle things, miniature lamps, containers—Louis and his Home Shopping Network obsession.

"Simon, wake up."

"I am awake." He pushes past me with a bowl. "What is that?"

"Fruit salad." He places the bowl on the table and covers it with a napkin, as if it were bread dough needing to rise. "Jaron has to eat something. He won't eat the eggs."

I fill a glass of water and chug it. Farmer says you

should drink a liter of water before breakfast. "Jaron will have a fit if you make a big deal out of him. You know how he hates to be the center of attention." And then I remember the trips to the hospital, the portable IVs, the tiny stitches running up and down his arms.

You learn about the body when you do what I do. How pain and pleasure are delicately interchangeable, often indistinguishable. How incredibly resilient we are. And how easily, sometimes invisibly, we slip away.

"Simon, you—"

"I'm grumpy in the morning."

"You're always grumpy."

"I like to be grumpy."

"Shut up already. Take a shower or something." He twists a rag and pops it on the back of my thigh.

Then, finally, Louis brings the quiche out of the oven for the last time, carrying it with two large oven mitts, and places it onto a wooden trivet. He pushes the other dishes aside, making room for whatever else he has planned. I lean against the sink, watching him move. Watching the vein pulse in his neck, the way the hair is growing back on his chest. Taking a quick, motherly inventory of his body. His injuries are healing. Slowly, but they're healing. I wonder what's going on in his head, however. Sometimes he feels so far away.

The buzzer announces their arrival. I scurry over and pick up the receiver. "Who is it?"

"It's me," they say in unison—the ubiquitous New York buzzer declaration.

I scratch between my legs and realize that I'm not wearing any pants. I slip into the bedroom. I pull on a pair of Louis's jeans, stuffing my boxers down into the leg so they don't bunch up around the waist.

The door opens and Jaron says, "Well, this place looks fabulous. Louis, you really have done a number in here. Quite the improvement." Of course, his place is a landfill. Stacks of never-used take-out menus and credit card applications. Only it's never stinky or dirty—no food waste that might cause that. "Farmer, don't you just love this tablecloth? Is this linen? Where's Simon?" Jaron herds us like sheep.

"It's very neat," Farmer chimes in.

I hear them chatting quietly, and I worry that I'm missing something. Like they're talking in code, or my shoes are on the wrong feet.

"Come on out. We've seen it all before," Jaron says.

All this polite blather makes me nervous. Why is everyone being so considerate, so gentle? Usually we're like a pack of starving baboons, gnashing teeth, a flurry of prehistoric birds. The violence, the fear perhaps, the crushing anxiety of one attack on the news after another has made us strangers.

"Good afternoon." I sit down at the table, figuring that's where I'm best suited. Any closer to the kitchen and I'd just be clumsy and in the way. "Jaron, what's going on?"

"Nothing. All is well."

Louis says, "I made a big fruit salad." He gestures at the bowl, snapping the napkin off like he's unveiling a work of art. I notice the way he's moving, the consciousness in his gestures—he's aware of the hurt in his body, and it pains me a little to watch him.

"Thank you for thinking of me," Jaron says.

"No nuts," I say.

Jaron says, "My grandmother used to put nuts in her fruit salad and it always felt to me like crunching a tooth."

Louis says, "Well, you know, I just—"

Jaron says, "Thank you."

Farmer bolts up. "I love nuts in fruit salad." We all look at him like he's from another planet. He recoils.

I lean back, annoyed by all the civil banter. I want to knock over my drink, dig my hand into the fruit, get naked. Louis's hand on my shoulder quiets everything, his touch like antibiotic—he can sense when I get like this. I calm.

"Farmer! What's doing?" I sound like some over-compensating father-in-law. Like some straight-acting family member from another dimension.

Farmer reaches into the bag at his feet. Farmer carries this blue zippered bag—I have never seen him without it. Once, on the subway, a drunken frat boy tourist had cut his finger, and was wandering through each car asking for a Band-Aid. Farmer reached into the bottom of the Blue Bag and produced not only a sterile bandage, but antibiotic ointment. He produces a glossy postcard. "Look," Farmer says. "The Museum of Natural History recently acquired a forty-seven-foot giant squid. Dead, of course."

"Really?" I'm genuinely interested. "Will you take me to see it?" The card is dark, with a jumble of suckers and tentacles surrounding hours and admission prices. And, of course, that lone gleaming eye, big as a dinner plate, staring out of the deep, staring right through me. The squid looks like he knows something the rest of us don't.

"Of course." He takes a sip from his glass. "They're having a hard time with things in the natural specimen departments. Especially the African mammals."

Jaron cuts his eyes at me. He mouths "boring" and rolls his head around. I watch him swallow a strawberry.

Louis says, "What do you mean?"

Farmer resituates himself, feeling more confident now that he's in a situation he can handle—exploring the goings-on at various scientific not-for-profit institutions. "Well, you see what kind of animals there are in those exhibits? Elephants and such. See, those are real animals. And they're very old, decades. Naturally, they're not doing so well. Fur is falling off, noses are pulling away from the faces, the skin isn't holding up like they'd hoped."

Jaron says, "Sound familiar?"

Farmer ignores him. "The museum is at an ethical crossroads. They have to ask whether they should go out into the wild and gather new specimens. Find a family of African elephants, kill them, taxidermy and all that, which, never mind morality, costs hundreds of thousands of dollars, and then replace the existing grouping. These animals are now endangered, threatened, or protected, mainly."

Louis says, "They can't kill living animals for the sake of a motionless zoo."

Farmer says, "No, of course not. That's why they're stuck. It's practically impossible to collect dead animals from the wild, I mean you don't find things lying around in salvageable condition. The question becomes, how do we preserve the current specimens so that future generations will be able to see an elephant up close? There won't be real living elephants forever."

Eventually everything goes extinct. Animals, technology, languages, fashion. Culture and community. Queers, maybe—these attacks are speeding us along.

We all look at each other. Jaron breaks the silence. "Way to bum everybody out."

Louis slices the quiche and I realize how hungry I am, not even remembering the last time I ate. My stomach growls. And this is what Jaron feels all day.

Farmer says, "I'd like to know how it's coming up there, but I can't seem to get anyone to get into it with me."

Louis says, "I thought you were well-connected there."

Farmer says, "Not in that department. It's very cliquey. I'm more of a stars and space guy and those people don't always get along with the life sciences."

I say, "Why don't the departments get along?"

Farmer says, "It's all about funding. Astronomy gets a new planetarium, world famous, and the agriculture exhibits still have the PRESENT labels noting the 1950s."

Jaron says, "I don't understand why they don't run out into the peaceable kingdom and jerk off a bunch of elephants, then bring the spooge back to the elephant fertility clinic and get some lonely old chick elephants knocked up."

Farmer says, "It's far more complicated than that."

Jaron says, "Anyway, how boring is this topic?" Farmer stuffs his mouth with quiche and gulps at his water, silencing himself. "Simon, what's up with you?"

I say, "Nothing."

Then the table goes quiet. The air gets sticky while we're all looking at each other and chewing. Silverware clinks down onto plates. The whirring white noise of the refrigerator. Are we going to talk about it? I decide to throw a wrench in.

I say, "So, what's up with all these people getting beat up?"

Louis and Farmer say, "I know."

Jaron says, "Seriously."

I say, "Pretty scary, huh?"

Louis says, "After seeing what they did to the other people, I know how lucky I was."

Farmer says, "Lucky is sort of relative here."

Everyone is looking at Louis, waiting for some kind of reaction. "Simon has found a new love interest, a bearded fellow across the street," he intentionally changes the subject. "Mr. Laundry, we call him."

Jaron says, "Tell me about him. Tell me everything."

"First of all," I say, "I never mix business with pleasure. And two, he's extremely hot. And the way I see it, it would be nice to have a regular who lived across the street. Easy money." I try to be vague here. I don't normally tell people the details. It helps me to forget them.

Louis says, "Tell them how you hang out the window on Friday nights and watch him go in and out of his building." Everyone smirks.

Farmer says, "You should be locked up."

I say, "He's hot. What can I say?"

Jaron says, "Oh, Simon, come on. Forget it. You're head over heels in mad sweet love." He flutters his hands around his face, like tissue paper butterflies on strings.

I say, "I don't even know him."

Louis says, "Exactly. You do better at unrequited love than you do at regular love."

I say, "Ouch. Thanks a lot."

Louis says, "Need I remind you of the imaginary liberal activist boyfriend?"

Jaron says, "What is this?"

I say, "It was nothing." Farmer laughs and leans back in his chair.

Louis says, "Simon had this client who worked at the United Nations—"

I say, "I never found out what he did there."

Louis says, "Anyway, they were doing it, what, a couple times a week on his lunch hour? This guy, he worked for the Anti-Defamation League, and he happened to always be sitting in the park on Simon's walk home. And so we went crazy trying to find out anything about him, we were all over their Web site, trying to find any shred of information."

I say, "I learned a lot, actually."

Louis says, "You talked about him all the time. And you used to drag me out there to see him and he would never show."

I say, "He was gorgeous. Real sharp jaw. Eyebrows. I spent all day fantasizing about his armpits."

Farmer says, "I forgot you were into that."

Jaron says, "You're so kinky."

I say, "I'm not really. Anyway, that's over."

Louis says, "We have replaced him with the bearded Mr. Laundry across the street."

I say, "I'd fuck him if it came to that, that's all."

Farmer says, "Good for you. At least if you're getting paid to fuck, it might as well be with someone hot."

Jaron says, "I know. You should see the creeps I do it with."

The fruit bowl is empty, the quiche has been devoured. And we sit looking at the plates and forks and glasses. Farmer is looking around at the apartment, sucking and crunching on an ice cube. Jaron is picking at his fingernails and Louis is looking at me.

Jaron says, "And I do it for free."

We all get giddy. I smile and Jaron smiles and Farmer smiles. Even Louis smiles. And everyone laughs.

While I'm standing at the window he appears.

Every Friday night the heavy door swings open and Mr. Laundry carries his dirty clothes to the Laundromat. He drags the army-green bag down the stairway and then, with one thick heave, using his shoulder like a crowbar, he brings the load to rest behind his head, arms stretching out to the edges of the bag. Tonight he's wearing a red T-shirt with the sleeves torn off and I can see a tattoo on his right arm. Worn jeans and frumpy tennis shoes. I want to rake my hands underneath his shirt, feel the soft warm fibers against the tough tight sinew of his body. Snake my mouth along the textures of his chest—smooth and hard near his shoulder, mushy padded sweaty near his armpit, the relaxed weight of his pectoral, the delicate change of flesh around his nipple, sensitive and flooded with blood. Slowness, a gentleness, pours out of every pore of his body. I wonder if this is who he really is.

I'm bored and kind of horny, but no more than usual. Then Louis comes in.

"What are you looking for?" He's half-naked, sucking on an unlit cigarette again, and the filter has gone all soggy.

"My Laundry Man is out again." I wonder what his name is, but I don't say this to Louis.

"How long have you been lusting after him?"

"About two months," I say, which is a lie. It's been four.

"Damn." Louis slides his hand down into his underwear, scratching at his dick. "Want to play Nintendo with me?"

"No," I say. "I'm going to bed."

"Did you see the new poster?" he asks. "At the place?"

There is a store about a block down that sells windows, screens, custom radiator covers. The owner is an avid member of the Republican party, and voices his opinions on the current state of the union by way of neon poster board and permanent markers. He has newspaper photos of the president, blown up to look like headshots, hanging on the walls, in the windows.

"No, what does it say?"

"Pinkos Go Home."

"Is that supposed to mean us?"

"Yeah," he says. "I guess."

Louis turns and walks back into the living room. I watch his ass. He yells, "I think if I were ever to commit an act of terrorism, that would be the place. Farmer could build a bomb." And I picture it: the storefront demolished, sparkling glass thrown into the street, blaring trucks, news cameras and gawkers.

Louis yells at me from the living room again, but I don't understand him, it all sounds mush mouthed and vague. Out on the sidewalk, life continues. A homeless man is lying half asleep on the steps of the bank. On the corner is a South American woman selling I don't know what from a plastic cooler in the bottom of a shopping cart. She lifts the lid, rearranging the curved shapes of steaming aluminum foil.

It begins to rain. Umbrellas open by the dozen, mostly black. Men with briefcases, women with the *Daily News* on their heads, enormous strollers with giant plastic covers. A woman, completely bald, ducks into a doorway.

When I look back toward the Laundromat, Mr. Laundry isn't there. I stretch my neck from one side of the window to the other, but I don't find him anywhere.

While I'm asleep I have a short dream. I have heard that your dreams, even if they seem to last forever, are all dreamt in only a few minutes. So all those times where you're naked in front of your high school reunion, or you're falling off a cliff, or you're screaming and no sound comes out, all that really only lasts a few seconds. Something about your REM cycle. Something about certain chemicals in your blood that calm down your muscles and program them to repair themselves. Something about how the brain needs to process the actions of the day. The way it decides what's worth storing in the long-term memory, and what can be thrown out.

Anyway.

Here's the dream: I'm standing in the middle of the street. And I couldn't say which street, because it was one of those nameless places like that—you don't know where you are but you're somewhere familiar, somewhere you might have been before. It's not a city street, it's a deserted highway, flanked by lush green fields, soybeans, rows of corn, and brown dirt in all directions. And I look up at the sky, which is purple and orange, the way the sky looks right before a tornado. Only I've never actually seen a tornado, but dreams can deliver truths to you like that. And it looks like there are birds falling down toward the highway, falling the way leaves fall, without any sense of urgency, pulled only by gravity and the moods of the wind. But as the birds get closer, I see that they aren't birds at all. They're typewriters. And they lose their lazy sway and fall faster, like they're being thrown down at me from the sky, fired from cannons. And they crash into the street, crumbling the pavement, digging craters into the dirt, shattering the wooden fence that separates the street from the field. And hundreds of them, lying there on the ground, start clicking their metal teeth. And the clicking gets louder. And louder.

Chapter Eight

The N train is not coming. It's after midnight and they're doing track work somewhere uptown from us, so it's going to be a while. Red and white posters are plastered along the columns, listing the places where they're working on the tunnels and telling you how to get to where you're going. The station is mostly empty except for the occasional garbage train rumbling slowly by, honking its horn. The workmen down on the tracks lean against the wall, waving lightbulbs at each other, waving their arms and talking. Jaron and I sit on the wooden bench, waiting.

I keep trying to suck up another drop of Coke from the cup that's long been empty, a three-dollar Coke I bought from the movie theater concession stand. The movie was vague—some romantic comedy piece of crap. A crazy mix-up about two characters who are in love and they're trying to keep it a secret. Doors were opened and slammed, names were called, jokes were made—or at least attempted. I think this weekend alone the movie made sixteen trillion dollars. Jaron and I couldn't figure out what made the movie so popular. Pretty faces?

Jaron is pale, and he looks like he's been awake for fifty-something hours. In my exhausted brain, everything he says to me sounds goofy. "Simon, how's Louis?" He pulls a sack of pills from his pocket and finds a medium-sized yellow tablet.

"He's fine. Still living with me." I poke my finger at the plastic bag. "What's that?"

"Multivitamin." He throws his head back and the pill vanishes down his gullet.

"I don't know why he hasn't gone back to his own apartment. He's still a bit creaky, but he's really okay."

"Who wants to be alone in the city? Fags are getting their asses kicked all over town." There were more reports yesterday. Three guys beaten up outside their apartment building in SoHo. One of them, all the bones in his face had been shattered. The doctors thought he had been in a car accident, thought he was thrown through the wind- shield.

"He could leave if he needed to," I say.

"You mean he could leave if he wanted to."

"I guess. What's the difference?"

"He's never going to go unless you make him. Quit being such a picnic in the park." I know this tone, which Jaron uses when he thinks he knows what's best for you and the rest of the world. "I knew this would happen," he says. "And Farmer, as soon as you called to tell us that Louis—"

"I don't really mind him. And his ribs are broken."

"Not anymore."

I know that Jaron is right, but right now he bores me,

and when I get bored I get nasty. "Shut up," I say. "Just shut up." I suck at the straw again.

"Of course." He shifts his weight on the seat in a way that tells me that if we're going to continue this conversation, I'm going to have to say something next. The workmen start jackhammering into the walls, cracking the white and purple tile. Concrete dust lifts into the air. The tunnels smell like water underground. Another garbage train rumbles past, this one loaded with black bags, bulging with last night's dinners, unwanted clothes, broken furniture.

"I don't necessarily want him there, but I won't tell him he has to leave. He'll go when he's ready."

"Fine."

"Jaron, why do you have to be so difficult?"

"You're getting the short end. Sooner or later you've got to push his ass out of the fucking nest. And toss that damned Calvin Klein underwear out after him."

"If you ate something you might not be so grumpy."

"And while you're at it, toss out those eternal stacks of headshots."

"Breakfast or something."

"Also his portfolio."

"Are you even hearing me?"

"Yes."

"Well then?"

"Well then what?"

"He'll go when he's ready. I said that."

Jaron's voice becomes violently clear as he looks into my eyes. "He didn't tell you that he's lost his apartment, did he? That his agent dropped him? He'll never work again, most likely. Nobody wants him." He sits back and tries to ruffle himself back together. He fiddles with his hair.

I say, "He's getting better."

"That's the way that industry works. Yesterday he's a superstar and tomorrow he's a nobody. The look is over. Beauty is fleeting, it's fickle, and they all know it." That tone begins again. "It's no wonder he doesn't leave. You let him hike a trail across your back. I know that you have a habit of looking pitiful and acting even more pitiful. But if you don't wake up you're going to find that he's got you in a cage."

I suck on the straw again, trying not to explode.

"And stop that incessant sucking, the cup is fucking empty."

I stand up and walk to the metal trashcan at the end of the small row of seats on the platform, and I toss the cup inside. Someone has thrown away a fashion magazine, and even in the darkness of the garbage bin the cover shines like perfect white teeth.

A rumbling begins inside me, pulsing out toward the edges. A tremor slides down my arm and I tighten my fingers into a fist. I take a deep breath, squeezing my hand and gripping the floor from inside my shoes. "Jaron, I'm completely sick of you."

"Well, sick or not, here we are in this forsaken subway station waiting on a train that's never going to come and that's that. Where are you going to go, Simon?"

I lean over and grab both of his shoulders with my hands, pulling him toward me. I'm a lot stronger than I thought. He's surprised also. The quaking expands, the blood pounding in my ears. I want to tear off his face and toss it into the dark tunnel. I want to close a bag of stinging bees over his head. I want to tear open his chest and look at his heart.

He feels like a rag doll in my arms. He makes a noise, a pitiful wincing. I'm screaming words that I can't understand, hardly even hearing my voice.

Jaron is so weak, so disgustingly complacent, I'm afraid I might snap his arms completely off. And I let go of him, sliding down onto my knees. The trembling subsides; I feel it draining out of me, disappearing, falling away. My head falls in his lap. Jaron rubs his hand across my neck, softly along the smooth part of my ear. He brushes the hair from my mouth. "Simon, the train is here."

Later, I'm with a sexy black guy from the Lower East Side. And when I ask him what he wants he says he wants to "try some new shit." He's got a bunch of piercings, some tattoos on the back of his shaved head. His apartment is covered in *High Times* and *Latin Inches* magazines. We're watching the eleven o'clock news and this talking head is blabbing on and on about a woman who was pushed from the subway platform onto the tracks in front of an oncoming E train. They had to shut down the line for a couple of hours and we agreed that if it had been another train it wouldn't have been down so long. What happened was this: Some guy asks the woman for the time. She's listening to her headphones and doesn't hear him. So he pushes her off the platform, right in front of the oncoming train. A businessman with glasses was on the news saying that he thought "random violence" was so terribly frightening. This black guy agreed, but that's not the way it is, is it? It's not random. The situation was perfectly clear: She was ignoring him, and he needed the time.

We get our clothes off. His fingers, coated with that nice kind of lube in the black squirt bottle, are stuffed into both ends of me at once.

I start to go to the place where everything is flat, to the place where nothing is. For a few seconds before the landscape appears, the noise in my head is unbearable, peeling my brain like a grape, and then the grayness opens, and the sky glows, bleeding pure light and brightness. Flashbulbs go off from above, cracking the real world in half, and in half again, over and over until the pieces flutter away like confetti and are gone.

The flat place spirals out in front of me; the horizon line emerges, like a closed circle, miles away in the distance. In the flat place it's quiet, like the sound of slow water, and the air smells like ashes, like sweet honeysuckle on fire.

A memory surfaces: Edward Burke. Blue Kool-Aid eyes and soft pink lips, so soft you could hurt him if you kissed too hard. Edward fucked girls. Mostly. I sucked his cock. His mother worked at a beauty shop. Sometimes I sat in the sticky plastic chairs, staring at Mrs. Burke and her emery board scratching back and forth, thinking that Edward had the fattest purple cockhead I had ever seen.

Then this black guy is moving looser than before, and I'm sinking into the bed, staring out into the flat place. The door is open and the TV is blaring *Family Feud* in the other room, the old version with Richard Dawson, and he kisses every woman on the whole fucking stage, even the teenagers. The volume is up really, really loud and they're all trying to guess America's favorite Italian food. Then something cold up my ass. A beer bottle, I think. I stiffen up and start to come hard, harder than I can ever remember, and my hips are jerking. When I look down there's a finger shoved up my piss slit.

Was this part of the deal?

I find it again: the place where everything is flat, the place where I can concentrate. Count to four. Focus on that electric buzz, the humming white noise of the wind and the open sky. The sugary smell comes first, brainwaves firing, burned at the edges. Fizzled out, cauterized, popping like a bad circuit. The tiny white hairs on the back of my neck stand up. Then the flat place emerges again, rising from underneath me like scenes changing at the opera: one moment this room, this man, and then next—the gray blank world where everything is safe.

Chapter Nine

I gather up my clothes, dividing items that can wait another week from the worst-smelling stuff, which I wad down into a drawstring sack. I scrounge up quarters from the change jar, walk down the stairs and out onto the sidewalk. More reports of attacks this morning. One of the newspapers has something about a "gay bashing" on the front page, one mentions a "possible hate crime," another mentions nothing.

I don't want to hear the details.

When I get to the Laundromat there is a short Mexican woman washing the tops of the machines with a rag and talking on the phone. She's chatting with whoever about whatever in a language that's all vowels, lugging a heavy cart of wet clothes behind her, rolling it through the aisles. Mr. Laundry is here, and he isn't supposed to be. It's Tuesday—not his day. His eyes follow me as I walk around the other side of the folding table. Part of me wants this to happen. Part of me is really horny. The other part can't even speak.

He walks right up to me. "Can I borrow some soap?" he says.

I know I've got a script somewhere for this kind of thing. How many times have I drummed up stupid conversation? But this is something different, and I'm nervous. *Flat, flat, flat,* I'm thinking. Find the place where everything is flat.

He says the line again. "Soap. Can I borrow some?" He tugs at his shirttail, a green cotton thing with a pocket.

"I don't bring it with me." Brilliant answer, Simon. What are you, a genius?

He leans against the vibrating machine, arms folded across his chest, his feet crossed at the ankle. Seeing him up close, the details appear: jeans worn at the cuffs, left leg more frayed than the right, skin wrinkled in the crook of his elbow, the tattoo on his arm only sort of visible under his sleeve, a lot of hair on his knuckles. I don't know what to say.

"Here's fifty cents. You can use the vending machine over there." I get two coins out of my pocket and stretch my arm out to him. He pauses, stands up straight, and walks over to me. He lifts his hand up and everything zooms in on this tiny moment. The part where my fingers drop the coins into his rough dark palm. The world slows.

"Thanks," he says, smirking, charming.

"Sure."

"Slow morning."

"Yeah." I notice my arm is still hanging out there in the open.

"So you live around here?"

It's an odd question to ask at a Laundromat, I think—is this supposed to be his pick-up line? "Yeah, right across the street."

"You like it?"

"I love it. Like my own little neighborhood, you know."

"I've been here almost a year. I see the same people walking around, same people coming home from work every day. Same people going to work every day."

"You start to recognize them and then you wonder if anyone starts to recognize you." We pause. He smacks his gum. I see his clean white teeth.

"So what do you do?"

"You mean for a living?"

"Yes."

I look over my shoulder for a hint as to how to answer this question. None comes. So I concentrate hard, pushing all the synapses in my brain to work together. Pushing toward a synchronized electronic buzz. I count to four. Like a brown blanket tossed over a fire, the world becomes flat. The air smells like ashes, molten marshmallow cinders.

"I'm a hustler," I say.

"You're kidding," he says.

"No." The flat place is wide and blank, and you can see for miles if you want to.

Mr. Laundry leans in close and whispers to me. "Can I ask you something?" I can smell the mint on his breath. The same Doublemint gum that my grandparents used to gave me in church, to make me stop squirming.

"Sure."

"How much for the whole night?"

The parade of spinning clothes pulsates behind him in a long syncopated line. I look closer at the squareness of his jaw and the stubble along his neckline. I want to touch his lips with mine, taste his tongue, smell him tomorrow on my fingers. "What do you want?" I ask.

"I've got five hundred in cash at the apartment. I'll get you more if you want it."

"My clothes," I say. He pulls some money from his back pocket and walks it over to the attendant. He talks to her in Spanish. "What did you tell her?"

"She's going to fold them and you can pick them up to-morrow."

"What a gentleman," I say.

"I do what I can."

"Do you speak Spanish?"

"A little." He opens the door and the cold air from out-side collides with the warm air from the dryers, blowing around runty dust-bunny tornadoes.

"You're not a serial killer, are you?"

"I don't think so," he says.

"You'll have to excuse him, he always does that." The dog, furry, brown, and dripping with slobber, nudges his face into my crotch.

"It's okay. I'm used to it."

He grabs the dog by his collar and tries to tug him away from between my legs. "He mostly sleeps all day. He's kind of old. Nine. I mean, pretty old for a mastiff." He scratches his shoulder, then his head, scrunching his face a bit like he's thinking hard. I can't wait to get my mouth on that tattoo.

"What's his name?" I say.

"Caleb. It means brave. Or victorious, depending on who you talk to." The dog laps at his face, covering his beard in drool. He smiles and kind of laughs. I'm going to have to kiss the mouth that just kissed Caleb.

"Right."

"It's stupid, I guess."

"No. It's nice. Fitting, you know."

Nervous again, I send myself to the place where everything is flat. The senses perk up, the vision clears, and the animal in you can float up to the surface. I'm sort of absently rubbing my dick, habit I guess, but it's not hard yet. I wonder if I'll be able to fuck him. I wonder if he wants me to.

"Yeah," he says. He picks up mail off the table, stuffs it under some junk in the kitchen. He snaps a dirty shirt off the back of the chair, like he's trying to impress me, and throws it into the bathroom where it falls onto the other heap of socks and underwear, a quiet lump. I sit down in a big leather armchair and open my legs. The leather feels like safety and goodness.

Caleb jumps on top of my lap. He weighs a ton. His paws are as big as my hands and some stuff drips out of his mouth onto my jeans. "I think he needs a bib or something."

"Sorry. Here." He hands me a towel that's only semidry. "You can wipe it up with this." It only spreads the goop around on my pants. "God, I'm sorry."

"Thanks. It's okay."

"You want a drink or something?"

"I don't drink."

"Smoke?"

"Or smoke either."

"Good, I hate cigarettes."

"Then why did you offer me one?"

"I don't know," he says. "I'm nervous."

"If I had said yes, would you have had a cigarette to offer me?"

"Never mind."

"So what's your name?"

"Aiden. What's yours?"

"Simon."

"Is that your real name?"

"Yes."

Aiden holds a knotted rope down near the dog's mouth, half playing with him, half talking to me, and Caleb slides off my lap. I wonder if he has bought sex before. Maybe.

"Well, I thought maybe you would use a fake name or something."

"No, just Simon."

"I guess not." He counts five hundred dollars in twenties and puts the stack on the table near the kitchen. He turns away from me as he counts.

"This is going to sound weird," he says.

"I've heard it all."

"No, I mean—are there things you won't do?"

"I told you I do everything."

"Because in *Pretty Woman* she wouldn't kiss on the mouth and stuff like that."

I laugh. "No. I'll kiss you on the mouth. That's fine."

"Sorry," he says.

"Stop apologizing." My dick is hard now, but I don't remember it happening.

He walks over to me. "What happened to your fingers?"

"Work," I say.

"Somebody did this to you?"

"No, I have another job that does this." I want to talk about medical records and files—maybe this would normalize the situation. Instead, this is what comes out, like self-terrorism, hijacking your own mind. And he doesn't push for anything more, so I leave it alone.

He kneels. He plays with my dick through the jeans and then unbuttons the fly.

"So, you're not going to beat me up, are you?"

"No," he says. "What gave you that idea?"

"You never know."

Next, we're in his bed and I'm naked. He rubs his hand up and down my whole body. I'm thrusting my cock softly and slowly into his mouth while he's got one finger in my ass. He feels like wet velvet. I lay my head back.

The flat place shrinks, pulls away first at the edges, begins to look a little like this room. The horizon bends to make doorways, and furniture appears. The burning marshmallow stink vanishes, leaving only the clean sheets, the hardwood floor. The change happens so slowly that I don't realize it's changing until it's different, the previous moment gone forever, and then I'm here. Right here with him.

The flat place echoes like a memory, its absence like a sickening déjà vu that amplifies the details, and the curious, gentle minutes spent with Aiden. If I wanted to remember them, could I?

Everything in the world is dissolving.

Aiden has his pants undone in the front. He jerks off and comes while he's sucking me, which isn't rare, really. After he gets his rhythm started up again, sucking harder on the upstroke and letting it slide on the down, I come. He takes his pants off and then the rest of his clothes. He lies down in the bed next to me and rubs his hand across my head where I'm sweating.

He closes my eyes with his fingers, then touches them, barely, to my lips. He pulls the sheets and blankets over us. I turn over onto my stomach and he reaches his arm around me. Aiden runs his thumb up and down my spine for a while.

Things settle and congeal. No noise. Only breathing. And the flat place is another country, inaccessible, a muddy Polaroid of a strange land where I once was.

I turn and press my face into his chest. I nuzzle my nose in the hair between his pecs, inhaling the moistness there. I burrow my head under his chin, both palms flat against his chest. I can't get close enough. Aiden bends his head down and kisses my forehead. His fuzzy chin tickles my face.

In the morning I get up and take the money off the table, taking only two hundred and fifty, leaving the rest—taking only my usual cut, feeling sort of bad about overcharging. Aiden is still sleeping, the sheet wrapped low around his waist, his shoulders spread out on the mountain of pillows. I stare down at the tattoo on his arm. A hollow hand, with a wheel of symbols inside—a tiny horse, a star, and a curvy line that looks like a river. Bluish green, smaller than I thought, and oddly soothing. I refill Caleb's water dish and let myself out.

Chapter Ten

Louis and I are watching television—something about people who used to be lesbians but who had sex changes and then became men who sleep with other men—I don't know exactly how this works. The reception comes in crooked and slightly off-color. The men, lesbian-has-beens, whatever, look green and pink and alien. It's just something to pay attention to in the morning, something that doesn't matter. Louis has poured wheat germ and flax seed on his cereal and he's wearing pajamas that I've never seen before. When he sees me looking at him he stops chewing.

"What?" he says. A dribble of milk escapes down his chin. He catches it with his sleeve.

"Flax seed?" I say.

Louis says, "Yes, it's good for you. And I found this Web site that will send you cartons of cigarettes on a weekly basis. And they charge it right to your credit card—well, I'm still charging everything to Calvin Klein. I wonder if they've moved someone else into the Tribeca apartment. I never paid the rent myself, you know."

"Where did you get those pajamas?"

"I bought them."

"I don't think I've seen them before."

"You don't see a lot of things around here." He keeps eating. The metal spoon clinking in the ceramic bowl rattles my teeth.

"What is that supposed to mean?"

"It means that things are different."

"What things are different?"

"Everything. Nothing. I don't know." He changes the channel to cartoons. Bugs Bunny is wearing a dress and trying to convince some other cartoon creature to fuck him, or something like that. Pooching his lips out and shaking his ass around in a blond wig.

"Talk to me, Louis." I get so impatient when he gets like this. "Why does everyone keep asking me if I'm okay?"

"You're different lately. Not in a bad way. It's still the same old you. You seem more, I don't know, something." He tips the bowl and drinks the last bit of milk at the bottom. Next, a Japanese cartoon is howling away in hyper speed. All the characters have the same eyes.

"Whatever," I say, and I get up and walk to the sink. There's even new silverware and new dishes.

"What's wrong with you?" he says.

"I don't know. Everybody's afraid I'm going to erupt or something. Like I'm somebody's drunken stepfather. I'm tired of it."

"Can I ask you something?" Before I have a chance to answer he asks, "What's bothering you?"

"Nothing."

"You're different."

"*You're* different."

"I was attacked."

"And what was I before? What was so different about me then? You're the one sitting around here buying kitchenware and pajamas off the Home Shopping Network."

"QVC, not the Home Shopping Network. There's a difference."

"It's all the same crap."

"Do you call that chair crap? The rug? That shirt you're wearing right now?"

"You bought this shirt off the television?"

"I hung it in your closet a few days ago. I knew you wouldn't know if it belonged there or not. What difference does it make anyway? You're wearing it, aren't you? Did you sit in the chair? It's very comfortable."

We're quiet for a minute, and I settle down into the QVC chair. It's not bad. The earth-colored upholstery looks like the soft side of Velcro. I rub my finger along the cushion and then sink back into it, like a memory. It reminds me of the soft brown leather of Aiden's chair. Which reminds me of the soft brown hair around his asshole. Which reminds me of his soft pinkish nipples and tender hands. Rough hands. Then I remember the guy who slobbered all over me and puked on the floor. One memory connects to another. You can link them forever, if you want to.

Louis gathers his breakfast dishes from the coffee table and sorts them in the sink. He turns around after a few seconds, walks over and opens the curtains, the new curtains, which are much darker than the old set, and the sun fills the room.

Suddenly, the tension between us is gone, and it's just plain old Louis and plain old me sitting around talking. As if whatever was disturbing and hard to talk about dried and faded in the light. I like this better. "Talk to me. I know it's coming. I can hear you breathing," he says.

"Louis—"

"Just say it, Simon."

"I was just thinking about this guy. We were fucking and he threw up everywhere. He took a lot of different things. Pills, mostly. I don't really know what. It was awful. He coughed and coughed and coughed. He said he thought he was going to be sick, and then he got sick . . ."

I stop telling the story.

Louis is at the window, clutching his side where his ribs were broken. For a second I'm lost in the memory of that disgusting guy throwing up and Louis vomiting in the hospital. Both feel too real. Or too unreal. It's like when you can't remember if something was a dream, or a movie you saw, or a story you read, or a radio blurb. The more you see, the more it floats away.

Louis holds his shoulders and closes his eyes. "Can I tell you something strange?" He sighs, like the sound you make before you try to explain something to a stupid person, which is, at the moment, how I feel. "When those guys were kicking me it helped me see what I am, in a way. It crystallized something. It was like a confirmation."

His words hang in the air a few moments. I look at the muscles in his neck, how they look so separate from the muscles in his chest. "You know I probably won't ever model again?" he says, looking at me.

"Jaron told me."

"My agent dropped me."

"But you look fine." I say this even though it isn't true. He's not as muscular as he used to be. His skin isn't taut and glowing.

"What can I say? Whether or not there are bruises on

my face has nothing to do with it. It's the business. People always want something new to look at."

"Louis—"

"Don't—" he says.

"I tried." My stomach cramps, and my hands feel so empty. "What the hell was I going to do? I was scared you were going to die, or they were going to kill us both. I wanted to—"

"No, you're not understanding me. I didn't expect you to help me. I know you couldn't have done anything. It's more complicated than that. Sometimes things simply are. Don't you see?"

"No, I don't see."

"They beat me because I'm a faggot. Call it by its right name. They busted my ribs because we're big flaming cocksuckers. It's as simple as that."

Then we sit quiet for a few minutes. The places where the sun touches the floor have become hot and when I hold my foot in one of the bright squares, it burns and feels good. For a second I think that the wood under my foot has become water and I feel like I'm sinking, my body dissolving in the brittle squares of light.

Louis breathes deeply, and long—like he's sleeping. I walk over to him and touch his shoulder. I don't mean much by it, but he holds my hand in his, changing it. What does Louis smell like? Branches, typing paper, copper. Metal buried in the earth for a decade.

He says, "I see them kicking me over and over. It's stupid. It's not like videotape, or a movie. It's not even a still picture, or a picture of a painting, or any of that. It's completely real." Something is fiercely awake in his eyes, pressing on his skin from the inside. "I want to forget it. I want to stop thinking about it. But I can't."

I glance out the window, hoping to see Aiden. The street is full of people. Tremendous baby strollers, men with cigarettes, children circling their mothers. I lean up against the frame of the window and stare right through my reflection. People are gathered around an ice cream truck in a long serpentine line, bodies of all different shapes and sizes. Someone for everyone.

Louis says, "What happened to that laundry guy you were stalking?" He pulls off his shirt, and the place where he was bound up is much paler than the rest of him. And he's lost a lot of weight. His pajamas hang loose on his hips and expose his pelvic bone, which looks like a drowsy slope pointing down to his cock.

"I had sex with him."

"For free?"

"No."

"Just once?"

"I hope not."

He leans his weight onto me, wrapping his arms around my shoulders, leaning his head into mine. Then he moves my hair out of the way, so it doesn't get in his eyes. There is a concrete pause between us, something you could touch if you reached out your hand.

We stand a few minutes together, looking out at the street below. The world passes by us, mostly unknowing, unaware. In the kitchen, I turn on the water and fill a glass, which is tinted blue and has spirals connecting at the bottom.

"Why the hell did you buy all this stuff?" I say.

"Everything was so boring."

"What happened to the old stuff?"

"I threw it out," Louis says.

I bring the glass to my lips. I miss my old plastic cups.

Chapter Eleven

These things happen when I'm lying on my stomach. Always when I'm lying on my stomach. Things come back into mind. Images, moments from the past. It's not terrible, it's simply a nuisance.

I was twelve.

He was sixteen.

We had been swimming.

There were lines on our thighs, the places where our swimsuits ended and our legs began, where our skin smelled like coconut suntan oil. We played Sunken Treasure, Sharks and Minnows, and sometimes, even though it wasn't allowed, we played Jump or Dive. One person gets up on the end of the diving board and, mustering up all the bounce he can, springs into the air. At that intoxicating moment when you're not going up, and you're not coming down, and the blues of the water and sky melt seamlessly into each other, the rest of the swimmers yell "jump" or "dive." You have to hit the water doing one or the other, whichever they yell at you. Midair you twist your spine or bend at the waist, hoping that by the time the water rushes over you, you're in the right position.

I liked him, and I wanted him to like me.

The days were longer.

We walked the long way home, past the green house with the broken mailbox, past the house with the fiberglass deer, past the place where they cut down all the trees and put up power lines. He told me the big metal structures that held the lines high off the ground were actually robot skeletons, left from a million years ago. They had immense battles—territorial armies in clumsy fight-to-the-death combat. After years of roaming and conquering, they died out, vanished. Their outer bodies decomposed and left the steel-frame skeletons to loom over future subdivisions. Then later, after electricity had been invented, he said, since there were so many of them, scientists hung the power lines up on their bones.

He had hair in his armpits.

I wanted to touch him there.

He smelled like chlorine.

We built mud and rock dams in the storm creeks behind his house. We cut out all the vines and weeds, using them to make thick green arches over the water. We found a forgotten birdbath basin and filled it with dirt. We mixed it with creek water and then added salt and pepper from disposable shakers we had stolen from fast-food joints. And when it was thick as concrete, we added pine needles, rotting leaves, broken bark, and grass. First we placed a line of long rocks across the water, then some mud, then smaller rounder rocks, then more mud. Over and over until the dam was high enough to make the water back up and pool out. It would hold for a few hours. Sometimes, if the water wasn't running too fast, it would hold overnight.

And once in late September, we built the rocks up so well that only the packing washed away. It left a heavy stone lattice across the widest part of the creek. He went on the other side of it to pee and I watched him tap the little drops off his dick, then poke it back into his underwear. The whole production must have only taken twenty seconds.

He was in high school, played basketball.

He tasted like sweat.

I met his sister, the one with Down syndrome, on Halloween. We were trick-or-treating and when we came to his house he ran inside to dump his candy. I was left under the yellow porch lamp with an eye patch, tiger-stripe bandana, and an eyebrow-pencil scar. She came to the door barefoot in a black sweater and black tights. Her face was covered in green makeup, and her hair was cut short and out of her face, her glasses thick and murky with fingerprints. She stood inside the house staring out at me. "I'm a witch," she said, and showed me where her teeth were missing. Then she smiled her goofy, crooked grin and crammed gobs of chocolate morsels in her mouth. We looked at each other for a long time. I tried to smile or wave back at her. But I just stood there, afraid she was going to open the door.

Last night I had the recurring airport dream. Maybe once a month this happens, if I'm stressed out or sometimes when I'm lonely. The airport changes—could be any place, any country—depending on what tricks my brain wants to play. But the rest of the story is exactly the same, right down to the cloud formations out the window, and the number of orange stitches torn out of the seat back in front of me.

This time it's Los Angeles International, and there's a man sitting next to me with one arm in a cast. We don't talk, just like usual, and I don't know him—even in the weird way you might know strangers in dreams. The plane starts to descend through the smog, blue fading into a rosy pink, then into the trademark yellowing haze. And I'm sitting there, swallowing hard, trying to correct the pressure in my ears, but all I can do is close my eyes, tighten my fist and wait.

That's it.

Then I wake up.

I always feel anxious and frenetic after, like I'm strung out on speed, unable to concentrate on the television, or the radio, or much of anything. So I stand in front of the closet for a few minutes, staring not so much at the clothes, but rather right through them, into the nothingness behind them, wondering how things got so out of hand.

Filing can remedy this. Sometimes. It's repetitive and mindless—or, I should say, it uses only the most basic of brain functions, which takes the load off somehow.

A pipe burst two floors above mine yesterday and this morning there is about an inch of brown, stinking water in the north side of the filing room—the whole place smells like the inside of an old tire. Since I'm already here, I take the new files from the basket and, careful not to slide around on the tile, organize them as usual.

One shelf is soaked, all the papers wrinkled and inky, maybe eight hundred incidents drenched from above and then left there wet and cold. The ceiling is torn open—wires dangling, insulation bursting out like plumes of cotton candy, and dripping, saggy plaster. Four or five files are laid open on top of the shelves, so they might dry out,

I guess. It's a futile attempt. The room is so moist even some of the clean files, even the ones six aisles over, are limp and wavy.

Near the epicenter of the incident—right under the ceiling injury—I pick up one folder and it falls apart in my hands, the weight of the water tearing it in half at the center. The forms inside go slapping into the puddle under me, so soggy that the writing has all bled away, and the crinkled edge is bright blue. The little boxes are empty, like they're fresh from Admitting. *Complaint,* it reads, and there are nine blank lines.

I'm walking by a door at one end of the filing room— this heavy metal door that's always locked—when I hear a voice on the other side: "So there are two cows standing in the middle of a field, talking to each other." It's a man's voice, Long Island accent. "And the first cow says, 'Did you hear about that awful mad cow disease that broke out down at the Henderson Farm?'"

Another voice, a smaller guy perhaps, whiny and nasal, chuckles in agreement. "Yeah," he says. "Okay."

The first guy, the bigger one again: "And the second cow says, 'Oh, I know, it's terrible. At least it hasn't caught on up here.' So the first cow says back, 'I'm just glad us ducks don't have to worry about it.'"

Dumb laughter, and the voices fade out, back into the buzzing of the fluorescent lights and the wet clunk of my boots on the floor.

I feel divided in half—one part of me wants to burst through the door, just to prove that I'm in here, that I'm not invisible, that what's happening on this side of the wall is completely ridiculous—all this water, all these ailments, all these human beings reduced to ruined, sopping paperwork.

The other half of me likes that nobody in that room has any clue who I am, let alone what I do in here, or what would happen, what would come gushing out if they opened this door.

And that's the quandary in everything—friendships, lovers, family, your entire life, the growing layers of electron shells. The question is: How much do you want them to know?

Another file has a torn scrap of notebook paper and jerky, scrawled handwriting, like the detailed, desperate work of a mad person. "I'm sorry," it says. "There is no way to express how much." No signature line, no way to tell who was apologizing, or for what. Perhaps the worst possibility is that the note was never delivered, or delivered too late. Maybe the note was a rehearsal—brainstorming for an important conversation, the kind people are having all the time in this place. Sometimes I think of all the whispering voices, and where they might go—up toward heaven, or somewhere else. Uptown, to China, to Mars.

There should be a better way to say "I'm sorry" in our language, this lazy busted-up American that everyone speaks. "I deeply apologize," people say—but that's so formal, so sticky with contempt that it makes my teeth hurt. There should be a sacred version of sorry, a word you save for when you are truly, incredibly sad, for when the amount of forgiveness required maybe doesn't exist. And you will instead have to bear the weight of that guilt forever.

If that word existed, I would say it to Louis.

Then, of course, only now do I find the note on the far door—the one that I never have any reason to use—that says for me not to come in while they "work to correct the damage." "Have a nice day," it reads, smugly. And other than the fact that the room looks like a field of World War I trenches, I manage to make it through the afternoon without any particular incident. And even better, I don't have to talk to anyone.

Chapter Twelve

The boys descend upon the house—DVDs, plastic bottles of orange soda, slick packages of red licorice twists, tubes of yellowed popcorn, stiff like bolsters. Farmer hands me three sticks, long skinny dowels, with clear bags of pink cotton candy tied to the ends, like something you'd hang in front of a slow donkey or a five-year-old with a mean sweet tooth. "They call this fairy floss in England," he says.

Louis says, "I like that better. Anything we make sound more gay, I'm for it."

Jaron says, "Darling, we've come to rescue you from your impossibility, from your dreamlike walk through this moment of shittiness."

The food fills Louis's lap. "What is all this stuff?" he says, like he's never seen popcorn before, like an old person who feels out of touch with modern things—then I think maybe he's actually surprised, and grateful. I'm not used to hearing him like that. "Wonderful," he says. "This is so amazing."

I say, "Jesus, guys, you could have called." I'm not really grumpy, it's just something I do. They see right through it.

Farmer says, "We brought movies."

I say, "*Hello, Dolly!*?"

Jaron says, "No, sorry to disappoint. We'll start with *Cruising,* that glorious picture where Al Pacino finds himself in a precarious position or two."

Louis says, "I've never seen it," already stuffing handfuls of popcorn into his mouth, crunching and swallowing.

I say, "Oh, *that.* Murders here and there, in the park, in bar backrooms. Great choice. Very topical."

Jaron says, "You know, I didn't even think. But Lois Lane is in it, and she's a real doozie, absolutely bonkers."

I say, "Yeah, she goes totally berserk."

Farmer says, "No, it's not Lois Lane, it's Marion Ravenwood."

Louis says, "Who is Marion Ravenwood?" Tiny white bits spray from his mouth onto his lap. "Sorry," he says, more spraying, and picking at his teeth with his fingernail. Sometimes he's such a mess.

Farmer says, "That was Karen Allen, from *Raiders of the Lost Ark.* Lois Lane was played by Margot Kidder."

Jaron says, "Well, who can tell the difference?"

Farmer says, "Karen Allen's face is rounder, and Margot Kidder is much more about the bone structure and the big doe eyes. Karen Allen is more motherly. You'd imagine her as somewhat solid, if a bit emotional. Margot, on the other hand, is fragile and, like, needs you."

Jaron says, "Are you serious?"

Farmer says, "What?"

Jaron says, "Listen to yourself."

Farmer says, "Whatever."

I say, "Is it true what they say about Billy Friedkin?"

Louis says, "What they say about who?"

Farmer says, "The director. They say Friedkin never gave any of the actors the entire script, so they were always wondering what was going on. Sometimes they didn't even know what was happening in the scene they were shooting, like, right then."

Jaron says, "What an asshole."

I say, "What happened to her?"

Farmer says, "Karen Allen? She teaches yoga somewhere in Massachusetts."

Jaron says, "How do you know that?"

Farmer says, "I read it somewhere."

I say, "If you saw her in this movie you'd never go near her yoga class, I can promise you that."

Farmer says, "She still works. She's had a long career."

Jaron says, "Well, that's nice to hear."

Louis curls plumes of cotton candy around his finger and pushes them down his throat. He devours a whole bag, and I can see him eyeing the second, probably wishing he could take the third and hide it somewhere in the bedroom. That would be weird. That would be like him. I wish one of them had called first, not because I'm annoyed, but I could have rearranged things. At this moment I'm supposed to be knocking on Mr. Bartlett's door, but now I'm late, soon to be very late. He'll forgive me. What choice does he have?

Jaron says, "What happened to Lois Lane?"

I say, "I think she started doing more television."

Farmer laughs, like this idea is a joke of some kind, like the word television is a punchline. He twists open one of the orange sodas, finds a glass in the cabinet, and pours, sticking his finger down into the foam at the top.

I say, "Why do you do that?"

Farmer says, "I don't know, it makes the fizz go down." I look over at Jaron, who rolls his eyes.

Louis says, "I could eat this stuff all day," meaning the cotton candy. "I mean you're eating, but you're not really eating anything, it just disappears, like, vamoose." His teeth are pink; he looks like the kids I used to see around my neighborhood back home, the ones whose mothers gave them plastic cups of cheap fruit punch bought in store-brand gallons. The whole block would light up with that particularly seasonal red grin. "What else did you get?" he asks.

Farmer says, "*Aliens*!"

I say, "Oh shit, really?"

Farmer says, "Yes."

Jaron says, "We figured you needed a little awesomeness. And who better to express the purest, most elemental awesomeness than—"

Louis says, "Sigourney Fucking Weaver. I haven't seen this in years."

I say, "I used to watch this on cable television when I was a kid."

Louis motions to the chairs. "Pull these around," he says. I wonder if he's hurting right now, if something in his chest is bothering him, the way he isn't standing up. He wouldn't say anything if it was.

I say, "I hate to tell you, but I can't stay. I have a thing."

Jaron says, "Oh, come on."

I say, "Really. As much as I would love to hang around and eat fag candy, or whatever, I can't stay." Farmer and Jaron start moving the furniture—twisting the TV around so they can all sit and watch.

Louis says, "But you—"

I say, "Or watch creatures burst out of chest cavities—"

Jaron says, "Oh, way to ruin the ending, Simon."

I say, "Sorry. If I had known you were coming . . ."

They glare at me, Jaron's eyebrows tilting down, Farmer looking a bit lost. Louis just stares. I put my keys in my pocket, tuck my hair under the brim of some hat that Louis got from doing some job for someone, and head out. I turn around and see them there for a moment, in the glow of the screen, settling in, narrowing focus, together.

Mr. Bartlett arrives at the door in a three-piece suit. He looks very pressed and clean except that his hair is not fixed, and his eyes are glassy and dark. I think for a moment that inside the deep, blank sockets he has no eyes at all. Despite all this he seems alive and alert. There are lots of candles lit and his place smells like peaches, cinnamon, and German chocolate cake all at once. The purple envelope is on the table.

"Simon, dear, would you like a glass of water?" He combs through the cabinets like he doesn't know what's in them—and it occurs to me that he might not. His hands pass over spaces where dishes, plates, and wineglasses should be. Instead, there's nothing.

"No thanks, I'm fine."

"Well, how are you these days? Been to see any good shows lately? You do go to the shows, don't you?"

"No. I don't get out much."

"Of course," he says. "A boy your age has very little blank space in his daybook. I'm sure it's easy for a boy like you to lose track of time." This is my punishment for showing up late.

"Yeah, sorry about that."

Mr. Bartlett says, "It's fine, Simon, I've already forgotten it." I'm hoping this will be the end of it.

"Did I sound silly asking you that?" he goes on. "About the shows?" All of this is less patronizing than it sounds. He means it sincerely. "In case you're wondering what that enormous white thing is, I had a service man come yesterday to put a new freezer in the extra room." He motions to the open doorway. The shiny new box switches on, humming and clicking. It's one of those horizontal opening things, like a coffin.

"A freezer?"

"I've decided that I won't do cooking every day anymore. Do you know what I mean? I won't do cooking for myself every day." The freezer sits against the wall, in the middle of the wall, not in the corner. There are two ficus trees on each side and he's hung a framed painting above it—a landscape that consists of mountains, trees, a lake, an uninhabited wooden shack complete with rusted tin roof. A place that could only exist in a painting. "Instead, I will cook very large portions and freeze them. For example, I might make a carrot dill soup that serves thirty, separate it into servings with this new Tupperware I bought"—he holds up some—"then reheat only the portion that I will be using. I will save time, and most important, money." His hands are trembling, and he smiles but it isn't real. It's like there are strings attached to his cheeks and someone has pulled them taut, showing his teeth, a marionette on display. "I've bought a cookbook entitled *How to Freeze Beautifully*. Now, doesn't that sound wonderful? That's exactly what I want to do, freeze beautifully."

I wonder if we're only going to talk today. That would be okay.

Mr. Bartlett brings two glasses from the kitchen. It's white wine with an ice cube. It smells awful, and the glasses are dusty at the bottom, who knows where he found them. I don't know what to do with it.

"What do you think of this foolishness?"

He means the attacks. I know this because since they began, gay men will say this kind of thing to each other, not saying much but knowing what the subject matter is. They exchange glances—not the way they used to, not interested in picking you up or checking you out. They want to know if, suddenly, you too feel a little bit like prey.

"I don't know," I say.

"Yes, I don't know either. I wonder why they're doing it."

"Because they hate us."

"Maybe so." Mr. Bartlett takes a deep breath; his hand passes in front of his face. He tugs at his hair and then his eyes run across the floor, up along the door frame, and then over my shoe. "Simon," he says, "do you think they'll come for me?"

"I doubt it."

"I don't really think so either. What do I have to offer them? I'm just a wrinkled old man. Rotten on the inside, surely." He pats his chest, soothing the fear, quieting the panic. "Now, my dear, I'm sorry for that. I won't speak of it again."

"It's okay," I say.

"Tell me something, how are your friends? Well, I hope?"

"They're fine." I stare into the glass, stare into the golden liquid.

"I feel as if you're not telling me the whole story."

"Really, they're good. You know."

"No, I don't know. You're not telling me something."

"They keep asking if something is wrong with me." There's a clock behind him, but the pendulum is stuck against the wall with duct tape. "Why did you do that to the clock?"

"I was sick of the incessant tick-tocking." He smiles again. "About your friends, what do you mean?"

"They keep asking me if I'm okay."

"And are you?" He doesn't look at me when he asks. He sticks his finger down into the wine and stirs the ice around. I do the same, and the water mixes with the wine in syrupy curls, the way air looks over a fire. "Are you okay?"

"Yes."

"Are you sure?"

"Yes."

"Then you have nothing to worry about. You can only trust your own instincts, Simon. Everything else is pretense. Your sweet little adorable stomach will tell you. Let me explain what I mean. I'm going to tell you a story about myself. Should I get you more wine before I begin or are you all set for now? It's not a very long story in case you are wondering."

"No. No more wine, thanks." I haven't even sipped it.

"When I was about your age, no, I was quite a bit younger actually, I was in love with an older boy. They're always older, aren't they? He was more beautiful than anything I had ever seen. He was taller than I was with dark hair and dark eyes. But, we were equals. He never treated me like I was less." The candles have mostly burned down and some wax has dripped onto the stout wooden chest. He uses his fingernail to pick at the drips while they are still warm and pliable. He molds little organic statues as he talks. "I was silly, you see, because he was not a homo-sexual." Mr. Bartlett makes the word sound like a scientific classification. "He was brilliant. I spent so many nights at his house, sleepovers and such. He would take a shower before bed, and I would lay my face down into his pillow. Just to smell him!

"But, what was I saying about the stomach? Here is the main point of this story. He went off to university. Which naturally meant he was leaving me. I was so racked with feelings for him that I thought I might, well, I don't know what I would have done. Then I sat down and wrote him a letter. I told him how much I loved him and how much he meant to my life, and it went on and on and on. I'm sure the thing was a rather bleak tome, and probably ridiculously young, do you know what I mean, young?"

"Yes," I say.

"He wrote back a truly touching letter expressing his sincere regrets that he was not one of us. He honestly did regret it, I think. He said the usual things. That our friendship wouldn't change, and we would continue on as if nothing had passed. Well, I knew that kind of thing would never be, but he almost had me convinced. He even quoted some of our favorite song lyrics. Oh, let me see if I can . . ." His words begin to float out and away from him, and he can't hold on to his thoughts. "No, I can't seem to remember." He sips the wine, desperately. It seems to help him focus.

"When he came back to visit me, the first time home from school, my stomach was in ruin. I was so nauseous. He hugged me and I thought I was going to vomit right there. It was the first time we had spoken since our letters. When he left I went directly into the bathroom and had diarrhea. Oh, dear, how embarrassing." He takes a long slow gulp from his glass and then looks over at mine, still full. "Simon, when your friends ask you if something is wrong, if something is bothering you, if you're okay, listen to your lower intestine." He smiles, and without opening his mouth much, he giggles. His eyes glimmer in the candle-light. After another mouthful of wine he gathers himself. "Now, did that story make any sense at all?"

"I understand," I say.

"Then let me ask you again. This time you can answer in a better state of mind, now that you've heard my story. Sometimes we only need to bring things to consciousness. Are you ready?"

He inhales, sits back slightly and then asks, "How are you doing?"

"I don't know."

"Try. Clear your head and then tell me. Be ruthless."

"I feel like I'm stuck in cement. Or I'm flying at the speed of sound over the fucking Grand Canyon."

"All those things, dear? All of them at once?"

"I can't tell the difference."

"One never can." Mr. Bartlett presses his hand hard into my knee. I don't want him to touch me. I want him to take his hand off. I jerk my leg away from him and set the wineglass down on the floor beside my foot. He looks star-tled. "Simon, am I pushing you too far? You've pulled away from me like I'm a scary old grandmother."

"I'm sorry."

"It's okay, I suppose. We'll let it slide this time."

I sit back and my foot tips the wineglass. It splashes across the floor and instantly seeps into the rug. "Shit, I'm sorry." I hear myself talking and apologizing. I hear Mr. Bartlett talking back to me and telling me that it's okay and that it will come out and that the cleaners will fix it, but I can't hear what he's saying either. The loud clanging opens inside my head. I try to go to the place where everything is flat, check out and stare into the horizon, but nothing comes. Why can't we just do what we always do? I wish we could just go to the stupid bedroom already and he'd tell me what he wants and I do whatever that is and then I can take my stupid money off the stupid table and go back to my stupid apartment.

More things Mr. Bartlett is saying: "It's okay. It will come out. The cleaners. Don't worry about it. The cleaners. The cleaners."

Then he stops moving altogether and shoves me down into the couch. I sit there stunned for a moment and then he sits across from me. The room has slowed. When I look down at the carpet to see where the wine has gone I can't clearly see the stain.

Mr. Bartlett presses his hands on my head, holding my face forward, focusing directly into my eyes, drawing us closer with his stare. He peers behind the clear surface and scans the front part of my brain. He's trying to find an answer in there somewhere. An explanation. I feel him prodding.

"Simon," he says, "do you know the word prestidigitation?"

"No." I feel his gaze latch on to something and begin to crop off the edges, clarifying it. A humming begins in the back of my brain, buzzing along my spine and shaking out toward my fingers. Blood rushing through the arteries, pulsing heavily through me.

"Do you want me to tell you what it means?" His eyes hurt like a scalpel.

"Yes."

"Magic."

"That's all?"

"Yes. Magic. Seems like an awful long mouthy word for something so simple, something so beautiful. Don't you think?"

A few seconds pass. Breath flows out of me, the vibrations in my bones slow. The pounding in my skull disappears.

And far in the distance, almost not at all, I feel something unlock, a door maybe. A tear in the surface, a tiny opening.

Chapter Thirteen

Aiden has fallen asleep in the chair with Caleb gnawing on the knot of rope at his side. He's wearing red boxer shorts and crisp white socks. The flap on his underwear isn't closed, and I can see his dick, barely. Earlier, before we were kissing and pulling off our clothes, he fidgeted around the apartment for a few minutes. He said he was looking for something. "Give me a second," he said. He went to the kitchen and brought a kettle full of hot tea and two teacups into the living room. "May I?" he said. As he poured he brought the cup down and then up again like a smart-ass waiter in a cheap restaurant. When I looked back up at him, his lips were on mine and he tasted like stainless steel—sweet and clean.

I'm sitting at the kitchen table, finishing the now-cold tea he poured hours ago. He stirs, and his hand falls lazily into his lap. His other hand is hanging slightly off the arm of the chair, waiting there. It's hard to tell if he's reaching for something, or laying it down. Caleb gnaws and chews, rubbing his gums against the twist of rope, until he is bored with it and lays his head between his paws. I smell my body, expecting it to be the smell of lube and spit, but it smells like nothing at all.

What am I doing here? When we fucked he didn't even come. He sucked me off and then lay his head down on my chest, rubbing his finger along my ribs, first with the middle and then his thumb. Then he ran his fingernail around the ring in my nipple. I shook from the sensation.

"Sorry, did I hurt you?" he said.

"No, I'm fine."

"You jerked away from me."

"No, I'm fine. My body hasn't calmed down yet."

"Was it good?"

I couldn't decide what to say—why do people ask that?—so I kissed him. He lay his head back down and drummed his fingers along my chest, nuzzling himself into my neck. "Can I ask you something?" He picked a hair out of his mouth, garbling the words.

"What?"

"Tell me what you're feeling right now."

"Oh, you're one of those, are you?"

"I guess I am." He smirks.

"I can't explain it."

"Try to."

"Listen, I'm not very good at this. Whatever I say is going to come out twisted and confusing and it won't be what I'm really feeling. So you should just take what you got."

"And what is that?"

"Me lying here naked." I didn't want to get into it—all the cloudy raging things in my head, all the reasons. I couldn't think right with his fingers touching me. And the smell of his hair. The taste of his brow.

Then Caleb tramped in and leaped onto the bed, lifting us both off the sheets momentarily. He lapped at Aiden's face and accidentally stepped one of his giant paws between his legs. Aiden wrenched his body in half, clutching his stomach. He moaned. Caleb slathered more drool on his hair and despite the stiff pain in his gut, Aiden began to laugh. Laughing and writhing and half-yelling at Caleb and laying his weight on me. I reached my arms around him.

"Fucking dog," he says. He turned over onto his back next to me so that we were staring at the ceiling.

"Can I get you some ice or something?"

"Caleb, boy, what are you thinking?"

That was a few hours ago, but it feels like a few months, a few dozen years. Sleep steals time like that, elongates moments, repeats them over and over.

Aiden sleeps quietly. I want to lay my head in his lap, but I don't. Everything starts screaming in my head when I try to think. My brain feels sugared in shattered glass.

Aiden is uncomplicated, soft, clean, painless—all those things. So I don't understand why, at precisely the same time, I want to place myself deep inside his body and also warp to some place where he doesn't even exist. I can't explain why I want him to put his hand on my thigh, then remove it immediately.

I walk over and press my mouth on his. His face smells a little like crotch, which seems sort of goofy and stupid. Caleb squints his eyes at me as I open the door.

Eight in the morning. Louis is already up and milling around in the kitchen. My bath towel is folded over the back of the chair. He must have been awake for a long while.

"Good morning," he says. I slide on a pair of blue pin-stripe boxers. They're the old-style short kind, and they make me feel like a geeky pubescent kid.

I run from the bedroom past the bathroom and slide with my socks. I glide swiftly across the wood and slam into Louis, who groans and yells at me with his arms full of bread dough.

"Ouch, dammit."

"What?"

"My fucking ribs, Simon."

"I'm sorry. I forgot."

"It's okay." He holds his hand delicately on his side, and then with the other flicks some flour onto my chest. "You're such an asshole sometimes." His hands are deep inside a bowl—giraffes galloping across a vaguely African savannah and those skinny trees that grow level on top. I wonder where he got that, if they sell them on QVC.

"Have some juice," Louis says. He offers me a glass. I take it. There're a few new appliances plugged into the wall behind the sink—ugly white chunks of kitchen convenience. I wonder what they'll do if I turn them on. The phone rings. We look at each other. "You're going to get that, aren't you?"

"I guess I am," I say. "Hello." I fiddle with the flap of the boxer shorts, a picture of Aiden flashing through my mind, and I kind of open it to look at my dick.

"Where the hell have you been? I tried to call you last night," Jaron says from the other end.

"Who is it?" Louis yells from the kitchen.

"Jaron," I say. He rolls his eyes and puts his hands back into the bowl. "Where are you?" I take another swallow of the juice, finishing it.

"Chelsea Piers." I can hear people laughing behind him.

"What the fuck are you doing at Chelsea Piers?"

"Batting cages."

I say to Louis, deadpan, "Jaron is at Chelsea Piers at the batting cages." Louis, equally amazed, stops kneading, and mouths "what the fuck." I cover the mouthpiece with my palm and say to him, "Jaron swinging a bat? You've got to be kidding me."

Chelsea Piers rests along the river at the end of Twenty-third Street. They've taken over five or six piers and built sports facilities on top of them. Something like three ice rinks, batting cages, bowling, roller-skating, tons of stuff. It's mostly hell—notoriously a place for straight people to go on dates, which is miserable to watch. (No wonder straight women are unhappy, look what they have to put up with. Look what they have to choose from.) But the driving range is pure heaven. It's one of those giant, stacked-on-top-of-each-other driving ranges, like you'd see in Japan, or somewhere equally modern and advanced. And if you stand out there on a not-yet-warm-enough-for-short-sleeves night, and stare up at the endless netting that keeps the drives from flying out into the river, you might think you've gone to a higher plane. It's a cage—like they might be keeping a dragon. And the light there is incredible, dozens of billion-watt lamps hammering down onto the fake green turf. The golf balls are launched into the empty space, fired like messages from the earth to the stars. And the whiteness glows like a dream. You can lose yourself. Forget all time. Probably just like heaven.

"Simon, are you there?" Jaron interrupts my train of thought.

"What are you doing there?" The events are all too incongruous. Jaron at the batting cages at Chelsea Piers at eight-thirty in the morning, at the end of November. It's a situation that only he could find himself in. The absurdity is ultimately appropriate.

"Why shouldn't I be here? It helps my stress level."

"Understood," I say. "What can I do for you?"

"Listen, I want to talk to you. I can't hit these balls like I wanted to, because of, well, I'll show you when I see you."

Louis is still looking at me. His arms are covered in flour and little ropey bits of dough. He looks absurdly handsome. Like a picture in a catalog that makes you want to buy what's being shown. Like a one-of-a-kind experimental car with someone sexy driving it. I don't mean to, but I smile at him. He turns his eyebrows in a funny shape, unsure of my grin.

"I just want to talk," Jaron says. "This afternoon?"

"Tell me where."

"Rockefeller Center. The tree is up. It's not lit yet, but the place is crawling with tourists. You'll love it."

"Okay."

"Gotta run. I'll see you there." The line clicks off.

I walk over to Louis and nuzzle my crotch into his butt, hugging him from behind, slight, barely there pressure. "Did you get me these boxers from the television? They're awesome."

"You look like a ten-year-old in them. I knew you'd like them."

"How did you know that?"

"I know." He scratches his nose with his shoulder. The air is moist with the simple smell of his shampoo, like fragile flowers, and the earthy tang of bread dough. "Want me to sew up the flap?"

"No."

"Are you sure?"

"Why?"

"Because your hard-on is sticking out."

Jaron was right. The tree is up, but it is not lit. People are crowding around it, taking pictures of each other, taking pictures and trading cameras. This one is a monster. I wonder where it was cut down, and what does that place look like now? When suddenly the tremendous trunk that held the ground together is sliced off the surface of the earth and carted into the center of town, what happens there? The empty space littered with wide-eyed animals saying, "What the fuck just happened?"

There is a little television repeating a time-lapse video of the tree being hoisted into place by a giant twinkling crane, with millions of tiny lights strung up its neck and along its massive metal belly. The video shows trucks backing up, beeping. A dozen heavyset men in oversize yellow gloves and cartoon hard hats, each too large for their heads, waving their arms in the air, like directing a plane to land, like calling the field goal good, a language of motions and signals. Cuneiform? Seraphim? Whatever sailors do.

There are some people ice-skating below, on perhaps the most famous skating rink in the world. The timid children reach their feet onto the shivering surface then dart across the indoor / outdoor carpet, squealing in delight.

I'm wearing a gray knit sweater and black leather coat that fends off the wind. I will not, despite the cold and the protests from Louis, wear a scarf. Scarves make me feel like I've been in an accident that involved a lot of whiplash. Or I'm some delicate statue that shouldn't move its neck much, locked into an uncomfortable but nevertheless healthier posture. The boxers Louis gave me seep out of the places where my jeans are ripped in little gray-blue stripes.

"Darling." Jaron emerges from the circles of chaos; the crowds part. "You're here. Some humdinger, eh? Did you see the movie of the erection?"

"What?"

"Don't get excited. I meant the tree."

Jaron sits beside me on the concrete bench. "I did see it. I love time-lapse photography." I sit up to adjust my pants and then I remember that my back pocket is stuffed full of soiled toilet paper sealed in a plastic bag. This guy on Central Park West asked me to save some for him, the same guy who stuffs hundred-dollar bills up my ass in his office. I suppose he'll want to do that, too. I like that okay. I can make a thousand bucks if I lie there long enough.

"Yes," Jaron says. "In time-lapse everything always looks so successful." He's wearing a thick black peacoat and clunky watch-out-here-I-come-and-I'm-a-big-flaming-queer boots. "Are you getting everyone presents for the holidays?"

"I haven't really thought much about it." Which is the truth.

"Well, you'd better rush out already. The lines will only get longer and longer."

Jaron wafts his hand around in front of us, a movement that's kind of talking with his hands, kind of batting away make-believe insects. "What are you getting Louis? Perhaps the lovely and seemingly everlasting Fruit of the Month?"

"I don't know. He's mentioned some movies he wants. Mostly Bette Midler."

"Figures."

"Or Joan Crawford, I think."

He moves a little closer to me on the bench, making room on the other side for a middle-aged man to sit. The man wears a smart brown fedora and a handsome, ample, kissable mustache. When I look back at Jaron his freshly shaved upper lip looks like a tiny wounded creature. "What does Farmer want? Only books, I suppose. Maybe I'll get him a huge dildo. Or a gargantuan set of fourteen-carat anal beads." Jaron laughs at his joke.

"Sounds inspiring," I say.

"What do you call those things for your nipples?" he says.

"Snake-bite kit."

"Right, of course."

The tourists float in and out of view, becoming one massive blur of windbreakers and bright white sneakers. The whole world is spinning violently around us, and we're here in the center, silly and excited.

"Maybe we shouldn't be so cruel," I say.

He fiddles with the buttons on his coat. "Oh, Simon, cruelty is all there is."

I laugh even though I don't think it's very funny. My instinct is to now apologize for screaming at him in the subway. Jaron and I are so infrequently alone, I feel like if I don't say everything that passes through my head I'll forget something. And I won't ever have the chance to say it.

Jaron nudges me. He cocks his chin forward, motioning me to look up. Above the tree, above the ice, above the crowd, an airplane has written in fast-fading smoke the words MARRY ME STEVEN. I wonder who and where this Steven person is, wonder if he'll answer yes or no, wonder how much something like that has to cost. Then there's a burst of excitement a few yards in front of us. Two men are cuddling together and one of them is pointing. I can hear them talking. "Honey, it's right there," one of them shouts. "Yes, yes, I'll marry you."

And that's when Jaron and I notice that this guy here, not Steven, not the one pointing, is blind. "It's right in front of us. Right there," Steven says, and moves his partner's head in the direction of the skywriting, even though he can't see it.

"How does it look?" the blind man asks.

"Beautiful. I love you," Steven says.

"Boy, that's faith," Jaron says. "I guess you don't hire a plane unless you're pretty sure they'll say yes."

"Sort of romantic," I say.

There is a chorus of well-wishers and happy people gathering around the couple. And I notice that people are quite glad to smile and wave at the older gay couple soon to be married (well, fake married, that is), one of them handicapped, and wealthy enough to buy a bit of skywriting over Manhattan. I guess certain kinds of gay people are nicer than others.

"What did you drag me out here for anyway?" I say. "You must have something up your sleeve."

"Ha," he says deadpan. He unbuttons his shirt cuff. "What do we have waiting for Simon behind door number one?" Jaron rolls his sleeve up, peels back a layer of gauze. He turns his arm over, laying his skinny hand in my lap. "Voilà!" he says.

It starts at his elbow, in the pale place where you test the temperature of baby's milk, and snakes down toward his wrist. A thick, purple wound. Sewn up with black thread that must feel like twine. The places where the torn sides of flesh meet pucker, wrinkle, and glisten. Jaron has sliced his forearm in half, a dark ragged stripe, elbow to wrist.

"Shit," I say.

"Please don't stare. I hate being the center of attention."

I pull him close to me and hide his arm with mine, like covering a tattoo you're embarrassed to show. As if through camouflage the damage might heal itself.

"Pitiful, isn't it? Could I be any less predictable?"

"When did you do this?"

"Oh, when? That's the strange part. I don't remember doing it." He knocks his elbow against mine like a hint, an inside joke. "I woke up and there it was. Mystery abounds. God, that sounds like something Farmer would say."

I feel stupid. Useless. Inept.

Jaron picks tenderly at the knotted threads holding his skin together. "Plus, I'm not eating, so it isn't healing. But I haven't eaten since 2001, so I guess that's no surprise. They did give me some Prozac, which is pretty common among cutters. I never take it."

"Does it hurt?"

"Not much anymore." The noise of the crowd rises, the laughing happiness, the horrible motion of Christmas all around us.

"You—"

"What are you going to say?" He laughs a little to himself. "I can't even kill myself successfully, that's what I overheard a nurse say. Don't they know this isn't about suicide? Idiots. You know, in high school I carried number twelve scalpel blades in my wallet. Or I'd burn myself with cigarette lighters, just when I needed a lift. What a bore." Jaron tries to make the moist cloud of his breath hover out in front of him in rings. He shapes his lips into a little circle and exhales. The wind carries his breath away from his face, like he might be driving fast, or riding a roller coaster. "One of the people in my support group was telling me about the way she erases her scars, so her family won't see them, but also so she'll have a fresh canvas for the next time. It's essentially the same technique rich women on Madison Avenue use to have their wrinkles undone. What do they call it?"

"Dermabrasion," I say, pulling the word out of nowhere. I didn't even know I knew that word.

"And can you believe this, this other guy in my group is convinced that his cutting is all some kind of autoerotic gratification. He said his cuts were supposed to resemble the female genitalia."

I say nothing.

He notices the little tears in my jeans and pokes his finger through into my thigh. "Enough about me, honey. Let's talk about you. Where did you get these shorts?"

"Louis bought them for me."

"I like them," he says.

"Me too. They're youthful, fresh, fun."

"Fresh my ass." Jaron tosses his coffee cup toward the trash can. It bounces off the rim and skitters out under the hooves of the crowd. "Shit," he says.

Winter arrives.

I'm walking home at almost midnight, there aren't any cars. My shoes make clean prints in the snow, crunching, that glorious, satisfying sound. When I turn and look to see where I came from I'm surprised to see how crooked I've walked—like a bug from one place to another, stopping here and there, gathering and depositing urgent information. The streetlamps cast a warm amber glow across the road and I can see the traffic lights change color in a line moving toward me. For barely an instant, when the lights are yellow and the streetlamps are yellow, everything is bathed in a golden glare. Even my hands look like they might be tinseled in bronze. I wonder how my face looks, if it too looks shimmering and young.

I asked Louis to shovel the sidewalk in front of the apartment while I was gone and he looked at me as if I had asked him to swear off masturbation. He hasn't left the house since he was attacked. He has everything delivered: food, clothes, everything. Now that he's discovered the video store will bring you anything you request, and come and get it when it's due, he's set. Last week he went through what Farmer and I call the "Lily Period." It was mostly old Lily Tomlin: *All of Me* (brilliant) and *The Incredible Shrinking Woman* (boring, except for that scene where she's in the sink). Before that it was anything with Bette Midler. He watched *Big Business* five times.

He won't smoke when I'm home because he knows that I don't like it. But the cigarette ashes in the coaster keep getting deeper and deeper. And now the windows have an inky film that won't come off.

If I open the door to go somewhere, or if I leave it open while I take out the trash, he stares out into the world, bleary and frightened. He even touches the mail cautiously, as if something poisonous is lurking in the credit card applications. He hasn't shaved in a long while and his semibeard, patchy in places, looks really sexy. He exercises as much as you can in a tiny apartment with no equipment (he can do some sit-ups and push-ups at this point, even though they hurt him). But he has lost most of his previous bulk. At least he still keeps his hair washed.

Louis's body was perfect. At the peak of his poster boy career, the shape of his torso was reproduced meticulously in clay and then turned into a bottle of fancy French cologne. Boite or Batik or something, I have a bottle of it somewhere. His face is the perfect blend of features—a hard jawline and soft, boyish nose. A little boy's beautiful eyelashes.

The snow is exquisite, especially as it falls—like a giant pillow fight in the sky, the flakes as big as half-dollars, bright and glittering like diamonds. As soon as the snow hits the ground, or I should say the pavement, it turns into a black slush that lingers for weeks. The city sends out the plows, which pile it up on corners, taller than people, dirty and spotted with street muck. And I don't know why people think that because there's snow on the ground they don't have to clean up after their dogs. Frozen dog shit everywhere, chunks of yellow ice. It can get pretty gross.

The winter sky is boring, it never changes. The sun rises and sets—still the same slate-gray empty. The buildings don't look majestic underneath it, the parks don't feel cozy. In July, when the sky is endlessly blue, the skyscrapers really do look like modern marvels of engineering, like the triumphs of man The History Channel says they are. In winter they stand there, cold and shivering like the rest of us. Big corporations string Christmas lights (always white) on the planted trees outside their entrances and hang red and gold decorations from the ceilings of their stark marble lobbies. Street corner planters are filled with white and purple "decorative lettuces," as Louis calls them, and that's exactly what they look like. Farmer says "ornamental cabbage." In summer the sky feels infinite and open, like you could take off into it. In winter it just feels like a lid.

Garbage freezes. Sidewalk life stops outside of everyone walking to work, walking from work. Instead of clumps of people, street sales, and hot chemical smells, the sidewalk becomes a vacuous place used only for transit.

Everyone stares into department store windows, pointing at mechanized polar bears and mechanized sledding children. People seem busier, more conservative. And having brunch at a restaurant seems not to last the entire afternoon.

Farmer likes winter. He likes coming in from the cold, in a thick woolly coat, to a steaming cup of coffee. He likes piling a bunch of people in a cab and hightailing it downtown for an open-mike night in a stuffy basement bar. Sometimes he reads when we go—and Farmer is amazing. The words spin off the page like from a catapult, on fire, lit for the enemies of his world. My favorite lines: *"And we talk of how anything is possible / because there aren't any words in this language / for anything that isn't."*

We used to have sex, Farmer and I. We even dated a little when we first met. Although I don't think either of us knew what we were doing. Everyone kept saying "Oh, and bring your boyfriend." By the time we got around to talking about it—making that an option—whatever it was, was over. Then we went for a while only fucking. He's a geek, but he's great in bed. Geeks are great in bed, because geeks have less at stake.

I'm staying busy. Mr. Bartlett has started seeing me more than once a week. He wanted to lay out a schedule so I could arrange my daybook as he calls it (never mind that I don't have a daybook), but he always changes his mind, says: "The last thing I want is for my life to be planned out like prime-time television. What's going to happen this season, what's going to happen next season? I'm too much of a reckless idiot."

That freezer in the middle of the room is starting to creep me out, all set up like a shrine. I'll come over and find him staring at it, glassy and content. We've had dinner out of it several times, which is fine, he's a good cook. If we're standing in the kitchen, he'll open the cabinet, reach for a glass, and say, "Simon, dear, fancy a dinner from the freezer?" Then he'll laugh, put his hand over his skullish face, and bare his beady teeth.

He talks more than he used to. He has always talked more than most, but lately he talks nearly nonstop. Sometimes we don't even have sex. He'll start telling me about whatever and practically take off. He does tell great stories. Funny things, stories he thinks will help me in some strange way or another. Sex stories, stories about himself, stories about New York before it got to be the way it is now. I don't mind the talking. If I see him in the middle of the day it gives me a break. A recharge.

Mr. Bartlett said to me yesterday, "Simon, do you wish to be happy?"

"Of course," I said.

He sipped his wine and swirled the ice around. "I don't mean happy like good weather or your favorite dinner. I mean the difficult happiness. Long-term. A rather blunt sort of happiness, I think." The clock on the wall, the one with the duct tape on the pendulum, now has tin foil crumpled around the hour hand like a swollen thumb. The second hand is bent, curving back out toward the world, drawing funny circles in the air. "You'll know it when it hits you. It hits you like a baseball bat."

"I don't get it," I said.

"You're sitting alone in a room, and you think you're feeling bored, but the more you feel it, the more you concentrate, you realize that you're not bored at all. It's the understanding that your life won't have any more surprises. You're settled." He folds the hem of his shirt down over his waist. "Sure, you may have friends and a job and

places to be in the afternoon, but that's it. Scary? No."
Mr. Bartlett looks down at his knees and rubs them together,
making little swishing noises with his pants. "Thank everything holy that there won't be any more surprises." Then
he sings, "Is that all there is?" He laughs and looks back at
me. "Yes. That's quite all there is." He winks. "But you've
got all kinds of years ahead of you before anything dread-
ful like that happens, don't you?"

Louis says that we're soon to see Mr. Bartlett with
firearms at the top of a clock tower yelling inappropriate
things at passersby below. Then he'll blow his brains out.
But that's not going to happen. When Mr. Bartlett goes,
he's going to go gently. And almost imperceptibly. Like
dropping a stone down a well too deep to hear it hit the
bottom.

Jaron says it's foolish seeing him so often. He says when
people are always giving advice you shouldn't assume
that, "A) You need it, B) They honestly care, and C) They
aren't quietly mutilating your psyche in the process."
Jaron's family is still sitting on the porch back in Indiana,
ready to set him up with the perfect blond housewife, expecting that at any moment he'll come tottering back. But
he won't.

Jaron moved to New York when he turned eighteen. He
lived with an arrogant Wall Street executive in his two-
floor loft for several years—a freshly shaved, thick-jawed
blond guy who treated the rest of the human race like shit.
Jaron's job was to lie around and look pretty, which he
does very well. Mr. Wall Street would take care of the rest.
Jaron was well liked among the ruling class—at any given
time he was sleeping with at least four of them. President
of this company, CEO of that one. They would buy him
away from Mr. Wall Street for the weekend, or however

long they happened to be in town. Once he vacationed in the Yucatan with some mucky muck from Focus on the Family. Mr. Wall Street was later jailed for embezzling several million, and Jaron was suddenly out of a job.

A year ago we were at JFK, waiting for Louis to arrive from London, and Jaron's brother passed us on his way to a religious retreat upstate. Jaron nearly pissed himself right there at baggage claim. Everything he had constructed collapsed in a few short seconds. All the questions were answered: Where have you been, why haven't you called. Then came the lecture about his mother. She misses you, she's lonely. Jaron stood there agape like a vegetarian in a sausage mill—you know this stuff is out there, but you never thought you'd have to look it in the face.

That's when we really started to notice his refusal to eat. He's been in the hospital twice in the last two years. There could be more episodes that I don't know about—and I won't know until the files appear. There are weeks where I don't see him. Months when he doesn't return phone calls. His closet is full of turtleneck sweaters.

Farmer thinks we should haul it all out into the glaring wide open—the cutting, the anorexia, a giant intervention. You know the type: Everybody sits in a circle and tells Jaron that we love him and we think he should stop. Then we empty out a garbage can onto the floor in front of him, show him the razors, the pins, hoping that the sight of all his mutilating tools out in the open might shock him into quitting.

Of course, this kind of thing would never work. He'd fade away into another dimension behind his thick black sunglasses and not say a word. He'd listen. He'd nod. He'd be very patient while we made fools of ourselves.

And the times when Jaron actually tells me that he's

landed himself in the hospital, I don't do anything except listen. I don't bother to ask why he does it, or when he does it, or how, or what would make him stop. I know that I'm not supposed to ask, it's the kind of arrangement he prefers. Because, after all, he continues to tell me about the biggies. And he never tells Farmer.

Yesterday I had an appointment with a disgusting mackerel-mouthed man, who smelled like wet cardboard and sour leftovers. He shaved my chest and my pubes and around my asshole—a pretty common request in men from New Jersey. Then he spread Icy Hot all over my crotch so it burned hysterically and when he raked his teeth along the place under my balls I swear he was going to chew them right off. He didn't really fuck me, he sort of poked at my ass with his dick. Was that boring or what? I tried to dissolve into the sheets, fade into the dried stains already deposited in obscure and complicated patterns.

I've seen Aiden a few more times. Each time he wants me to stay longer than before. He cuddles against me from behind and kisses my shoulders until I'm asleep. Sometimes he doesn't kiss me, he just touches his lips to my skin, which is really better than a kiss. He'll rub his thumb along my brow and press his half hard-on along my bumpy spine. I'll ask him if he wants to fuck me, or if he wants me to suck him off. He'll say, "Just because my dick is hard doesn't mean that I want to come," which is something I completely cannot understand.

I can't remember much anymore. Only smells. (What does Aiden smell like? Fresh-cut wood and spearmint.) I can't remember the simple look of something. Never the way a hand might stretch. Never the feel of something. An eraser on my skin. The bluntness of metal. My brain is missing its gray matter. The soft liquid that holds it secure and upright has dried up. Or perhaps it's dripping out of my ear. I feel like my central nervous system has morphed into a little jack-in-the-box in sickly sweet colors. Someone turns the crank, the cords strung tighter and tighter until the universe explodes, ugly and grinning.

I feel strange sexual pressure. Every man I pass has become a sexual option—violence can make you very horny. I have an incredible want for men I don't know, men I pass on the street, straight men I bump into on the subway. I don't feel the pressure in my crotch. I feel it higher, around my mouth and in my jaw.

I want to taste them. I want to close my teeth around their biceps. Mostly to prove that they're real, and that I'm real. I need to feel the tightness of knuckles around my face. Cram my head against their chests and listen to the unusual sounds inside—their stomachs humming and griping about what they had for lunch. I want my palms flat against their bodies. To make sure that they're whole and human. To make sure they don't dissolve, evaporating into billions of weightless carbon and oxygen particles. Hold them down, so they don't float away.

Chapter Fourteen

I meet Aiden on the corner by the Chinese food place that serves the best dumplings in the known universe—possibly the unknown as well. His choice. We debate as to whether we should eat there, among the steamed-up windows and miscellaneous meat (duck? pork?) hanging on metal rods, or at his apartment where, inevitably, Caleb will finish what we can't. Or don't. We opt for take-away.

"I'm going to get some beer," he says. "And I have to stop at the bank." Sometimes they say this resentfully—about the bank—even though *they* called *you*. But Aiden says it plainly.

He moves through the heavy plastic flaps that dam up the warm air inside the store. Then straight to the back, opening the sliding glass doors and selecting an imported six-pack of bottles. Thinking that he'll hand me something to carry, I step forward as he opens the door, and he actually bumps into me. I can feel him underneath the coat and scarf and sweater and shirt. My body remembers him. My mouth. As we walk, I think about peeling the layers off, skinning him.

Then we arrive at the bank. The brightly lit room shows the redness of his cheeks and the pink of his nose. While he waits for the money to slide out of the machine, he turns to me and smiles. "No receipts!" he mouths to me, and then pretends to smack his forehead. He looks stupid and cute. He steps away from the machine after folding the bills into his wallet. A headline in the stack of newspapers catches his eye and he pauses to look more closely at it. I watch his face. It's something he doesn't understand, or can't make out—probably something horrible. He leans in, picks up a torn piece of the front page. Then I really see him. I see him confused, all the cogs grinding in his head.

I wonder if I'll take the money that he just stuffed into his wallet. Or if this one I'll do for free.

"All done." His arms full of beer and Chinese food, he manages to get keys out of his pocket and unlock the door. Caleb shakes his slobbery face, pawing at the floor near Aiden's feet.

He hands me the bag. "Get plates and stuff." He bee-lines to the bedroom and then into the bathroom. With the door cracked I hear him pissing.

"There're plates already in the bag here," I say.

"I don't like the paper ones," he shouts over the toilet flushing and the noise of the faucet. I get dishes out of the cabinet and lay two plates on the table. "And I hate that plastic silverware. Can't cut a damn thing," still shouting.

"Okay." I place a fork and knife beside each place, and I line up the bottoms so it looks even. The fork I put at my place has one tine missing, so I get another one to replace it.

"Let me feed Caleb," he says, coming out of the bathroom. As he passes me he leans his face over to mine and kisses my mouth. He does it so suddenly that I'm not able to kiss him back. The taste on my lips after he's gone is sweet like toothpaste and I wonder if he brushed his teeth while he was in there. Mouthwash?

"Dinner. Come on." A few seconds of silence. Then the clinking of dog food into the bowl and the heavy steps on the linoleum. Then the pressure of his hand on the small of my back. And the closeness of him against my hips.

"Sit," I say. And he does.

"How is your roommate?" He stuffs a dumpling, still steaming, into his mouth.

"He's afraid to go outside. He's not really my roommate. He's just staying with me awhile. I think."

"Why is he afraid to go outside?"

"He was attacked by those gay-bashing jerkoffs. They broke a few of his ribs. That's all, basically."

"Shit. That's terrible."

"Yeah. Motherfuckers."

"Did they catch anybody yet?"

"No."

"They probably aren't trying too hard."

"Yeah."

"You don't sound very upset about it."

"Sorry." I realize that I don't really know how I feel about Louis. I don't really know how I feel about the whole situation. I only know that I feel helpless.

"Don't apologize," he says, his mouth full of moo shu pork. A drop of plum sauce drips out onto the back of his hand, onto the place where the hair from his wrist changes to fine and light.

"He used to live in Tribeca. I brought him to my place when they released him. His underwear contracts fell apart—"

"You live with an underwear model?"

"Yes."

"Does he have a big cock?"

"Aiden—"

"I'm kidding, kidding." He holds up both hands, palms out. Then he pops another dumpling into his mouth. He leans the chair back on two legs. "Really."

"Did you see that huge Calvin Klein ad in Times Square?"

"The one with the monkey and the kayak?"

"That's the one."

"That's him?"

"That's his crotch, yes."

"You can see his dickhead in the picture," Aiden says.

I spread the brown-purple sauce around on the pancake. "He can't work out like he used to. His abs aren't that ripped anymore. And his thighs aren't quite so skinny. His ribs are okay, though. The bruising has healed." Aiden hunches over his plate like a hawk guarding its kill. He wipes the side of his mouth with his finger. "Or maybe he doesn't want to work out anymore. I don't know. It's all very confusing."

Aiden reaches for a fortune cookie. "Here, let's do these." He starts to tear open the plastic wrapper.

"Wait, there are rules to these things," I say.

"What are those?"

"You can't choose a cookie for somebody else. And you can't read them out loud. You can pass them over, but you can't read them out loud."

I take one and crack it open. The sweet crumbs dust my fingers, and the paper feels cool and ancient. It says: "What is hidden in an empty box?"

Aiden reaches his hand out, and I pass him the bent fortune. He reads it. "Yeah, mine is just as shitty." Aiden's fortune says: "You will have an opportunity, if you wish to." I smile at him. When he smiles back his teeth line up like little squatty football players. "Want something else to drink?" He gets up and walks into the kitchen. He hitches his jeans up onto his hips and pulls his shirttail out. A fuzzy brown fan of hair splays out on his lower back, gathering together and disappearing.

When he comes back to the table, he's holding a cold can of Coca-Cola and an empty glass. I lean my head down and kiss his wrist. He smiles that goofy smirk. "What was that for?"

"Want to go to the bedroom?" I say.

He stands up and moves toward me. He unbuckles his belt and unbuttons his shirt from the top down. I kiss his belly button. I lick his cock through the moist cotton, and he tucks his thumbs in the waist of his underwear and pulls it down, his balls pulled tight against his body by the elastic waistband. A grunt oozes from his lips, sticky clear stuff already dripping out of him. Our bodies curl together on the floor. I get on top of him and put my cock inside, both of us swaying in one solid motion, him pressing back into me more than I'm pressing into him. His mouth tastes like ginger. And I come.

"Are you going to stay over?" he says. "I want you to stay over."

"Okay. I can."

"You're all cut up again." He pulls my hands to his face and kisses my fingertips. "Does that hurt?"

"No, I'm used to it."

We move into the bedroom and I get him off with my mouth.

Christmas comes, goes. Gifts were exchanged and, pleasantly, we all got something that we really love. Farmer gave me a book about the history of the subway from its initial ground-breaking about a hundred years ago to its current urban marvel status today—tons of dense history. He gave Louis a set of Provence-inspired dessert plates, which was exactly what he asked for. He got Jaron a leather case for his sunglasses. I thought it wasn't that great a gift, but Jaron loved it.

Jaron bought all of us museum memberships. Mine to the Museum of Modern Art, Farmer and Louis to the Guggenheim. He told us that we were seeing far less art than a person in New York should. It was a nice thought, but I can't see myself at the MoMA, among a sea of black clutch purses and landowners with pocket watches. Unless they did some kind of Georgia O'Keeffe retrospective. Because I love to see the jet set staring up at incredibly beautiful paintings of vaginas disguised as flowers and bobbing their heads up and down. Actually, I did see a few things there that I liked: Jackson Pollack, something Picasso that wasn't paintings, something French and blurry, but nonetheless good. In the gift shop you can find the entire collection reproduced on umbrellas, coffee mugs, stationery sets, magnets, sweatshirts, mousepads. Jackson Pollack cellular phone covers.

Louis, apparently, has taken up knitting, since Farmer and Jaron got scarves, and I got a hat. It was all a great surprise. And I imagine that there's nothing more hilarious than Louis chain-smoking, watching Montel Williams lecture some unwed teenage pregnant girl, while muttering "bastard" out of the corner of his mouth and knitting a long, twisted clump of yarn that eventually stretches out into a scarf. Like a freak show of a grandmother. Like a freak show of himself.

I bought Farmer some poetry books he asked for. I

couldn't say what they were, I didn't recognize any of the names. He gave me a list. I took it to the bookstore and handed it over. The guy walked up and down a couple of aisles—reminded me of my job, actually—and came back with a few choices. I picked two of them. Louis wanted more dishes, so that's what I got him. Tomatoes and garlic painted onto the bottoms of the bowls, very Italian look-ing. We ate Thai food out of them. I got Jaron a book about homosexuals in the Holocaust. He loves anything pink triangle. This book he swore he hadn't read before. I read the one chapter where the prisoner gives an SS guard a blowjob for extra bread.

The N train is mostly empty. The man sitting across from me stares down at his palm, where he's tapping the flashing red buttons on an obnoxious electronic poker game. Everyone in this car curses him under their breath, glares at him with their tired eyes. The clicking of a slot machine's tumbler, the high-pitched beeping of five cards turning up, he keeps three, throws away two. Clicking again, two new cards come up. He loses, cusses under his breath. Somebody holds the door open at Fifth Avenue, yelling at somebody else on the platform, making a plan to be in touch later. The conductor over the intercom: "Stand clear of the closing doors." Then everyone's eyes up at the door-holding guy. The conductor again: "Gotta let those doors close. Come on, man, let 'em close."

Then, later, this guy takes his shirt off and pushes my head down onto his nipple. I suck on it for longer than I want to because he keeps pressing my head down and I think that he must want me to bite down the way he's holding me there. So I bite down and he just squeezes me harder. He takes the dildo from the foot of the bed and stuffs it up his ass while I play with my dick. He fucks himself, watching me. He doesn't tell me how fast to jerk off, so I have to guess. I eventually figure out what he wants and this goes on for a while until I tell him that I'm ready to come.

First there is the magnetic buzzing of machines and the clanging of wooden spoons on metal pans, but I suck air through my nose again, forcing myself lower into the flat place. Distance, I'm thinking. Get some space between you and everything else.

He lays me on my back and sits on top of me with my dick up his ass. He pumps up and down really rough, hurting my hips, but my dick feels good. I won't be able to hold off much longer. He grabs my hand, rubs it on his chest and stomach, licks my palm, and sucks on my wrist. I start to feel the warm tingle deep between my legs. He pushes my fingers into the back of his throat and rubs them against the slimy tissue there. And I feel his throat clamp down on my fingers and his ass tightens on me like a vise.

His body heaves, spurts. Watery and clear, hotter than mine, all over my stomach. I close my eyes, hold my tongue to the back of my throat trying to reduce the stink in my sinuses. I start to come. I grind my teeth.

And far away, that small rip in the fabric of the sky appears, moving closer this time, exponentially, like shifting lenses on a microscope. Then the rip bulges and a drop of clear fluid seeps out into the flat place. And from the other side, a finger pokes through—pink, healthy, and wet with life.

Chapter Fifteen

"What do you think of this eggplant? I don't know how to tell a good one from a bad one." Mr. Bartlett holds up a bulbous purple vegetable, bloated and ripe, his other hand resting on the handle of the grocery cart. He turns the other side toward me, and then peeks his face closer to mine, as if he were whispering a secret. "What's that thumping business? Not for eggplant, right? Only melon." He smells the stem end. Then I notice that he's wearing eye shadow. His hair is tied up in a lime-green rag that hangs down to the middle of his back, where it splays out into a fringe with pink beads. His fingernails are painted green to match the rag. Fuzzy house slippers tie-dyed pink and green. White pants and a white T-shirt that says JESUS IS COMING, LOOK BUSY. He's folded all our coats, gloves, and hats into a woolen mound at the bottom of the cart. All the food piles up on top of it. None of this really bothers me, how he looks, I mean. He does what he has to do to get up and out in the morning, right? Besides, nobody looks at us funny. Maybe he does his shopping here all the time, and the bagboys are used to freakish Mr. Lime Rag drifting through the aisles smelling the stem ends of egg-plants. People probably think he's my father or something. Grandfather?

"I don't know," I say, meaning the eggplant. "I think as long as it doesn't have any yucky spots on it. Maybe you could thump it. I don't know."

I filter through the zucchini, bagging several, the ones that look the firmest, healthiest. But I don't know what I'm doing. I haven't bought a vegetable in months. Glow-ing red radishes are bunched up against yellow squash, tiny blue rubber bands announcing that they're completely, one-thousand-percent organic—only they're almost rot-ten. And I know that they're not as perfect looking as the ones that aren't organic, and we're supposed to forgive this about them, take what nature alone gives us—but who wants half-rotted vegetables, organic or not? I toss some radishes in the cart even though Mr. Bartlett didn't ask me to.

He likes the planning and shopping more than the eat-ing itself. It's true—he does make a carrot dill soup that serves thirty, only he never eats but about six servings. The rest lies in the freezer until further notice. Dozens of plas-tic baggies in carrot-orange, split pea, tomato. He sug-gested last week that he might want to buy another one, another freezer. If he had his way the whole fucking apart-ment would be filling up with freezers.

"Simon, be a dear and get me some celery." Mr. Bartlett motions toward the piles of stalks. "Celery is wonderful. And, in fact, if you wrap it in aluminum foil, it will last for weeks in the cooler." I hand him the celery; he tosses it into the cart, where it lands on top of onions and ginger root. "You know, I was meaning to ask you, would you

like to go to a show with me? I have an extra ticket because of my subscription. I don't even know what it is, to
tell the truth." He blinks his beady eyes at me, looking
pitiful, but not too much more pitiful than normal. "Oth-
erwise, I'll feel like I've wasted all sorts of money."

"Sure." He'll pay me for the time spent.

"Oh, wonderful." He slides past me smiling, his head
bobbing up and down like a dashboard toy. "I really
thought you'd probably have plans. A boy your age usually has lots of plans." His face elongates, his eyebrows
rise.

The grocery store radiates light like a giant magnesium
experiment. If we weren't used to the excessive use of fluo-
rescence, we'd think the place was toxic. Because something about grocery stores, I think, is anti-human nature.
Some Cro-Magnon gene in us is never quite satisfied by
the tall shelves of boxes, anything that comes presliced,
this place where people come only to take things away.
And no one bothers to worry about how everything is
shrink-wrapped in plastic. Or coated in wax. Or whatever.
It's almost as repulsive as the organic stuff.

Mr. Bartlett is hovering over the lettuces. He holds one
red leaf and one romaine, balancing them in each hand, as
if to judge which is heavier. He chooses the romaine, and,
turning toward me, points vaguely in the direction of
potatoes and garlic. I gather up some of each, not really
knowing what I'm supposed to be doing. But it's not like
he's going to get mad at me for getting too many potatoes,
or too few. He doesn't even know what we're shopping
for. Everything is a grand experiment.

I walk over, dump the stuff in the cart, and we move on,
out of the veggies and into the aisles. I pass a pyramid of
creamed corn, and Farmer loves creamed corn. I put a can

in the cart, the store brand, then another, figuring I'll hoist them out later when Mr. Lime Rag and I are putting things away in his kitchen.

"Simon, dear, tell me, how are things with you lately?" I knew he was going to ask this. He always asks. "How are your friends? I think at our last conversation there were some things that you were trying to deal with. Am I wrong?"

"No, things are okay." In theory, I don't mind talking about it. However, when Mr. Bartlett and I drum up this subject I never can quite articulate what I'm feeling. The language comes out wrong. More so, it's that I never really understand what he wants to hear. When I'm sucking somebody's cock and they say "more on the head" or "suck my balls," at least that way I know exactly what they're looking for. But with Mr. Bartlett and these little how-is-Simon-feeling conversations, I have to guess. I never know if this is some kind of role-play fantasy in which he helps me with my problems while secretly getting his rocks off, or if he's making small talk.

"You know, same old stuff." I say something that means nothing.

"Of course," he says. "Same old everyday."

"You got it."

"Because since we talked last, I thought of another story that might help a young person." He pushes the cart past me, an offensive move that means if I'm going to hear this story, if I'm going to get my hundred bucks, I'm going to have to run after him. Behind him the air smells of lavender.

I walk quickly along, catching up to him before he turns the corner.

"Yeah, okay, let's hear it." He looks at me funny. I wonder how much my impatience shows.

"Let me see. I'm going to tell you about a love I once had." Groan. How many times do I have to hear about his unlucky-in-love melodramas? "He was a good twenty years older than I was. And I was just your age. Perhaps a bit younger, at twenty-one or twenty-two."

Periodically, between sentences, Mr. Bartlett reaches into the shelves, picks out a food item, and lays it gently in the cart, which is filling fast. "We made love a few times. And we lay in bed all night and talked about the silliest of things. Things that were, oh, what's the word? The word for something that has no answer? You know, a topic you could go on and on about but never reach a conclusion?"

"I don't know." Now I'm pushing the cart behind him as he zigzags from left to right and back again.

"Well, whatever those subjects are called." Mr. Bartlett pauses a moment, bleary and sick with confusion. His eyes wander across my face, my torso, the tiled floor, the stacks of canned goods, like a neurosurgeon is working in his brain, pressing on the specific spot that is supposed to remember that specific word. Mr. Bartlett is at the unfortunate mercy of a whole load of unseen forces. Something passes over him, a consciousness, and he returns to the world. "Where was I?"

"Topics of conversation."

"Oh, yes! Topics of conversation. We talked about what made people homosexual, what was the purpose of art, what was the very nature of humanity. Timeless things. Subjects that become all the more romantic when spoken of in the afterglow of a wonderful sexual experience. You know, topics that might be dissertations at Harvard, or Yale, or places of that sort."

Parmesan cheese in an aluminum green can, tomato sauce, tomato paste, stewed tomatoes, all of it goes down into the cart. What the hell difference does it make? Another can of cheese. "Planning a lot of pasta nights?"

"One can never have enough tomato products. I use them in everything." He cuts his eyes at me, upset that I've interrupted his glorious and educational speech.

"Oh."

"He had not a hair on his entire body, except for the natural places, of course. This was before everyone started shaving everything off, before everyone started trying to look like twelve-year-olds again. He was not a boyfriend, nor a date, but an affair."

"A summer fling." I push the cart along. We turn the corner, facing a long pink row of meat.

"No, it was the dead of winter. I remember so clearly because I wore this skimpy little shirt thing under my coat because I knew I looked good in it. I suffered through that awful New York cold so that I would look attractive. Can you imagine?"

"I can imagine."

We move on to the cereal aisle, Mr. Bartlett walking ahead of me like something rejected from the Rose Parade, slow, flirtatious and excessive. Cartoon animals with fruit-shaped eyes, cheerful and toothy, wait next to Olympic champions, promises of hidden toys, and mail-in offers. Sad plastic bags of vaguely named, unbranded wheat puffs, or rice crisps, or fruit wheels line the bottom shelf, sagging like flounder, some bursting. Along the top shelf, cellophane-encased conglomerates of tiny cereal boxes.

He flips the frayed end of his do-rag through his fingers. "Of course, in my head I built it up to be this great soul mates kind of operation, and if it weren't for the horrible constraints put upon him by his family, and his job as a film actor—our society at large—we would live and love forever in a cramped but comfortable apartment in the West Village." Then he stops talking. His face glazes serious. In the meat section, he reaches for a plastic-wrapped Styrofoam plate of beef chuck and holds it out at me. "And then do you know what awful thing happened? Can you foresee the awful series of events that are about to unfold?" I drop the chuck onto the cans of Parmesan.

"He left you."

"Not exactly. I mean, yes, he left me. But that was part of the whole thing from the beginning. It wasn't the leaving that was so terrible. When one is left by one's lover because of a social situation, one can curse the whole world and take on a hermit's appearance. It offers a great advantage."

I'm watching a Latino kid carry crates of milk down the aisle. I'm watching him rub his nose on his sleeve, watching his gloved hands grasp three gallons each. The pale curve of his bicep and the snarl of his lips as he lifts. "So, what happened?"

"Later on, it was practically months later, I found out that in the same period of time that he was sleeping with me he was sleeping with this awful creature that I knew sort of through some other people. Actually, I'm not sure if it was the same period or not. I heard from someone that it was, and even then it was only rumored. So, potentially, all my self-loathing and my head-over-heels business was for nothing, which is sort of the point of this story." He straightens the rag on his head, patting himself to see if he's forgotten the house keys.

"Oh," I say, still eyeing the Latino kid and the milk.

"I know. Terrible. You should have seen this thing, skinny as a branch."

"Sounds pretty bad."

"I was devastated. I thought to myself, how could that beautiful man I loved, if you could call it that, want to be naked in the same bed as that disgusting cripple."

"He was crippled?"

"No," Mr. Bartlett sighs, "I meant that he was ugly. People seemed to find him interesting. But it is New York and people will act like you're interesting even if you're not."

We've made it to the checkout. We place all the groceries onto the rubber mat, rolling the fruit and canned goods down to the end. A can of medium whole beets gets caught in the perpetual spin, a hypnotizing purple barcode.

Chapter Sixteen

Step one: Pick a moment in your life. Press your finger down onto it, holding it like you would the first loop in a square knot. Step two: Find a moment that represents where you are now, something separate, current and different, and touch another finger to that, too. Step three: Measure the distance from one to the other—in lovers lost, furniture stolen from street corners, estimated electric bills paid, early morning phone solicitations, car accidents you witnessed. Band-Aids on fingers. Step four: Figure out how the hell you got here now from where you were there then.

Sometimes the first moment I choose is my cheesy orange fingertips in the propped-open back end of a station wagon parked on the tire-tracked sand of a crowded Florida beach. I must have been three years old. I don't remember it, but I have seen the photograph of me sitting there—blue and yellow tub of cheese balls between my diapered legs, hand stuck inside. Blond hair, just like now. When you look at pictures of yourself doing things that you don't remember, the image freezes and becomes part of your history, even though it seems invented. A memory that forms who you are without you knowing it. Like genes, unconscious but familiar.

Sometimes the moment is foamy orange Circus Peanuts melting on the dashboard of a pickup truck. We were driving without anyplace to be, or any place in mind to end up in. He bought a Mountain Dew because it was my favorite. I should tell you about the way his hands moved when he talked. The way words seemed to burst out of his fingers. The urgency, the way he made even garbage seem like quantum physics. But it all gets screwed around in my brain. Memory serves only to fuck things up. And photographs can lie to you, because if you have a picture of someone, and they go away, die, or disappear, the photo becomes the only thing you remember about them.

How did this start?

Shredded carrots at a salad bar, on some school trip in a shopping mall?

A completely mediocre, but still-your-favorite orange-tinted album cover?

The smooth spine of an unread paperback book?

Other times, like this time right now, right here in this guy's bedroom, it's greasy, orange clean-up wipes, the kind that he rubbed up and down his arms before climbing up behind me. "Do you like to get fucked?" he says.

A giant of a man, six-foot-plus-something. Huge, but not alien looking, still handsome, still attractive. A tiny line of mustache. He's bulky like a sack of flour, his body dense, smooth like rising dough. Forearms thick as a coffee can, covered in what I guess is car grease or engine grime, a shiny ultraviolet glimmer. Smells like steel. Skin brown underneath.

His lips are drawn on so beautifully, that I can't help but look right into his mouth when he's talking, and not into his eyes. He kisses my hand.

He's holding a white plastic tub. Tearing off the lid, he pulls out a strip of creamy orange-colored cheesecloth. A powerful knock-your-ass-on-the-floor kind of scent. The most fake, plastic, outer space, movie-smelling orange. Good though. The orange-powered grease cutter is pasted into the spaces of the cheesecloth. He rubs his hands, detailing the knuckles, the cuticles. And the smell of it hangs around through the entire act. Through the rough fingers, unclipped nails tugging at my warm knot of skin, before he's climbing up behind me.

Once again, I end up on my stomach. And I realize that when he reaches his arm around my face, around my neck, and grabs onto my shoulder with his hand—starting to really fuck me hard—that I'd better get fucking control of myself. I start to flatten out. In my head, I mean. I start finding that pre-aware, rocklike place where I can concentrate. I go to the place where everything is flat. I'm inhaling, looking for that sugary ashy smell, and suddenly, uncontrollably, my brain begins its hyper-journey back to twelve years old. Memories hijack my neurons. Memories of taste, touch, of fake orange, and when I place my mouth on this guy's arm, it all becomes clear. I'm no longer in this place, in this bedroom. My head, my brain, myself, it's all somewhere entirely different.

We're pushing our bikes up this giant hill, and the bugs are swarming around our heads. Hot Southern summer, with salty beads of sweat around our brows and upper lips. Slapping our necks with our dusty hands, smashing black gnats. Sometimes one will fly into your mouth. But we don't care when they do. And when we get to the top of the hill we find a beat-up old cassette tape, cracked open and spilling its threads of sound onto the pavement. And we unwind the tape, a huge, hundred-foot string. And we snap it in half at the middle, tying the pieces onto the seats of our bikes, and ride back down the hill, watching the glittering of who knows what on cassette flowing behind us like a tail, like a stretched-out wish, like a thin brown destiny.

We're driving a beat-up white car through a rainstorm at three o'clock in the morning in the middle of Mississippi—or maybe we'd made it to Alabama without seeing the sign, or maybe we were still in Louisiana. And the rain is coming down so hard that we can't see the street in front of us. And we're both thinking *tornado warning for all surrounding counties,* but we don't say it out loud. So for three hours we travel what adds up to be forty-two miles on the low-shoulder freeway. We pass a few cars parked on the side, determined to wait it out. And in those three hours, the loud, wind-shaken hours, we don't speak. I squint, my eyes low along the top of the dash, and he drives, tapping the gas pedal, not braking, easing on, rolling back toward home. Then, crossing the state line, we see the brightness of the morning. I look over at him; he stares ahead.

And when he loosens his grip around my neck, around my head, when my mouth breaks free from the inside of his elbow, the awfulness of the present returns. This guy, this orange-smelling grease monkey barks in my ear about how he wants to tie me up. Haven't I heard all this before? You would think it was tattooed across my forehead: TIE ME UP, TIE ME UP!

He knots my hands to the bed frame, rope made of

something natural, cotton I think. Blocks my legs apart with a short two-by-four. So I'm spread-eagle on this bed, on my stomach, of course, and the knots rub raw places into my wrists. And I know that if I didn't tug so much on the rope, then it wouldn't rub so much. But he asks me to struggle a little, and I don't know how much is "a little." So I do it until he starts going, "Yeah, yeah."

We used to take drives out to nowhere on weeknights. He'd smoke and we'd put a mix tape on and take turns talking. About what we wanted to do when we grew up, even though we were sixteen and didn't know what we wanted to do when we grew up. And didn't really care. And what we wanted to do would change every few miles, every few minutes. And we were grown up already. We'd pass rusted farm machinery, crumbling frames jutting out of the browning grass, leaping out of the dirt. Out near the deserted factory that you'd ride past if you went far enough. He'd take pictures of me in front of it. He wouldn't let me take pictures of him; he said he didn't like his picture taken. I wouldn't smile because I knew what we were doing was serious. And he knew it was serious. And so he didn't ask me to smile. We didn't have to pretend. It was too hard to pretend. And mostly it still is.

We were fifteen and hiking up the part of the trail that was marked DO NOT ENTER. Because the best parts of the mountain were marked DO NOT ENTER. We'd stand at the tip of the rock, where the trail went shooting straight out into the air, over the waterfall, the canopy. The place where red-tailed hawks spiraled in circles, heavy wings lifted by the fast and beautiful air. The place where he put his arm on my shoulder. And we stood quietly. I could hear the thumping of my heartbeat in my ears, in my chest, in the tingling pulsing pressure of my fingertips. Some nights we slept outside in heavy nylon sacks, drowning in the half-light of the moon. Some nights we climbed trees, or burned pine needle shapes in the road. Picked blueberries and ate them in the dark.

And I see him pull open the drawer from the bedside table, noticing the grease mark he missed on the back of his elbow. The orange air thick and clammy around my head, stuck inside my nose, taking my olfactory canals hostage. He opens the drawer, rustles through the dog-eared *TV Guide* (what is that, a compact?), the Q-tips and wadded up tissues. He pulls out a syringe. And the needle goes down into the side of my arm, a warm yellow energy flushing out my veins. If pain and happiness were mixed together and held in liquid suspension, that'd be almost what it felt like. And here's where everything comes slamming back into me, tearing open the little fear pockets in my head. I jerk hard on my wrists and there's nothing. No response. Like waking up too fast and you fall down. Only here the falling feels so fucking good. All of a sudden, falling without impact. So I slam my face back into the pillow, like a fool trying to re-enter a dream. Saying softly to myself, "Come on, come on, come on."

And he pushes the needle (a different needle?) down into my arm again.

And like two trains colliding, *all 142 passengers are presumed dead or buried alive in the wreckage,* I'm on my stomach and the arm wrapped around my face tastes like a gritty lemon paste, smells like orange bubble gum, like circus peanuts. Light breaks open in my brain and shines on the back of my eyes, exposing broken vessels, tired retinas. Shock therapy in my arteries, buzzing like a blank radio and numb like a sleeping foot. I'm stuck here, roped and blocked with his fingers up my ass. No, wait, did I tell the fucking part already? How did I start this story?

Late at night, I drive out to the docks and stare out into the lake. And it feels like I'm drifting out, away from the shore, away from everything. I lie on my back, settle down in one of the concave places, rub my fingers against the wood. And the night gets so dark that I can't see anything. Even my hands, inches from my face.

And then I start falling asleep, but it feels different than this in-and-out stuff. I feel my body letting go. Uncontrolled, unconscious, uncomfortable. And no matter how hard I try, no matter how much I tug and grunt at the stupid ropes, I know that I'm about to go under.

And this beautiful creature with the tiny mustache, orange-scented forearms, and perfectly drawn lips breaks open another bottle of clear something and stuffs the needle down into it. "Want another one?" he says.

Then in one choppy, movie-edited segment of brain activity, I see everything at once:

Louis, across the East River, across the Queensboro Bridge, on the second floor of a three-story building, sitting, lonely in my (now, reluctantly, our) apartment, huddling his limbs close to his body, a scraggly ashy cigarette passing from his lips to his fingers over and over and over. Walking periodically from one room to another, peeking out from the places where the curtains don't quite meet. Rarely bathed, sleeping too many hours, shopping uncontrollably through the Internet, randomly subscribing and unsubscribing to cable TV and pay-per-view movies.

Farmer, on the Upper West Side, at the American Museum of Natural History, sitting underneath a half-plaster, half-real skeleton of a long-dead terrible lizard, its toothy mouth thrown upward to the mosaic ceiling. His eyes tired, raking across the ivory pages of a used hardback book. He comes to a passage that feels all at once awful, human, and hurting. A series of words so strong, current, and true that he cries. And between the roof and his fragile face are the tiny, worthless arms of the world's most infamous predator.

Jaron, among his papers, boxes, and endless stacks of mail. He pauses, looming over his own arm, pressing the razor against it so slowly he can feel, like the clearest ringing of the clearest bell, the sharp edge push through. And then the coldness of the metal inside his 98.6-degree body. The blood moving, the change of texture, the satisfaction that comes with breaking that second sweet layer of skin.

Then Aiden. Asleep, wrapped in loose white sheets. Drawing breath in, slightly stirring at each new dream world. Holding a pillow close to his chest, close to his neck. The kitchen lamp left absently on, pouring orange glow onto his back, the light catching each tiny hair, like iron filings, bursting with beautiful color.

I roll my head back, willing it all away, trying to scream into the void, but nothing comes out. All the hairs on my neck bolt upright, continuous crackling of dendrites in my brain. And the finger emerges from the tear in the sky, then another, then the wide palm of the entire hand, slick with clear fluid, fresh and newly born. It reaches toward me, clamping down on my wrist, squeezing until my knuckles go numb. I try to jerk away, and then—

Quiet.

I come out of it, shaken and unsure. The borders of the room materialize again, walls and windows and doors. And this grease monkey climbing up on top of me. And the hand is gone, the air sealed again, impermeable, like a see-through plastic surface.

And once more, the blazing white light of the needle going down into my skin.

My arms go limp, the rope slacks.

My eyelids atrophy, fail.

Part Two

Part Two

Chapter Seventeen

When I was little, my mother told me that inside everyone, at the absolute center of us, there is a tiny golden kernel, our essence distilled down to something pure, elemental, something very close to a soul. She told me that radiating from this small kernel are thousands of vaporous strings, impossibly thin, like the rippling pink licks that float inside a plasma globe. And those strings hold us all intact like a magic anchor, tied with minuscule square knots to our organs, our bones, our skin, which pull our bodies back toward that absolute center, toward that precious kernel, like our own unique gravity.

I used to stand in the middle of my bedroom, arms splayed out, looking at my naked body in the mirror, wearing the cheap X-ray glasses mail-ordered out of the back of a comic book, trying to see through my flesh, trying to locate that shining golden center. I would squeeze my eyes closed and open them quickly, as if to sneak up on the real me. I would curl into a ball under the sheets, the bedroom dark, the curtains closed, and the lamp turned off, expecting the light from that kernel to shine out from my insides, a flickering orange glow like a far-away candle.

But as I got older, passing involuntarily through the summers as a horny, lanky teenager, somehow those pink strings began to stretch and break. Imagine your body growing larger, inflated, ballooning out—imagine time as physical distance, your edges moving ever farther away from the core that holds you together.

It never occurred to me that I could make money doing what I did. Sleeping with men wasn't a pastime, it wasn't a hobby. It was who I was. Or it was the way I figured out who I was. Sex was how I learned to read myself. It was where I learned to disappear into the other side of the known world, sink into that flat place. It allowed me access to my hidden self, that unknown person that comes scratching its way to the surface, unexpectedly. It unlocks a space, a landscape, a perpetual wind.

The first time I got paid for sex, it was an accident. I had picked someone up, or maybe he had picked me up—however that mutual glancing is decided. He was rich (so he said), and happily married (so he also said), and he poised his pen over his checkbook after I had finished. "One hundred dollars," he mumbled, as if he were speaking to nobody in particular—and at the time, I didn't know what kind of money I was worth. I was still breathing hard, my temples moist with sweat. He wrote it out, tearing along the perforated line, a clean, satisfying sound. And I took it, foolishly I know now—who takes checks? But he stuck a twenty in my pocket and asked if I'd come back in two weeks. So for almost a year there were one or two appointments a month. One time we fucked on the sofa, and

I accidentally knocked a lamp off the end table. I didn't stop—he loved it—and he said he'd blame it on the maid.

I got better at it. People traded my number around.

Men called with hushed voices, confused when one of my parents answered the phone, and I became weary and anxious—afraid of being caught, I suppose—each time it rang. There were so many hang-ups that they considered removing the line entirely. But more than anything else, more than the phone calls, the wads of cash lying suspiciously around my bedroom, my coming and going at all hours, what really became the central issue—or, I know now, what *had always been* the central issue—were the growing differences in what we wanted from the world. It was the surfacing of a fundamental alienation which had been there all along—the reality of our lives suddenly made visible.

"Why don't you want what we want?" my mother actually asked.

My parents were full of disappointments. In me, of course, but in their own lives too. And my desire for something more meaningful (at least meaningful to me) in this life than fifty-minute church services and potluck dinners with chitchatting strangers was somehow taken personally.

We tried to "make it easier on everyone." Their words, not mine. We had gone through the usual steps. First, a promise to be where I said I would be (never mind that they didn't *really* want to know where I was, and so I lied to save them from it), and to be home at "a reasonable hour," though it was unclear what exactly that meant. Second, my own separate, side entrance to the house, that sort of controlled freedom. They were slowly kicking me out, pointing out along the way that "you're only doing this to yourself."

They stopped speaking to me unless it was absolutely necessary, preferring instead small notes stuck to the kitchen counter, as if left from hotel housekeeping. Even the notes were stilted and shallow, cryptic, as if language was strange to them, as if they simply lacked the words. "Your father has gone for a few days." (Gone to *where*, I thought.) "Turn off the pot roast when you wake up." And sometimes, as if it were her punishment: "We love you."

All my mother wanted was for me to be happy—whatever that means—and all my father wanted was to think about his queer son as little as possible.

All I ever wanted was someone who would stay.

I bought a train ticket to New York City, and the trip felt like a new beginning—the inauguration of an altered, unaccustomed life. I wondered what the other people on the train were trying to get away from. Because that's what trains were to me then—escape—and that's how everything looked, speeding across the land. Nameless places, small Virginia and North Carolina towns that exist for what purpose? As we got closer, people got more excited. Even at three and four in the morning, reading lamps were on; people were whispering to each other, quietly laughing.

That memory is very clear to me, those moments locked inside the train with strangers. My head seems to document those anonymous moments in more detail, in an easily retrievable, up-front kind of way. Like being all alone in the filing room, combing through the private records of hurt people, the incessant flood of sickness. The vastly democratic reality of the body—how it fails, and how we heal it. And so many private moments in the company of men who want, among other things, to get off.

When I arrived in New York it was just past dawn, a quiet Sunday morning. I grabbed my bags and climbed up the stairs stained with the decades of city muck, emerging. There was a specific quiet, an uncomplicated city sound. And I was alive, nauseous with sleep deprivation but buzzing with presentness, newness. Sometimes, if you're lucky enough to be up at that hour, that early Sunday sunrise, you get to see everything frozen in a loose opaque haze, like everything is coated in a lustrous numbing powder. The buildings here are huge, leaping out of the ground. Billboards as tall as buildings. Radio towers on top of buildings. Everything wants to rocket launch itself into the sky. Escape the concrete. Fire off, soar away.

I asked around, found out where people like me hung out. Which bars, which corners, where we could stand without being chased off. There are plenty of places. Of course, I never need to do that now, I'm busy enough with repeats. In fact, there are the messages I got today—three calls from people who want to get fucked—potentially six hundred easy dollars (assuming I can get hard enough to fuck three people in one afternoon).

And then there's Aiden. I don't even know what he does when I'm not around: job, hobbies, TV watching—all the seemingly banal details that make up a life. Jaron says I'm in love. I could be. The way love can be a temporary insanity, the kind of madness that sounds like your only defense in a courtroom. "I'm sorry, your honor, I didn't know what the hell I was doing."

Farmer says I'm stuck, frozen with ten thousand options in front of me and therefore choosing none. I believe him. Or I want to believe him. But am I capable of that? Capable of wanting, finding, and successfully sustaining a love of that warm and fuzzy universal magnitude? It's an interesting word to use: *capable*. As if it were a dexterity that could be learned, practiced, and executed. A sport or a skill.

Aiden does cause strange sensations, things that I haven't felt before. Stirring things deep in my stomach, a whirring of distant noises in my head. A room full of faces, whispering rumors that may or may not be true. The pressing of personalities against glass.

Can you pinpoint when this sort of thing happens? Can you pry through the layers of skin and blood, isolating that precious golden kernel, protect it, save it, let it glow brilliantly inside you? Can you press your finger on a moment, holding it down, and say: Here, this is where it all changed?

I still hear my mother asking that question, not in my dreams exactly, and maybe it even comes from inside me: "Why don't you want what we want?" I think she thought I might have the answer.

Chapter Eighteen

I open the door. Louis sits curled up in the armchair, muttering something under his breath at the television (which is muted) and smoking a cigarette. Beside him are two ashtrays, both full. One is transparent green glass, the other is a clear plastic bubble surrounding a pink plastic lotus blossom. Seems odd to me—tapping your cigarette ash into a lotus blossom. I am learning not to ask questions. Our relationship is changing, becoming an odd tolerance, a convenient safety net, a place where truths are ignored but clearly visible. Perhaps all close relationships are this way, I don't know. We pretend that nothing is different.

But it is.

"There's mail for you on the counter," he says. "More credit card applications. I started to fill them out, to see how many they would give you before people started making phone calls. But then I thought about how many credit cards you already had and figured that no self-respecting company would give you another."

This is what Louis has turned into. The kind of person

who seals the TV remote inside a plastic bag and refuses to leave the house for any reason whatsoever, period. He watches QVC with the sound turned off. He straightens pictures that aren't crooked. Why do your friends sometimes turn into people you hardly recognize?

He stamps the cigarette out, changing the channel to something that looks like *Entertainment Tonight,* but in Spanish, until I realize that it's not Spanish at all, but Portuguese, and it's not *Entertainment Tonight,* but a talk show whose topic today is how to lose weight. Enormously fat people in loose, dark-colored clothing talk into the camera while a woman with a microphone, a fake blonde, dabs a wad of tissue at the corner of her eye and, between sniffles, rolls her Rs when she says things like: "You can take control of your own food," and "Food will not control your life." Only I can't understand any of this, of course, seeing as how it's Portuguese. But what else do they say to people like that on shows like this?

"Louis, you have to stop smoking in the house." Sometimes you never know what kind of mood you're in. Sometimes you wake up thinking you're okay and suddenly basic human interaction seems to be just beyond your reach. You find yourself acting like a shadow of yourself. Like Bizarro to Superman. Was I always so sensitive?

"I'll try to cut down," he says, not looking in my direction. Still, I think he absorbed the comment and will genuinely make an effort. Louis is never as distracted as he wants you to believe. "So, Simon, what's the story?" He changes the channels, flipping fast, registering only a few nanoseconds of programming. I wonder if his fingers are ahead of his brain. Like maybe if something caught his interest, he'd have to flip back a few stations.

"What's the story about what?" I say. "Why do you have the remote control in a plastic bag?"

"Dust can ruin a remote." He clicks the TV off, crinkling the baggie, the remote sliding around inside its embryonic sack. "You're not hustling much," he says.

"I'm slowing down. I want to concentrate a bit more. All those strangers leave me strung out."

There's a pot of steaming water on the stove, whole sticks of cinnamon broken up in the brownish water. Louis has taken to boiling cinnamon sticks, something he saw on a TV show somewhere. They said that if you want to sell your house faster you should bake bread in the oven right before people come to look at it, because people will associate the smell with home and think your house is really homey. They also said that boiling cinnamon sticks would do basically the same thing. It smells good, but it's a little overdone. We're not selling my apartment, it's just another behavior that Louis has taken on since he was attacked. So don't ask me why we're always boiling cinnamon sticks. My apartment smells like cinnamon sticks and cigarette smoke.

We look at each other for a while, the way people who have known each other forever will, in silence. "Something happen?" he says, reaching for the pack of cigarettes and tapping the bottom against his palm. *Tap, tap, tap.* He looks over at me.

"Nothing happened." I try to say this as honestly as possible. I don't exactly want to get into the whole dumbass story about how I got myself into the kind of situation that I did. I just wasn't careful. Wasn't thinking.

Okay. It's true that I feel less myself as the days go on. Contrary to what might seem like the crucial, shifting moment—that incident with the guy and the needle and the, well, everything—my decision to stop having sex for money, at least for now, was more cumulative than direct. How can I say this so it makes sense? See, the needle itself was less scary than my lack of planning, or my inability to stay in control of the deal. The details are, believe it or not, sort of trivial. Some part of me lost its quickness, its lucidity. The rest was just fallout. I could see everything happening—the rope, then the two-by-four, the next thing, and the next—and did nothing about it. Frankly, I've spent enough years compartmentalizing.

And that's the truth, as much as I know of it right now.

Though I don't want to tell all of this to Louis.

"New Year's resolution," I say, which really isn't true because I hate that stuff—any kind of holiday-based decision-making.

Tap, tap, tap. "It must be more complicated that that."

"Nope, it's not." Also, I don't want to talk about Aiden.

"Well, whatever you want to do," Louis says. "I mean, who am I to tell you how to behave? I can't even leave the house." I smile at him. It's an easy smile for me, and it sort of happens without me trying. Reaching my hand in the refrigerator, I inadvertently knock over a stack of empty plastic water bottles. Why are those in there?

I saw a show once about this new therapy called "Radical Honesty Therapy" that seemed to be catching on in places like Los Angeles. Couples would come in and sit across from each other. They would say all the awful, judgmental, angry, stupid things that they didn't like about their partner while looking right into each other's eyes. Stuff like: "I resent you for your nose," and "I hate the way your hair looks," and "I wish you had better lips." Saying all this stuff out loud was supposed to erase any problems they might be having in their relationship—or indeed were having, since people sought out (and paid enormous sums of money for) this new kind of therapy. Of course, all the things they complained about were superficial, how-you-look stuff. As if the reason that they hated each other was because her nose was too big or his hair was all wrong. I have considered that perhaps these dumbass reasons *were* the root, which is so fucking *Los Angeles,* and another reason why I fucking hate the place.

So I dive in for some Radically Honest Conversation: "Why is it that you refuse to leave my house?"

"Because I'm scared of being attacked again. Because I'm ugly. Because in here I don't have to be responsible for anything I can't control. Because I'm bored with my life, and I don't want to have to think about that for more than a few seconds, if I have to think about it for any number of seconds at all."

It hasn't occurred to me that Louis believes he is ugly. He still has the stone-cut jaw and the million-dollar cheekbones. His hair is still rich. His skin is pretty pallid and unattractive, but that is easily cured. Everybody's airbrushed now anyway.

"I wasn't quite sure you were so aware of your decision." I fumble through the cabinets, looking for something to eat, finding only a bag of dried banana chips that taste good initially, and then coat my mouth with pasty banana-film, which quickly becomes unappetizing. "You're not ugly. You're actually the type they're looking for now." I fold the bag down over itself and stuff it back up into the cabinet.

"Yeah, doesn't that make you sick?"

"Yes, actually," I say, meaning the banana chips and then realizing that he means the models.

He gets up from the chair and walks around the apartment, collecting catalogs, the phone books, some stiff cardboard boxes that contained some sort of mail-order happiness. He makes a stack in front of the chair, sits back down, and props his feet up. The stack crumples a bit, but holds. He starts to light a cigarette, again, but I stop him just before I have to suffocate in this tiny room. "Okay, just a habit," he says.

"I hate smoking," I say. "I think it's one of the most disgustingly selfish things a person can do. I don't think it's right for a person to invade your space in such a way that it makes your eyes water, your skin itch, and your chest seize up."

"Wow," he says. "Okay."

"I try to take up as little physical space as possible. And I hate smokers because they end up taking up the whole fucking room. Like asshole straight guys who sit on furniture and spread their legs open."

"Fuck you. You sound like somebody's dad." Louis puffs his chest out and furrows his eyebrows into a frumpy line. "Now, uh, Louis, listen here, son. So long as you're staying under my roof, it will be my rules that you live by. When you grow up and have your own house with your own children, you can make your own set of rules, but until then, blah, blah, blah."

"My dad always said that if he ever caught me smoking he would assume that I was on fire and pour a bucket of water on my head."

I pull out a chair, blue painted wood with a woven straw seat, and sit down. I push aside cartons of cigarettes, stacks of unopened mail, catalogs, Kinder Egg toys, other things that Louis has bought. The stuff covering the table shifts like those awful quarter-eating games they have in video arcades—you plunk your coin into one of the slots up top and it falls through a complex series of flags and whistles and then lodges itself among the other four billion quarters hanging on to the edge by their toenails. The cigarette cartons push against the mail, which pushes against the catalogs, which push against the little things, and it all creates this eerie continental shift across the table. But not a single damn thing falls to the floor.

"What even happened to that guy you were stalking? From the Laundromat?"

"It's not stalking."

"You practically preyed on him from the window. It's the dog, isn't it? You turn to putty."

"Aiden."

"Oh, he has a name now."

"No, he's always had a name, I'm only telling it to you now." He gets up from the chair, and the makeshift ottoman sags and falls over. He empties the ashtrays into the trash, knocking them against the side, and scrunching up his face. I walk over to the cabinet and take down a box of Triscuits. "What about him?" I say between the wheaty layers filling my mouth.

"Have you seen him again?"

"We see each other at the Laundromat. And we've been out a few times."

"You're not interested in him anymore?"

"I fucked him. So what? I fuck everybody."

"Well, you don't exactly talk about him like it's work."

"I don't talk about him. You asked. Since when do I talk about him?"

Here's where I decide to drop the whole cooler-than-ever act. I figure that Louis isn't going to let up no matter how much I avoid the topic. That's the difference between us: I'd rather not talk about it and Louis would rather send it over the airwaves, simulcast in stereo and streaming hi-fi audio.

"Okay. I am interested."

"I knew it. I could totally tell."

"The sex is different." Then, reluctantly, I add this: "It was soft. It was nice."

"Since when do you like it soft?"

"I don't really. But this was okay."

"Hmm," he says.

"He wasn't using my body. Like he expected to connect in some other way. It wasn't an out for him. Or a release. Do you know what I mean? An out?"

"Yes."

"Or an excuse."

"I understand."

"He meant every touch."

"Probably good for you," Louis says. He begins picking up, stuffing a stack of papers, probably junk mail, probably credit card applications, into the trash. "Farmer asked me if you'd cracked yet."

"Farmer said that?"

"Yes." And we both smile, remembering that Farmer is out there defying all notions of human nature, seeing things far ahead, living with hope and joy. This is what I'm feeling at this moment, wonderment. I realize that part of it has to do not with Farmer, but with the thought of Aiden. Only I don't realize that until a few seconds later when I imagine us walking along the banks of some river in the middle of a huge ripple of green mountains and something else equally as invented. What has happened to me?

"So what are you going to do about those?" he says.

The blinking light of the answering machine: eleven messages. "There aren't enough sick people in all of New York City to allow you to live off that crappy filing job you have. Maybe you should get a new job. Give your fingers a rest. They look like shit."

You think if you pick at the pale, dead skin that it will get better. You think that if you peel off the dry bits, it will all blend back into pinkish pleasant healthy looking. But it gets worse. Remedy the symptom and you're still where you started. I know the answer is that you have to cure the cause.

"One time I had a job at an ice cream place. My forearm was huge from all the scooping."

"Oh?" he says.

"Yeah, in the winter everybody smoked pot in the back room. And every fourth customer thought it was fucking hilarious to ask us how many flavors we had."

"You could not work at an ice cream place."

"I so could."

"Could not," he says.

"Could too."

"Simon, you could not."

Chapter Nineteen

Aiden and I meet at the Laundromat—not on purpose. Though, of course, I know which nights he'll be here (Fridays and sometimes Tuesdays), so perhaps I'm trying to torture myself. The possibility that I have been torturing myself for the last twenty-four years has crossed my mind. It has yet to be confirmed. The tests are still out.

The short Mexican woman is again wiping down the fronts and tops of the machines, talking on the phone with the cord stretched across the room, pouring pink liquid detergent into the dual compartments on top of machine number fourteen. A Russian woman, tall and dark haired, takes up two folding tables. She snaps some men's underwear in the air, trying to jerk out the wrinkles. Underwear dust floats around her, drifting to where I'm standing, to where Aiden is leaning against his machine. Everyone is crowded around the small row of dryers with rolling baskets full of wet clothes, waiting their turn. One load out and another one in, mere seconds separating their sticky presence inside the tumbling cylinders. Is all this sanitary?

I choose to act like this is just an ordinary day where you're at the Laundromat and the person who you're crazy for walks in and starts a conversation. And when Aiden asks me if I "wanna hear a kickass story," which he does as soon as he sees me, I just about want to leap into his arms and go trotting off to the Poconos to sit in the heart-shaped bathtub.

But I'm cool. And I hold it together.

"Yes, I want to hear a kickass story," I say, fiddling with the washer dial, choosing hot/warm over warm/warm or hot/hot or cold/warm or cold/cold—as if any one of them made any fucking difference. I flirt a little, smiling and then not looking at him, and he smiles back, sometimes touching his upper lip and smoothing the coarse hairs there.

"So I'm driving through Florida with some friends, right?" His beard is freshly trimmed, jeans ripped at the knees and frayed around the pocket edges. Reddish orange sweater. He looks like an orphan. I want to press my face into his neck, touch my lips to his nipples, the delicate flesh like a blister. He's going to ask me to come home with him and I haven't decided what I'm going to say.

"I swear I'm telling this exactly as it happened." He says this the way a person will when they're about to tell a story, one they've told a million times, and that people often refuse to buy into. An overly truthful tone. An excessively sincere patience.

"I believe you," I say, and I wonder if he can hear what I'm thinking when I say it. It sounds like a confession rubbed out of my mouth with a soapy washcloth, or a blurry crayon transfer. Some kind of evidence.

"We're driving out of Florida and Amber is in the backseat. I'm driving and Leanne is flipping through the radio trying to find something that isn't a rock ballad. You know how radio is at the beach, am I right?" He pauses, like he's waiting for me to absorb this, or for a certain comprehension to pass across my face. And I get the feeling that he's really excited about this story and it's taking all he's got to tell it without jumping ahead, to stick with the details, to tell the little side stories and embellishments that make a good story.

"And Leanne puts on the Sugarcubes CD and rolls down the window."

I stuff all my clothes in the machine, squishing them together, not separating whites from darks. The clothes have been washed so many times there's nothing left to bleed out. I throw my underwear in the back of the machine, snatching it out of the bag. Everyone hides their underwear except the people who should be hiding their underwear. The Russian lady has a huge, lumpy, grayish stack of underwear.

"And what pulls up alongside us but this huge station wagon with all its windows open, right? Leanne starts laughing her ass off, pointing at the kid in the backseat who's got this orange cat in his arms, big ugly kid with glasses. Big head and two giant teeth."

I plunk quarters down into the five slots, sliding them into the machine. It clicks and makes a metallic farting sound and the wad of clothes starts spinning inside, slowly getting darker with the hot/warm water and soon the window gets foamy and white. Aiden pokes my arm.

"Listen to me," he says.

"I am," I tell him.

"I'm driving right alongside of the car, right at the exact same speed, and the kid holds the cat up to the window and starts waving the thing around at Leanne, shaking its paw so it looks like it's waving at us. And then, all of a sudden, the cat jumps out their window and into our car, but into the backseat, right? He could have thrown the cat out the window for all we know. Or maybe the cat chose death-by-highway over a lifetime of this Kool-Aid kid cutting all its whiskers off." Aiden rips open a one-load serving of powder detergent, and I notice that it's Cheer with extra Color Guard, or whatever they call it, making a mental note—that's how he gets his clothes to smell like they do.

I'm completely involved in looking him up and down, wondering if he notices, and not really caring if he does, and also a little bit hoping that he does. I'm smiling, I know, but the story is awful, and I can't help laughing because he's so into it, throwing his arms around and doing his hands like a steering wheel, turning ten degrees, alternating directions, the way people do when they imitate driving. If anybody really drove like people imitated driving, they'd get arrested so fast.

"So the cat lands on Amber's lap and then jumps up into the front seat and runs all over our legs, then up the dash and making this horrible cat-squealing noise. Like when you try to start your car when it's already running, you know that sound?"

I fold my arms, plant my feet, overly aware of my posture.

"And then, and then," Aiden says, "it jumps out of Leanne's window and onto the hood of the station wagon and they brake really hard and the kid in the backseat yells something and then I brake really hard, scared that I'm going to run it over, right?" He motions in the air, leaning to one side and then the other. "Amber slides off onto the floor of the backseat behind us and gets all tangled up down there. And we're in the two right lanes and I can see this big Mack truck is speeding up behind us in the fast lane. I'm thinking, oh, please, oh, please, and the truck runs over the cat but doesn't squish it on the tarmac, right?"

"This story sucks," I say.

"Wait, it gets worse." Aiden bends his knees, really getting into it, rigid with tension. "The wheel flips the damn thing up into the air, like, launching it up. Leanne and I start screaming our asses off. And like two seconds later there's this huge *whomp* and the smooshed kitty parts land on the station wagon's hood. BAM! And Amber sits up, all twisted around and confused. 'What happened?' she says. Leanne and I just look at her. She had no idea what went down."

"Wow."

"Yeah."

"Intense."

"Yeah." He leans back on his heels, leaning against the machine, which shakes so hard that I think it might leap off the tiles and gnash him to death, crushing the annoying Russian woman and snapping the Mexican lady's phone cord. He stands up straight again, giving the machine an odd turn of his eyes, laying his hand on top of it like a healing gesture or the first offensive move in his plan of attack. "Hold on there, buddy," he says to the big metal box. "That's my clothes you got in there."

My machine clicks again, whirring and then draining, starting the second of what feels like a hundred thousand cycles. Water sprays through the little compartments on the top, and since I've forgotten to close the rubber flap, it spumes a fine soapy mist over the surface.

"Hey," he says. "Do you want to come to Vermont with me?"

"What?" I say, the way you do when you heard exactly what someone said, but you're trying to get them to rephrase it, in the hopes that you'll have some other kind of emotional reaction than the one you had immediately. And people know this tone when they hear it, so they comply, not rephrasing, but giving you more information, detailing the parts that they think you've had trouble with. In this case, the possibility of me going to the lovely state of Vermont—where there are no billboards, Farmer tells me, and where it's fucking freezing right now, covered in a good two or four feet of snow—most likely.

"I have a house up there, well, I'm building a house. It's mostly done. Just need to get the insides in. I'm going next week and I thought you could come with me."

I can't imagine the look on my face. Louis always says I have a hard time disguising the way I feel. "I don't know," I say. "It's the middle of winter."

"I know."

I pause, digesting the invitation.

"Come on," he says. "I'm taking Caleb."

"Let me think about it," I say. I want to go, but it's hard to admit that. And trying over and over to refuse yourself is like trying to escape gravity, like tearing yourself away from yourself. It hurts like hell and it's a colossal waste of time. I get this feeling a lot.

I'm clicking the buttons on the machine next to mine, hot/hot and cold/cold back and forth in maniacal, obsessive despair until one of them actually pops off and the Mexican woman glares at me from across the room and even comments about my little tantrum to whoever she's talking to on the phone—or at least that's what it looks like from here.

"Stop doing that," Aiden says.

"Sorry," I say, like a kid pushing to see how far he can go and feeling sheepishly embarrassed because he didn't go nearly as far as he imagined he could.

"I'll pay you."

"That's not the issue."

"I want you to come."

"I said, let me think about it."

"Come on."

"I'm nervous," I say, releasing something inside me, the way honesty can be a release. And for that one second it feels nice to tell the truth. But then the overwhelming state of reality sets in and I realize that I've admitted to Aiden what I don't even admit to Louis, Jaron, and Farmer, even though they know it already. People say that the truth will set you free. What they forget to tell you is that once you're set free, you still have to deal with the fact that you fucking told the truth.

"So am I!" Aiden says. At this point we're yelling.

"Let me think about it for one minute!"

"Okay!"

I turn away from him, walking to the garbage cans in the corner, crossing behind the Russian woman, who's now taking up three rolling carts full of warm, puffy clothes freshly tumbled and scrambled with wadded anti-static sheets and mismatched socks, the long sleeves of once-bright-colored button-down shirts faded to the color of somebody else's, some anonymous laundry. She pulls the socks from the corners of the wire baskets, flipping them inside out in a fast, jerky movement. Like pulling the skin off a rabbit.

"Okay, how about now? Did you think about it?" He shouts across the whole place, and hardly anybody turns their head, this being New York City. Studies show that

New Yorkers are as attuned to their surroundings as people who live in constant fear of being attacked by wild predators. Like, for example, in parts of Africa. Body language becomes the basic system of communication, even though you're not aware of it. You watch for muscle tension in the neck, legs, and shoulders. You hear tone instead of conversation. You learn to shift your eyes without being seen. So for about forty-six nanoseconds Aiden and I are the most interesting thing in the whole world, especially during my infantile hot/hot cold/cold button performance. But people quickly lose interest and begin to wish that we'd simply go away. Here we are, howling at each other from across the room, excited, our stomachs fluttering.

The Russian woman stares at me through her brown eyes, snapping T-shirts in the air, tucking waistbands down into the folded underwear dumplings she has stacked on the table. She looks down at her piles, then back up at me, over to the clock, and then back at me.

"Now will you go with me?" Aiden says.

"Yes, okay, fine."

Chapter Twenty

Jaron's voice squeezes through the keyhole and out into the hallway. "And then I told them to get the fuck out of there before I called the cops." I pause. Farmer is laughing. The cigarettes stain the air, even out here in the hallway. Louis still smokes too much when I'm not home, I can tell by the way the clothes smell when they come out of the closet. The way the windows go gray and filmy. The smoke has probably found a home in the layers of once-shiny paint.

All Jaron's stories, his small performances, are a puzzling combination of utter honesty and elaborate, almost impossible exaggeration. You never know what's real. Because at the same time that you know he'd never get himself into such a situation, there is a huge percentage of his personality that is simply unpredictable. In the way that you watch an actor on television playing a rogue fighter pilot, or an undercover agent with a knack for sharpshooting, and then you see the actor, not as the character but as himself, on some late-night interview show and you say to yourself: "Hey, that guy's not like that character at all . . . no, wait, he does look like he knows how to make a pipe bomb."

I open the door. They all look at me, as if I'm the strange one. "What's up?" I say.

"Hey," Farmer says, happy to see me.

"What are you guys talking about?"

Farmer answers, "Jaron in the kitchen with the candlestick."

"Nice," I say.

Jaron has a candlestick, chunky blue glass, lifted into the air like a stabbing instrument, re-enacting his Lower East Side drama. "And then when they ran away, the one guy trips on the curb and falls on his face," he says. "Dumbass."

Louis is enthroned in his armchair-stack-of-magazines-ashtray fortress. He stamps out his cigarette, blowing the smoke out of one side of his mouth, fogging the air near the window, which is barely open. "Sorry," he says quietly, just to me. The wind outside draws the smudgy threads through the slit. "Jaron was mugged," he says.

Jaron says, "Well, not officially."

I say, "What is officially?"

Jaron says, "They didn't really ask for my money, so I'm not sure if it was a mugging exactly. They would have, maybe, but I kicked the Crocodile Dundee knife out of his hand and threatened to kick his ass."

"Open the goddamn window," I say. Louis obliges and as soon as it is open the pressure in the room changes and the smoke is sucked out. A soft, persistent breeze slips through the crack, which turns the air from warm and stuffy to cool and clean. Oxygen is a wonderful thing. This reminds me of a lecture that Farmer and I went to years ago at the Museum of Natural History. Something about how the air is actually tiny solid particles, and those solid particles interact with similar particles in your lungs, and how your lungs are made of small particles themselves, and so they get mixed up with the oxygen ones. And that's all we are, in the end. Swirling atoms, giving and taking from each other, sharing electrons, borrowing and stealing. Flowing, restless, and never ending.

Jaron says, with a bow, "I have survived." And he waves from the wrist, like a beauty queen riding on the back of an open-topped convertible, all sparkling crown and Vaseline-slicked teeth. Jaron does this imitation well.

I open the fridge, nosing around, trying to figure out what to do with my apartment full of people. Hanging out in this room means being part of the conversation. And hanging out in the other room means listening to the conversation go quiet at times, louder at others, and knowing that they're in there talking about you and you can't do a thing about it.

Louis says, "What did you do with the knife?"

Jaron says, "I put it in a trash can."

I pull out the orange juice, unscrewing the top and drinking a long gulp. The boys give me a few disgusted looks, as if this wasn't my house and this wasn't my orange juice.

I say, "Probably the same creeps that attacked you."

Louis nods. "Could have been."

Then for a few seconds, nobody says anything.

"Did you see the posters?" I say, meaning the conservative propaganda plastered all over the windows of the radiator shop. " 'Pinkos Go Home' has been replaced with—"

Farmer says, "Happy Birthday, Nancy!"

I say, "And there's a picture of her with a cake, candles, the whole thing."

Farmer says, "There's even a 'Just Say No' button stuck on the window with packing tape."

Louis says, "I hate that guy."

I remember the bomb that could have been—the storefront exploded, smoke pouring from the gaping, crumbled bricks. Farmer and I look at each other. His eyes change, the way you'll be looking at someone but not really looking at them. You're really looking through them, and then you realize you're staring, and you're sorry, and the other person is confused. "Simon," he says, and the violence in my head disperses. "Wake up. Where are you?"

I put the juice back in the fridge and open the freezer. There are a few bags of frozen peas, which I won't eat, but Louis buys them anyway, stacked up with some awful-tasting pizzas in badly chosen flavors—at least for pizza, like salmon with dill and spicy lentil. This makes me think of Mr. Bartlett.

Louis says, "Any news with the laundry guy?"

I say, "Aiden. He's taking me to Vermont."

Louis says, "He's what?"

Jaron says, almost interrupting, "For how long?"

I say, "I don't know. A few days."

Louis says, "For what?"

I say, "He's building a house up there. He wants me to see it."

Louis says, "Don't you think that's a little strange?"

Here's where I'm reminded that your friends hate it when you make other friends, new friends. They don't trust the new ones and they begin to stop trusting you.

Sometimes they move away to places that you've never even heard of—probably for good reason—and change careers or political parties. The once-vegetarians begin to eat meat. They call you up, or write a scathing letter, wanting to know why you deserted them, why you abandoned them. They try to reconcile what was done (or left undone), and what was said, or more often not. They break open old photo albums and scrapbooks, tracing your common histories through news clippings, photographs, and ticket stubs, as if the paper trail were proof of something owed. Then, raising their hands above their heads and calling out at you from across the room, they bitch and moan about what's different and lost and wrong about *you.*

I say, "No, I don't think it's strange at all."

Jaron says, "Don't get so defensive."

I say, "I'm not."

Louis says, "Yes, you are."

Louis gets up and brushes the chair where he's been sitting, as if he's eaten a stack of crackers whose crumbs are suddenly attacking his backside. He gathers the ashtrays from around the apartment.

Farmer says, "I think it sounds like fun."

Jaron says, "It does sound like fun."

On the counter is the plastic wrapper from a pack of cigarettes. I pick it up, wad it into a crinkled ball, and toss it into the trash. Everything inside is covered with ash: unwanted magazine blow-ins, circular cardboard bottoms from frozen pizzas, junk mail addressed to former tenants. On the countertops are dirty and clean dishes, some rubber bands, a day-old baguette hard as stone, bottle caps, and plastic swords from grenadine-soaked drinks—saved from a disgusting shellfish binge at the Red Lobster in Yonkers where Louis and I had dinner prior to fucking this straight-acting landscape artist from Northampton.

I say, holding them up, "Remember these?"

Louis looks over, smiles, and says, "Most certainly."

I say, "How did we end up—"

Louis says, "We drank Shirley Temples."

I sit across from Farmer, who is picking at the frayed edge of the bamboo placemat. Louis rearranges the stack of magazines beside his chair. Jaron looks at me, then down at his fingernails.

"There's talk of a demonstration," Jaron says. "A protest of some sort."

Louis says, "The Million Fag March."

Jaron says, "Something like that."

Farmer says, "They'll have to disguise it as a pride event if they want anybody to come."

I say, "With a big stage and dancers."

Farmer says, "Open bar and corporate sponsors."

Jaron says, "I read somewhere that gay people are the most brand-conscious demographic in the world."

Louis does the "gag-me" thing with his finger.

Chapter Twenty-one

What do you pack for a place you've never been to?
All afternoon I've watched the rain from my window, the women with plastic bonnets running in and out of the drugstore buying light bulbs at half off and unsold bulk bags of Valentine candy. I like the sound of the rain, especially while I'm sleeping. The quiet tapping against the air conditioner mixed with the sound of Louis breathing and adjusting the sheets. The weather people say that it will rain off and on for at least three more days. What do people say? *If you don't like the weather around here, wait five minutes*. The truth is they say that everywhere.

Aiden, his flannel shirt spotted by the rain, pulls his car—actually a banged-up blue pickup truck with a faded camper cover—around to the front of my apartment building, slamming the door when he gets out. He walks around the back, opens the tailgate, and Caleb flops out onto the sidewalk, lifting his leg at a parking meter and urinating, foamy drool sagging out of his jowls. He shakes his head when he finishes, the slobber slinging off his face, and smiles, the way a dog will. Aiden reaches down and pats his head.

"Okay," I say, "I'm going." Louis is watching the muted TV and fumbling through some catalogs.

"Want something to eat?" he says.

"No, I don't think so. Maybe we'll stop along the way."

"Maybe," he says, and then presses his face into the pages. "There's this place in Florida, Key West I think it was, where all they make is sandals and the whole place smells like the inside spine of a *National Geographic* magazine. Did you ever smell a tannery?"

"No, it must be something in the finisher."

"The what?"

"The finisher. The chemicals they use to print the pictures."

"What do you know about finisher?" Louis says.

"Nothing really."

"That's all you're taking?"

"Yes."

"You'll freeze your ass off," he says.

He returns to his catalogs, already reaching for a cigarette. I take an empty plastic Evian bottle out of the refrigerator and fill it at the tap. "That's sacrilege," he says, and turns off the television. "Enjoy yourself."

"Thanks," I say, "I will."

I shut the door behind me, honing in on the airtight *shh-chunk* of the rubber seal against the metal frame, and then pausing in the hallway to resituate my hand on my luggage. I walk down the stairs, which are still, two months later, covered with dried, brittle pine needles: Someone upstairs dragged their Christmas tree to the street, and failed to vacuum. It smelled nice for a couple of weeks—now the hallway smells again like stale bread and cigarette smoke. And the constant tinge of yellow curry, something they're always cooking across the hall from me.

The passenger door is hanging open. Caleb has situated himself in the back part of the cab, staring out at Aiden through the glass. "Here, let me get that," Aiden says, and takes my bag out of my hand. I stand there, watching him put my bag in the back of the truck, closing the tailgate and locking it with a key. He looks back at me. "Did you bring a coat or anything?"

"Just this," I say, meaning the denim jacket I'm wearing.

He looks back at the truck, as if to make sure the luggage hasn't dragged itself away. "Okay, you can borrow something of mine. Vermont is colder than that."

"I didn't really know what to bring," I say, crawling into the truck and pushing tools and coils of rope underneath the seat to make room for my legs. He gets in, slamming the door, which changes the pressure in my ears, and Caleb leans in, trying to lick Aiden's head. He succeeds, and drools onto his arm. Aiden grabs a wadded-up rag from the dash and dabs at the wet spot.

"Let's get this show on the road!"

"You're such a geek."

"I know," he says. "Thanks for coming."

"Sure."

"Do you want me to pay you before we leave?"

"I don't want you to pay me at all."

Aiden says nothing. Then, slower, "I thought that we agreed that—"

"We didn't really. You offered, but I don't want you to."

"Are you sure?"

"I'm sure. I'm trying to be a little more selective these

days," I say. I mean for it to be a joke, for my winky grin that comes right after to be the punchline, a little flirty, but Aiden seems to miss the point.

"Good," he says, proud and happier than I suspect he thought he'd be, surprised. "It's probably not safe these days anyway."

And here's where I'm thinking: *You have no idea.*

He clicks on the windshield wipers, which drag soggy leaves across the glass, dripping a brownish red stream as they go. "I'm glad you're coming because you want to," he says, and starts the truck. It rumbles around me.

"I want to."

Riding in a car through New York changes the way you see it. The streets are again unfamiliar, the people are again a blur of colors and moods. You miss the details— the cracking sidewalk, the neon glare, the clipped conversations. And New York becomes simply an idea, a façade, not a real place. (Jaron and I have argued over this detail before—whether or not New York *ever* begins to exist as a real place.)

We pass a parking lot—more like a giant holding facility, like a train yard—full of school buses, all in slightly varying shades of that trademark, cheesy yellow. "Welcome to New York," Aiden says in this thick, put-on Brooklyn accent. "On your left, ladies and gentlemen, forty-fucking-million buses."

"You're funny," I say. I lean over and fiddle with the radio. The thumpy sounds of hip-hop fade in and out of focus, like listening to the consciousness of an entire generation—boiled down, angry, and somehow empty. The sounds of product placement, self-righteousness, and image. Jerky, catchy. Disposable.

"Why does this music always feel like it's trying to sell me something?"

Aiden grips the steering wheel with both hands, aligned at the perfect ten and two position. "Because it is."

"Oh yeah," I say, faking surprise.

Leaning back, I drag my finger on the outside of his thigh. He reaches to adjust the rearview mirror, and I watch the tendons in his forearm as he does this. The wind pushes the rain into horizontal lines, silvery beads stretched out into brushstrokes. The window begins to look like a painting.

Caleb every so often sneezes, or blows air through his furry, saggy cheeks, as if he's bored of us already, as if he's made this trip a thousand times. As soon as we get through the stop/start of traffic lights and curving on-ramps he quiets down and eventually starts to snore.

The first real exit is marked by a McDonald's, sharing the building with a gas station and a touristy trinket shop that sells all sorts of New York paraphernalia, even though we're a good half hour out of the city by now. The same store, set back from the busy lanes of cars, sits opposite, a mirror image of itself. The parking lots are full, the gas pumps busy with lines of station wagons, raincoated children fidgeting underneath their umbrella-toting parents at the rusty restroom door. It is easy to forget what America looks like. New York can fool you in that way.

"McDonald's puts chemicals in the french fries to make them taste like beef," I say.

"When they cook them?"

"No, before."

Aiden settles in, adjusting his weight and cracking his neck back and forth, something I notice him doing often. "You're going to get arthritis," I say.

"Not true. Rumor." He looks back at Caleb, like check-ing on a child, tugs at his beard and smoothes his mus-tache.

The time passes. A few hours. We talk awhile, then we don't. We play the radio. We watch for out-of-state license plates. Farmer was right—no billboards. And when we stop for gas and to let Caleb relieve himself, Aiden kisses me (briefly) as I sit (barely) on the front bumper.

"Someone's going to see you," I say.

"Maybe," he says.

Then we're off again. The orange needle on the gas gauge slowly rises as we pull out of the parking lot. The smooth, flowing lines of road, curves and straightaways, passing near-invisible exits one after another—strangely named places like Brattleboro and Bellows Falls and White River Junction. Hand-painted signs for maple syrup and goat cheese, fresh lamb. The cars change. The speed of life changes. And the farther north we drive, the darker it gets. Then complete darkness. Only the headlights beam-ing out in front. First the tapping on the hood, on the roof of the car, the sound of ice, different from the sound of rain—pitched higher, faster tempo. We pull off the inter-state onto a two-lane road.

"Will it be like this all night?" I ask.

"No, it will probably change in a couple of hours. Soften up."

"It feels nice to get away."

"Yes, it does."

Streetlights throw down their amber-green light in dim circles on the road, each visible for fifty yards ahead. To the left I can see rows of farmland and a fence, broken here and there. To the right is black, the limbs of trees and then more black behind them.

"What's over there?"

"That's the ridge where my house is." He leans over to me, trying to see out the passenger window. "We have to drive this road for a while. It's not far now." Caleb sits up, touching his muzzle to my arm, his tail wagging behind him, thumping against the floorboards and the back of Aiden's seat.

"He's excited," I say.

Then the sleet, which has held on for so long, changes itself into snow, as if with a gentle wave of a hand, a magician's flourish. The snow crunches under the tires as we turn onto a dirt road.

The steep curves must make me visibly nervous, because Aiden keeps looking over at me. "It's okay, you know," he says. "I do this all the time. In worse weather."

The snow falls harder now, and we finally come upon the clearing. I can make out a jutting boxy shape against the sky.

"See my house," he says.

"Yes," I say. Then, for whatever reason, I think of Louis. "I hope Louis is okay."

"This is the model?"

"Yeah, used to be." And it's not *for whatever reason*— it's because we're delicately connected, maybe forever, and he's always in my mind for one reason or another, lurking in the background, or screaming at the surface.

"What will he do while you're gone?"

"Smoke. Order from catalogs and complain out loud to nobody about the television." I set my feet up on the dash.

"He was attacked?"

"Yes. It was months ago."

"What did the police say?"

"Nothing. They did nothing."

"Why don't they do something?" Aiden says. "I hate them."

Aiden invokes the mysterious and invisible *them* to do something, which hundreds have done foolishly before. As if *them* were a visible enemy. As if *them* were a few guys in suits and penny loafers sitting around a table stacking up bullet points, outlining a comprehensive plan of action. *Them* is what we call the guilty, too, when we talk of it— the ones who beat us and corral us like animals. And when they talk of us, around their dark poker tables, around their parked cars, that's when they begin to hate us—if they didn't hate us enough before. And then we become *them*.

Them is worthless. Who is *them*?

I wake, tangled in musty sheets and lying in what I discover to be a fine, barely-there layer of sawdust. The sun pours in from a giant window, one perfectly clean sheet of glass as wide as the room, as tall as I am, and nearly invisible. The view is perfect. The house sits on the edge of a great ridge where rocks jut out of the earth, like launch pads, thrusting out into the open air. Not another manmade structure in sight, except for the road. A huge drift has formed at the base of the road, where it turns into actual pavement, with a spotted line down the middle and remnants of power lines. The old wooden poles are still here, standing upright next to the new metal ones, nearly identical. Two sets of tire tracks—ours maybe, half covered from last night's dusting, fading back into nothing, and fresh treads on the other side, deep and wet, somebody on their way to town for breakfast, maybe a newspaper. Snow covering everything, and big, big sky.

I lay my hand on the cold glass. How many shades of light, how many variations on white.

Then I smell cooking. Aiden, of course, though it takes me a moment to recall what it is I'm doing here. I am used to waking up in other people's houses. Waking up to the smell of someone else's daily routine. (You'd be amazed at what horribly tedious and intensely methodical things people do to themselves in the morning.) And I remind myself that if I want this to be something different, I can't play it the same. If I want this to do anything, go anywhere, be great, I'm going to have to give in to it. So, okay, Simon.

Relax.

While I'm rubbing the green crust from my eyes, Aiden knocks on the door, which isn't closed, but hanging halfway open. I tug on a clean shirt.

"Want some breakfast?" he says.

"Mmm," I say, following him, walking into the kitchen, my tongue feeling tacky and sour in my mouth.

"Grumpy in the morning, are we?" I look over at the stove, reconsidering. He raises his eyebrows, watching to see what I'll do—like a zoological experiment. "There's eggs and bacon," he says. "And granola."

"How charming. If I didn't know you better I'd say you were trying to impress me."

"Don't speak too soon. Are you forgetting that we always order out?"

He pulls a plate down out of the cabinet and loads it up. I scoop up a forkful and shove it into my mouth. He's right, the eggs are awful.

"Pretty bad, huh?" he says.

"How did this happen? Preschoolers can make scrambled eggs."

"I need more practice."

"Tomorrow I'll cook the eggs."

"The bacon is good."

"So you're one and one." He brings me a glass of orange juice. "Where's Caleb?"

"Downstairs. He likes his Vermont bed. He'll stay down there all day if I let him. Do you want to see him?"

"No, whatever. I don't—"

"Caleb," he shouts. "Get up here." He doesn't talk to the dog like most people talk to their animals. He talks to him like another person, another human. No baby talk, no goochie-goo, no high-pitched squealing, and I like this. Caleb lumbers up the stairs, turns the corner and stops. He looks at us, once over at me and then back at Aiden, as if to say *What?*

Aiden says, "He's a big fan of yours."

"Right."

"I'm serious. I wouldn't say it if it weren't true."

"How can you tell?"

"Just look at him." Caleb ambles up beside me, pokes his head into my hip. I scratch his ears and give him a good friendly whack with my palm on his side. "Bass dog," I say. It makes a deep thump. "So what do we do here?" I finish the juice, stack the dishes in the sink, run hot water into the glass. "What plans do you have for me?"

"We're going on a walk."

"This is what you do for fun?"

"Yes."

"It's freezing outside."

"You'll bundle up. Were you cold last night?"

"No," I say. "How did you manage that?"

"I had a friend come over and turn the heat on before we came."

"Well done." He leaves the room. Caleb watches him go. "So what do I wear?"

"This," he says, returning. He holds out a blue hooded

sweatshirt and a pair of red coveralls. Then he produces from behind his back a wad of multicolored wool items—socks, gloves, and a hat. "Put these on." I take the coveralls from him, start to put my bare leg inside. "No, silly, over your jeans."

Aiden's house is E shaped. A central room, a corridor, filled with boxes and tools and coils of electrical cord, and doorways leading to three long, rectangular rooms off of that. The first is the bedroom, covered in sawdust from some sort of shelving project that hangs above the bed, and a closet, mostly empty. The second room is the bathroom, with the stairway leading downstairs to a semifinished basement full of boxes and sheet-covered furniture. The kitchen, all yellow and orange with an avocado fridge, is sunlit from the same side as the bedroom. There is hardly anything here, only the bed, the kitchen table, and the chairs. No useless knickknacks crowding shelves. No TV, no couch, no place to let your brain rot. Outside the kitchen is a deck, nearly as large as the house, where Aiden says he sits to watch the sun go down, or come up, which I think is always more spectacular. ("Sunsets or sunrises?" he said. "Accomplishment or possibility.") High ceilings and hardwood floors that seem older than the house, recovered perhaps. But this feels less like aesthetic, more like the floors were a practical, useful, even cheap or haphazard solution. The wood is scarred in places, like the basement floors at St. Vincent's, where the giant filing shelves have been moved around over the years—the miserable and the dead carving out their suffering into the floor. This floor, Aiden's, looks like that.

"Got your clothes on?" he calls to me from the bottom of the stairs, standing at the door. We yell through the house.

"I'm working on it." I'm wearing so many layers I feel stuck inside a soft armor, prepared for battle. "Why don't you have any furniture?"

"It's all down here. I haven't brought it up yet. I'm lazy."

I walk down the stairs. Caleb cocks his head aside first, then wags his tail. He's dressed in dog coveralls and dog shoes.

"He's wearing booties," I say.

"They keep his feet dry in the snow."

Aiden is bundled up as well, only he makes it look agile and practiced. I asked him on the way up here what happened in the dead of winter. I asked him if people just stood around in their houses, watching the snow pile up outside, and calling each other on the phone. "Of course not," he said. "People have to go on with their lives."

He flashes his adorable grin at me. "Oh, Simon. You look so cute."

"I feel like a twelve-year-old."

"I could eat you up," he says in a pathetic Southern accent, a bad, overdone imitation. It makes me blush, and the warmth flushes out through my skin.

Caleb leaps out into the open space, bulldozing out a chunk of snow. We walk behind, letting him choose the way. Or maybe he's following the usual route, some basic sightseeing itinerary that Aiden takes every morning, a cleansing ritual. I do the same thing sometimes, through Astoria Park, back toward the Beer Garden along the brick wall, taking note of how the graffiti has changed—what's been painted over and what's been rewritten. The snow makes moving difficult, but we walk down to the road; it's not so deep here, and easier. Caleb runs ahead awhile, then stops, chewing a stick, or peeing, or patiently waiting. After a while, with my blood moving quickly through me, my body figures it out, and I don't notice the cold at all.

Woodpeckers. They sound like a machine gun firing rubber bullets at something stiff and resonant. They're nearly impossible to see, and when you do pick one out, after minutes of standing still, fixing your eyes and concentrating on movement, you can watch their little red crests vibrating against the wood. Perched in the trees that grow close to the road, announcing their presence from every direction, on the top of the ridge and also farther away. Their sound carries forever; cold air is better for that. Vermont natives must tune it out, or it could drive them crazy. Like the city sound. Like the beating of a waterfall, or the sibilant sound of strangers talking, something your inner sieve discards, or makes inert.

"How are you doing?"

"Good," I say. "I like this."

"Me too."

The wind blows, whistling through my hat and in my ears, one tone pitched high and whispery, the other low and vibrating. Snow shakes off the branches, like a falling cloud of cake flour. Then more machine gun pecking, two of them, from opposite directions, loud and syncopated. I stand still, looking up into the trees.

"You like the woodpeckers?"

"Yeah," I say, and he pats me on the butt, like we're baseball players. Then he hugs me like they do in movies, both of us facing forward, my back to his front, staring off into space. "They're so determined."

"This one here," and he points, his arm angled out from my shoulder. "Melanerpes erythrocephalus." I turn around and push him away with both hands, a firm, happy jolt. He laughs. "You asked."

"What's the civilian version?"

"Red-headed woodpecker. Common name." His beard is flecked with snowflakes, and I reach up to brush him clean. It's really an excuse to touch him. Even in this weather I can sniff him out: leather. Not the dyed black sex leather that gay men wear in dark bars and under their business suits. This is more natural, softer. Brown suede perhaps.

"They're sort of rare. We're lucky to see one like this." He starts to sound like Farmer, with heaps of useless information logged away in the wrinkled, folded creases of his brain, retrievable like a card catalog. "There were some more at the house this morning, but you were asleep. Picoides vilosus and Picoides arcticus."

"Vilosus?"

"Hairy woodpecker."

"Like you," I say, and poke him in the belly.

Then, with a shove, he pushes me down into the snow, climbs on top of me and pins my hands back over my head. He kisses my head, my neck, my face. And I squirm, trying to roll away, but not trying too hard, and I'm laughing and he's laughing and the snow seeps into my pants and into my hat and melts, dripping into my ears. He kisses me over and over, fast and light.

"Get off," I say, flushed, excited, and turned on.

"Make me," he says.

So I push him up, throwing him to the side, where he thumps against the ground. Caleb comes running over, slobber flapping off his face as he trots through the snow. I leap on top of Aiden. Caleb barks, barks again.

"Caleb," he shouts through fits of giggles and twisting

his body underneath mine. "Get him, boy." And the dog barks more and more, wagging his tail and pawing at the ground. I grab Aiden's hand, pinching tight the tender chunk of muscle between his thumb and index finger. Pinching just hard enough to keep him here.

"Ouch," he says. "Simon, you're—"

"Oh, yeah," I say. And then I grab his crotch, pushing my hand up. "Try it now, huh? Think you're so tough, huh?"

"No fair," he shouts, laughing and smiling and eager. "Okay, okay, I give up. I give up." And I know that if he wanted to, he could throw me ten feet in one direction. Because I've held his muscles in my hands, kissed his forearms and felt the rippling of his back when he comes. "Foul play," he says.

I kiss him, pressing my lips on his, pushing my tongue into his mouth. The snow is all over us, powdery, stuffed down in our pockets and shoes, quickly melting, the cool water tickling our fingertips through the gloves. The wind blows bits of ice in between our faces, catching in our eyelashes and in Aiden's beard. I grab the back of his head with my freezing wet hands and hold him close to me. His mouth is so warm.

After dinner—burgers, mashed potatoes, and slightly strange spinach salad (more of Aiden's cooking)—I do the dishes. I like to have my hands in the water, the soap bubbles on my wrists and elbows, a towel thrown over my shoulder, giving me some kind of image, like a blue-collar dishwasher, something silly and subconsciously sexual. Oh, what we wish we were!

Aiden brings boxes and empty picture frames upstairs, putting things away, sometimes measuring, writing down lengths, and eyeing up the shape of the room with furniture. This is when he is the most beautiful, when he is mentally occupied to the extent that he is no longer watching himself from the outside, when the task at hand takes him over. I open a bottle of Corona for Aiden, stuffing (with minor difficulty) a wedge of lime down the neck. It soaks my fingertips, the juice seeping into my cuts, stinging a little—the cries of the infirm, whose existence has been reduced to numbers on paper. Their pain muted, perhaps, by the distance.

"Here," I say, handing him the bottle.

"Thank you," he says, leaning against the door frame, sipping the beer, wiping his mustache with the cuff of his sleeve. "Tomorrow we'll carry up some furniture." I fill my glass with water from the tap, reconsider at the sight of the cinnamon color, and pour it out.

"Oh, I get it. Do the dishes, move the furniture."

"No, of course not," he says, as if I were serious, and I consider for a moment that he doesn't know I'm kidding. I am not as good at sarcasm as I think. "You can finish the orange juice. The water here's not so great, I know. I have to get somebody out here to look at it," he says, an afterthought, spoken to no one in particular. He picks at the label on the beer.

"I'd rather save that for breakfast."

"Have a beer then."

"Actually—"

"I know. You don't drink."

"Right."

"Why don't you drink, if I may ask?"

"Sometimes people ask me why I don't drink and I tell them that I'm a recovering alcoholic. Or that I'm the designated driver, which always gets a laugh. Or I look down at my shoes, touch my fingers to my temple and say, 'Uh, I don't drink,' and let them make up some reason. People would rather make up their own reasons anyway."

"So which is it?"

"There is no reason. It's something I decided I would do years ago, and it stuck. Stupid, I know." And I wipe my hands off on the dishrag, folding it over the sink. I hop up on the counter, my legs hanging off the front. "Sometimes you make choices for yourself. You figure they're practical, or economical, or spiritual, or whatever. You come up with elaborate schemes, an entire gridwork of reasons and excuses. And it works for a while. Then you forget all the rationalizations. Your mainframe blows. And you realize that nothing is what you thought it was. Yourself, even."

Aiden walks over to me and stands between my legs. His arms are around my waist as he leans in to kiss me.

"Wait."

"What's the problem?"

"Listen," I say, pushing his arms off me and leaning my head back, as if from heavy glare. "I don't make a very good boyfriend."

"I don't imagine that you would."

"I need to know what you expect up front. This is how I work."

"We're just exploring something." Aiden folds his arms, and I stare at the bottom edge of his tattoo. "Are you completely unaware of what's going on here?"

"No, I'm not."

"Well, what's the problem?"

"This isn't the time for me right now."

"Bullshit," he says, near shouting. He moves away from me, pulling a chair out from under the table and sitting on it backward. He smoothes his hair with his hand and rubs his fingers through his beard. "You're scared." He says this as if naming it were the cure.

"Don't you think I know that?"

"Yes, I think you're aware of it. I think if you would loosen up, you'd be fine."

"How am I supposed to relax? Louis, who used to be tan and muscular, is now pale and skinny because a gang of gay-bashing fag-haters decided that he'd be their next victim. And they're not stopping, are they? I might be next, you might be next. Jaron practically cut his arm off last week, and he expects me to keep it a secret." I'm talking with my hands here, emphasizing the cutting motion, holding up my arm so he can see. "The world's not safe. It's too fucking hard to relax."

"But I make you relaxed."

"Yes," I say, hesitant. "You do."

"So quit worrying so much about what's happening. Whatever's going to happen will happen, no matter what you talk yourself into believing."

"Whatever."

"Okay, say 'whatever' and roll your eyes at me, like I've said something completely impossible and stupid." And he walks out of the room. He goes down the stairs, starts moving boxes again. Immediately I'm freaked out, afraid that I've done something permanent. I don't have any practice in these kinds of real conversations, where you're talking and he's talking and you're saying things that you don't much say out loud.

After a few seconds I figure I'd better go say something. I stand in the doorway leading down to the basement. I can hear the shuffling of tools, the moving and stacking of boxes.

"All right," I say. "Are you going to come up here and talk to me?"

"Come down here," he says. I roll my eyes, realizing then that I do that a lot, that people notice, and it's not nearly as invisible as I might think. So I go down the stairs, sitting myself near the bottom. Caleb sleeps soundly in his Vermont bed, ignoring us.

"I keep telling myself, 'don't screw up, don't screw up.' Because that's my habit. Mostly I fuck things up."

He doesn't say anything right away, but I can see his brain working, turning over the tumblers, formulating a response.

"So then don't fuck this one up," he says.

"It's not that easy."

"Shut up a minute. I never said it was easy. It's not." He stuffs his thumbs down into his pockets, bunching his jeans up in the front, showing the spray of hair below his navel—the place where he loves to be kissed. "I just want you to try."

"Why me? Why spend all that money and then try to make it something different?"

"Stop it—"

"I want to know."

"Just accept the fact that I like you."

"Tell me the truth," I say.

Without a pause, without even a heartbeat: "Because I always fall for broken people." Aiden looks down at his feet. "I have this thing. Like I can fix them."

It feels like someone pulled the plug out, and everything slips slowly away, flowing off of me with the quiet rush of gravity.

"And now you know," he says.

Broken, I think. *That's about right.*

Then we go for a minute without talking.

Aiden walks over to me. He touches his hands to my forehead, and I lean into him, my face rubbing against his thigh. I squeeze my hands around his leg and he pushes his palm down the back of my shirt, rubbing his fingers along my shoulder blade. "But that's my own shit," he says. "You never know."

"You should meet my friend Farmer, you'd really get along. All that useless woodpecker shit. Farmer's the same way. You both should go on *Jeopardy!,* because you could really rack up. Take home the big one."

"I'd like that."

"One time he took me to see the peregrines on Fifth Avenue. It was great. They were so fast. They practically throw themselves off the buildings." The more I talk, the easier it gets.

He scratches his head, as if shifting to the reserve tank, performing a reboot. "Do you want to go upstairs?" he says.

And I turn and go, without answering, pulling off my shirt as we go, unbuttoning my jeans and trying to kick my shoes off as I walk. I lie down on the bed, Aiden lies on top of me, a cloud of sawdust puffs up around us.

"Aiden," I complain, "why didn't you—"

"I know, I know."

He kisses the soft inside part of my elbow, the part close to my body. He runs his tongue along my wrist and through the center of my palm and then up to my knuckles.

"Wow," he says. "Your fingers taste like lime."

Aiden starts the water running in the bathtub. He twists at the knob over and over until it catches. The showerhead sputters, then works fine. He drops the towel around his waist, and it lands in a heap at his feet. He kicks it to the side. From the back he looks older. He steps into the water and closes the glass door behind him.

We go on long walks through the woods, along the ridge and up to the lookout, which isn't a lookout exactly, but a bare place in the trees where you can see all the way to Canada, he says, though it's only half an hour away by car. We eat again and again, and each day's events revolve around when and what we're going to eat—as if we had nothing better to do than think about food. And each time we sit down at the table, we're hungrier than we expected. His cooking improves—not that I could do any better. We move some furniture, heavy wooden things that look handed down and important. A Chinese apothecary cabinet with a hundred tiny drawers, some taller than you can reach, empty but smelling like moss and black tea. A green leather-topped coffee table, a lamp, two armchairs, and a rug for the bedroom—actually a random piece of carpet, with a crooked side and an unfinished edge. We brush the sawdust out of the sheets. We listen to the woodpeckers, and he tells me about their mating habits, their migratory patterns, and whatever else he can remember, which is a lot, I think. Aiden builds a mailbox at the base of the hill, a project that leaves him beaming with happiness. We lie bundled in blankets on the deck and watch the sunset. We have sex twice, good, focused, and compact, letting our bodies make the decisions. What more could you want from a vacation?

He emerges from the shower steaming and soft, like a slightly undercooked, hairy pink monster. He towels his head, flinging water everywhere. I'm lying in bed, listening to the morning, curled up in the mountain of pillows.

Caleb lies at my feet, his head nearly hanging off the edge, watching Aiden's hands move around, as if he might have a treat, or a ball to throw.

"We'll eat something and then start back. Okay?"

"You have to work tomorrow?" I ask.

"I don't work much."

"So how do you afford all this?"

"Mind your own business. I inherited some money."

"I knew it," I say.

"It's not a lot. Only enough."

"Why do you do your own laundry?"

"I said it was just enough."

This happens all the time in New York—you meet someone and say "what do you do" and they say "I work for a nonprofit agency that provides free services to the poor / sick / dying / underserved community of whatever neighborhood." And then, months later, you're invited to something at their apartment that turns out to be two floors of a stately brownstone and you're looking around at all the artwork on the walls and the huge furniture and you say to yourself: "nonprofit, my ass." Then someone informs you that they have a lot of money socked away, trust funders or smart investors or lottery fucking winners.

He stands in front of me naked, his chest hair still wet and matted down. He runs the towel across his stomach.

"Don't give me that soft liberal bullshit about rich people. It's tired." Aiden snarls his lip. Then, imitating one of those tree-hugging, tofu-eating, Birkenstock-wearing, raw-foodist types he says, "Who knows if it is good to have riches?" Then he blows his nose into the towel, wiping his hand on his thigh. For a moment I'm turned off by the crudeness.

"Just an observation." I sit up, wrapping the sheet around my waist, picking at my toenails.

"Don't do that," he says, meaning the toenails. He leans over the bed, nuzzling his head into Caleb's belly. He whacks him on the side a few times, and Caleb starts grumbling, chewing on a pillow.

Aiden looks up at me. "Do you want to have breakfast in town?"

The counter is filled with burly Vermont men and burly Vermont women drinking steaming cups of coffee and putting forks into ham and cheese omelets. They pour maple syrup on buckwheat pancakes and hunch over, propped up by their elbows. They watch the fuzzy black-and-white television behind the register as if they could see right through the grainy static. I can't see what they're watching—news, weather, maybe a morning show beamed in from a big city. We take two stools in the corner.

"Coffee?" she says, the waitress with crinkled lips, like a thousand tiny tears, like handmade Japanese paper. Her hair is dyed blond, that older-lady shade that's more yellow-gold than anything natural, and it's all pushed up away from her face, held there by a pink hat with a dirty brim and some pins. She rattles her fingernails on the countertop, tapping out of habit it feels like, something to pass the time.

"No, thank you," he says, polite as always. "Pancakes and sausage, well done."

"I want a grilled cheese sandwich, two eggs scrambled, and a strawberry shake."

"Also," he says, "can I get a vanilla Coke?"

She doesn't answer yes or no, just walks away, scribbling on her pad and waving two fingers at the cook, who seems to understand her, already cracking eggs on the grill and stirring the batter, laying out plates. One constant motion.

I lean over to Aiden, poking his side with my finger. "Not a chatty kind of place, I guess."

"Guess not."

She brings the soda, setting it down in front of him and then pulling a straw from the pocket in her apron. She lays out two napkins to our right, then a fork and knife on top of each. He stirs the Coke, pushing the heavy syrup around in the glass, and it swirls upward, mingling with the ice and then settling again at the bottom.

"Excuse me, can you give me quarters for this?" I pass three one-dollar bills across the counter, landing them near a napkin dispenser. She looks down at them, then cuts her eyes back at me. Out of her pocket, she fishes out quarters and stacks them on the counter in front of me.

"Here," she says, and takes the dollars.

Aiden smiles at me, like he knew this kind of thing would happen, like all morning he's been dying to see what I'll do down here. "It's not going to be that much," he says. "One dollar, tops."

"What if I have to call back?"

"Whatever you say, dear." The mention of this word, *dear,* surprises me, and I say it a few times to myself, quietly and with no breath at all, like trying on a piece of clothing that doesn't belong to me, or going by a different name, if only for a moment. *Dear* sounds like a foreign language.

"I'll be right here," he says.

I trust him, I realize this now. Not with everything—but I can feel it, a smoothness spreading out, an ease. To put it simply: I'm not trying so hard. I read a book once (or maybe I was reading about a book) that was supposed to teach you how to "open yourself to people" by using a series of fill-in-the-blank pages and workbook assignments. By admitting your vulnerability, and writing its "layers" down on the paper provided, you would learn how to create "genuine" and "memorable" relationships with others. The goal was to be "fully open" by page one hundred. Not a lot of time to get there, I thought. And what are you supposed to do once you've uncovered all your layers? You're supposed to go around all vulnerable and open, sharing yourself with everyone. That's exactly what we need—legions of vulnerable readers parading around Manhattan. The book was very popular, so there must have been something right about it.

The phone is back in a hallway near the bathroom, which is labeled with both male and female stick figures, plus a separate—I guess neutered—figure in a wheelchair. The door hangs open like an installation in an art museum, wads of paper towels covering the floor near a violet garbage bin, stuffed to the top and overflowing. I can see myself pick up the phone in the vanity mirror, like sneaking up on something private, like voyeurism without the scandal—is there such a thing?

I dial the number, then plunk the quarters in the slot. Louis is there—possibly alone, reading the newspaper, another beating maybe, smoking a cigarette with the television stuck on The Weather Channel. He's probably barely dressed, the clothes hanging off him, chosen by accident. He's opening boxes sent from various Internet establishments: kitchen supplies, bed linens, and cigarettes in cartons. It rings twice before he picks up.

"Hello." Not a question, or a greeting. Merely a comment.

"Hey, it's me," I say, already noticing a tenseness in my voice, already afraid of being found out.

"Where are you?"

"In Vermont. What's going on?"

"Jaron is in the hospital. He's okay, but—"

"What happened?"

"He cut his arm awhile back. It got infected and it's all through him now."

"Is he eating?"

"He says so, but I'm not sure." I hear the rattling of glass ashtrays in the background, the whistle-clang of the radiator. "I can't imagine the nurses aren't making him eat. Isn't that their job?"

"Louis," I say, "did you go see him?"

"Simon—"

"Go down there."

"I don't know. Farmer's been down there every day. Sometimes he spends the night." A few seconds of silence, then the sound of the television, a news program I can't make out. The clicking of the cigarette lighter and the fuzzy distance of the telephone wires. "They said only family should stay with him."

"Louis . . ."

He says nothing. Then, "You're right."

"I'm coming home."

"Okay," he says, exhaling. "Come home. I think you should."

And then the grinding clicks of wires and connections closing. The dial tone clicks on, droning out at me like a sad ancient instrument. I place the receiver back in its cradle, look back at myself in the bathroom mirror. Sometimes I look so tired.

Aiden shovels pancakes into his mouth, sipping Coke

from the straw and dragging the sausage pieces through the syrup. "So what's the news?"

"I have to go home."

He stops chewing. "What happened?"

"My friend is in the hospital."

"Okay," he says, putting the fork down. He waves two fingers at the waitress, who begins scribbling on her notepad. "Get in the truck. I'll do this." And he pulls out his wallet.

I stuff my hands down into the gloves, pull the hat on, zip up the coveralls in front and push open the door. The truck is quiet, away from the sounds of people eating and the oily sputter of the grill.

My head is empty, sunk deep into black water, whiffs of that charred marshmallow stench. And nothingness—not like a sheet of paper waiting to be written on, or a vase you think should be filled with flowers. This is the sound of a blank cassette tape playing loudly on a car stereo—air and dust and the sound of nothing.

I've heard this sound once before.

It was ages ago, my grandfather's death. I must have been six, maybe seven. The phone rang and my mother went to get it. He had suffered a heart attack. He was in the hospital. Or on the way to the hospital. Or he was still at home waiting to go to the hospital. There was no panic in her voice, only a cinching kind of fear that was all details and logistics. She walked around the counter and gathered her purse. She had this sense of resignation, an understanding, a veil of preparation. She told me to stay at home in case someone called. That horrible sound of nothing that happened at the funeral, where no one spoke of him, or cried for him—he was not a particularly pleasant man. I admit that I cannot remember too much of it clearly. I only remember my great-aunt's dress hem ruffling against the ground near the curb where she stood.

I do not want to hear this sound ever again.

"We'll get Caleb and then we'll go," Aiden says.

"I'm sorry."

"It's okay." Aiden lays a hot pouch of aluminum foil in my lap. "That's your breakfast. Grilled cheese sandwich and scrambled eggs."

"Thank you," I say, even though I'm too sick to eat. I touch his leg, fingering the line of stitching in his pants.

"They didn't have anything for the shake."

"That's okay."

We start up the road, snow falling down on us, and the warm air soon pours into the cab, almost burning my hands if I hold them close to the vents. Aiden unloads stuff from the back of his truck into the basement—I have barely anything. He makes a phone call. I can't hear what he says, and soon enough we're driving back to New York. Caleb seems unfazed, happy as ever to be in a car.

"Who did you call?"

"The neighbors."

"I didn't see any neighbors."

"They're a few miles away, but they're still neighbors." Caleb drools onto my sleeve and I towel it off with the wadded up T-shirt on the dash, not even thinking about it.

"Are you ready for this?" I say.

"Ready for what?"

"You get to meet all my friends at the same time."

"Except the one who won't come out of the house."

"Louis. He's the model."

"Was the model," Aiden says.

"Yes, was the model."

We pass the same exits, the same strangely named places

where people's lives are different. I do not believe that they are easier—ask anybody if their life is easy and see what they say—but I would guess that they are quieter, slower, and somehow closer to what was originally intended: more grass, more dirt, lives squeezed into shape by the seasons. Maybe I have romanticized it. I still believe that it's true.

Eventually we make it to New York. The snow has again turned to rain, slower this time, and the water darkens the street to black, pours off the buildings. People buy umbrellas on their way to the subway station and toss them in the trash on their way to their apartment buildings. The cast-off umbrellas poke their limbs out of the garbage, broken like leggy insects by the wind. Sagging and dripping and lonely and meaningless.

Chapter Twenty-two

The helmet-haired ladies at the main floor reception desk recognize me only slightly as I walk through the electric doors, then return to their word searches and nail files. I'm another nobody to them—could be visiting a sick grandmother, scheduled for some kind of treatment, here about some blood work, it doesn't matter. As long as I don't bother them, right?

I leave Aiden in the waiting room—uncomfortable chairs, coffee-stained carpeting. The television that no one watches, flickering with bad reception. Flimsy magazines, useless like secondhand sneakers, pages of once-shocking celebrity gossip. He grabs my hand as I go, squeezing it once.

Jaron's room is the fifth on the left, through a set of double doors down a bare beige hallway. And though it is bright and alien out here, among the numbered doors and metal rails, the endless blank corridors, his room is lit by orange-colored lamps, and it feels more organic, more like a place where a person could heal. A cheap glass vase of pink and yellow flowers stands in one corner, like the consolation prize from a low-budget '70s game show.

"No guests," Jaron says, waving his palm back and forth at me and blinking, as if to take in more of the room, zooming out to a wider view. His arms are perforated with tubes, carrying solids in liquid suspension into his body, refilling the tired organs, reminding the cells that their job is to keep him alive.

"Get over it," I say.

"Well, you can get rid of this dinner tray. These nurses can't do a damn thing." He points in the air, a finger lifted in no particular direction.

"Good to see you, too."

"It's true. I hate them."

"Don't bite the hand that changes your intravenous."

Jaron's eyes roll back, his head tilts to the ceiling, and he lifts his arms, an almost religious pose. One arm is bandaged up, wrapped in gauze and fluorescent pink tape. "Oh, great traveler from afar, share your wisdom!"

"What were you—"

"So there are these two guys in line waiting to get into heaven and a limo drives up."

"Is this a joke?" I say.

Farmer steps out of the bathroom to the sound of the toilet flushing—a grand entrance, something out of a sitcom, a late-night talk show gag. "You're here," he says. He rubs some paper towels around on his hands, wads them into a ball, and tosses it underneath the table into the garbage.

"I'm here."

Jaron says, "And the door to the limo opens up and this man gets out. And he's dressed in these long flowing white robes, and he has a big beard and glowing white light behind him."

"Did you bring him?" Farmer says. He moves a pea-colored plastic chair over to the side of the bed, motioning for me to sit.

Jaron continues, never missing a beat, "And he's got a stethoscope hanging off his neck. The one guy says to the other, 'Hey, who's that?' And the other guy says, 'Oh, that's God. Sometimes he thinks he's a doctor.'" I laugh, sort of.

"Here he goes again," says Farmer.

Jaron continues: "Let your soldiers ride out from the fiery mouth of your lair and dislodge this sagging flesh. Let them remove the feculent chicken soup the nurses have placed before me." He presses a red button on a long cord that winds up the arm of his hospital bed and disappears into the wall. It makes a boring, vague, hardly persistent *bing*. "Return my body to its primordial state, all gurgling parameciums and what have you."

"Well done," I say.

"That was the short version," Farmer says. "The paramecia are a nice touch, although scientifically impossible."

Jaron says, "See what I've put up with for the last hundred hours? It's like Trivial Pursuit that never ends. My own personal hell, endless *binging* up and down the hallways and Farmer telling me, among other things, all about the dwindling number of Trappist monks."

I say, "You should be thankful somebody showed up."

Jaron says, "Such a sharp tongue."

I lean over and kiss him on the head. He absorbs it, the way a child will humor your affection by sitting still until you're done. His hair smells like antiseptic, like recycled airplane air.

"I thought you told me you were on medication."

"I was. It didn't work. Maybe I forgot to take it, I don't know." He shifts his body, sitting higher on the bed, reaching behind his head to tousle his pillow. "Oh, well, here I am."

"I brought a friend," I say.

"No, no, no. Not at this most delicate of times. I look like an abortion!"

Farmer says, "The drama today, I swear."

I say, "I'll send him home if you don't want to meet him."

Farmer says, "I want to meet him."

Jaron says, "Okay, all right, bring him in already. I couldn't look any worse." I shut the door behind me, stepping out into the hallway, ready and yet not.

Fear of hospitals is pretty common—the lingering veil of dying, of old age, of losing control of your functions. And despite the fact that I have potentially spent more hours at this place, deep underground among the aisles of the nameless afflicted, than I have in any other one place since I moved here, I do not like walking the cinderblock hallways past the ever-busy staff looking down at their feet, shuffling off to the lab, or the nurses' station, or wherever. Some patients (the most lonely, the most incurable) keep their doors propped open. They gaze out into the hall, waiting for someone to come in and relieve them, finally, of their ails. I don't look into the rooms. I don't want to see what's lying in the sheets, limbs piled on each other, plastic tubing crisscrossing the air above them, the television stuck on something they don't want to watch, but are too out of it, or weak, or hurting to change it.

"Follow me," I say, glancing back at the helmet-haired

ladies, who are stuffing tri-folded sheets of yellow paper into envelopes.

Aiden stands, hitching his hands up off his hips, retucking his shirt, rubbing his fingers on his hairy face. "All right," he says. "Let's do it."

"Jesus, why does this feel like an audition?"

Aiden pats me on the butt, a somehow alarming display here at the hospital.

I open the door. Farmer sits in the chair next to the bed. He smiles as we enter, an unfamiliar meeting-your-biological-mother kind of grin, the look you give someone you're supposed to like, but might not. "Nice to finally meet you," he says.

Aiden says, "You too."

Farmer says, "We've heard so much about you." Only coming out of his mouth it sounds like a question.

Aiden says, "Only good things, I hope."

Farmer says, "Of course, of course."

Jaron and I look at each other. "This is so corny," he says.

Farmer says, "Shut up."

Aiden says, moving his hand over to Jaron's bedside, "It's nice to meet you."

Jaron says, "Yes, it must be," and laughs at his joke.

Aiden laughs too, covers Jaron's hand with his other, the way churchgoing people will do when they want it to mean something. "I'll take this," he says, and picks up the tray. Farmer opens the door and Aiden steps back in the hallway.

Jaron says, "That was short."

Farmer says, "Hot."

I say, "I think he's nervous."

Jaron says, "No wonder you're so goo-goo all the time."

I say, "I am not goo-goo all the time."

Farmer says, "Yes, you are."

Aiden returns and Jaron immediately launches into something about his stitches and medications, a seamless change of subject, like a casino magician using the age-old technique: palm, flourish, and misdirect. Farmer pulls a chair up next to Aiden and they sit, descending into babble about whatever, subjects that prove they've known each other in a former life, like they're best friends forever, like sisters. Farmer has this effect on people.

Hospital beds are always longer than they need to be, and the extra space dwarfs Jaron's body, shrinking him. I flip through the pages on his chart, the colored tabs, the scratchy handwritten complaint, the nearly illegible record of medications given. "You're not supposed to have this," I say.

Jaron says, "I know. It's new. Some kind of power to the patient initiative they're running around here."

I say, "Really?"

Jaron says, "People were complaining. They said they didn't have any idea what kind of treatment they were getting. They wanted some kind of record." He smoothes the sheets over his legs. "Of course, it's not like anybody can read a word of it."

"I can read it," I say.

"Well, duh," he says.

"They've pegged you as a nutcase."

"Really?"

"That's what this paperwork means. Well, a more complicated version of that." And I point to a special string of numbers on the side of the file. I point to the handwriting on the tab.

Jaron says, "Idiots."

The hallway *bings* about ten more times, from all different directions, like a warehouse full of animatronic birds, exact copies of each other, announcing the urgency of pain, of hunger, of boredom, and confusion. "See what I mean?" Jaron rolls his eyes.

I say, "When can we take you home?"

Jaron says, "Right now."

I say, "I'm serious."

Jaron says, "I don't know, ask the doctors."

I say, "They seem to be getting along." I motion to Farmer and Aiden.

Jaron says, "Was there any doubt?"

I say, "They're probably talking about endangered woodpeckers."

Jaron waves. "Hello?" He produces a small white towel from somewhere and waves it around, like a pitiful, almost feminine S.O.S. "Hello?"

Farmer says, "What?" He and Aiden look at us, holding their thoughts, not moving away from their conversation just yet.

Jaron says, "Turn on the television."

Farmer reaches for the remote and points it in the general direction of the TV. The blank screen, dusty and pointed slightly askew, brightens into the local news. We all look up, like we're waiting for instructions. A woman appears, a pinkish business suit, gold clip-on earrings and a pearl necklace, plus her stupid, sexless hairdo. She stares ahead, addressing the teleprompter.

"A vicious hate crime today in the Financial District,

where two men were attacked in the early morning hours outside the Wall Street Sauna, one of the few remaining gay bathhouses in the city. Police have not yet released the names of the victims. Both men were taken to St. Vincent's Hospital with substantial head injuries, and both are said to be in critical condition."

She continues, more details that I don't hear, something about *blunt trauma to the chest,* pieces of information that slide in and then immediately out of my head. My stomach does a massive plunge, an elevator crashing to the basement.

"Let's go out to our *Eyewitness News* correspondent who is live at the scene." A firm, emotional pause, telling the rest of the viewers (the ones who aren't likely to get their heads bashed in with crowbars on their way to work) what to think, and how to feel about the situation. This seems to be the job of the local news no matter where you are in the country. The anchors chitchat about the weather and say "gosh" and "isn't that something" after the piece about the Boy Scout with perfect attendance—all this in between stories of abandoned babies, forty-car pileups, and failing school systems. They laugh when they're supposed to, appear reverent when their teleprompters say they should. I used to think that hollow-souled people were destined to become only toll takers and adult video store clerks, but I know now that they become fixtures in the local news.

The screen splits into two boxes, a faded map of the boroughs underneath it all, giving the scene a kind of non-location, like they could be anywhere, hovering over the city like fictional narrators. The pink business suit on the left, a gray suited man on the right. He holds a microphone topped with a cartoonish blob of yellow foam, his other hand holding an umbrella, the water dripping off it lit by the blaring light of the camera. He is haloed by the silvery beads. "Tell us what it looks like down there," she says, and looks up into the camera. "As you can see, it's rather quiet here right now," he says, "but right behind me is where the incident occurred early this morning."

Jaron jumps in, practically screaming at the television. "That faggot?" he shouts. "Fuck you."

"This tragedy, believed to be committed by the same group of attackers as the previous assaults—"

Jaron says, "That guy won Best Chest last year at The Lure."

Farmer says, "No way."

Jaron says, "What an asshole."

The rain continues, and the news guy steps aside and waves his hand in the air, displaying the entrance to the sauna, like a game-show model pointing out the state-of-the-art features of the item up for bids. "Police say they were on their way to work after an early morning tryst just inside these doors."

Aiden says, "Good-bye Wall Street Sauna."

Jaron says, "They always ruin everything. What's a tryst anyway? I guess they can't say suck and fuck, can they?"

Aiden says, "Or handjob."

Farmer and I look at each other. He says, "I'm going to get some ice." And he stands, opens the door, and is gone. His missing energy leaves the room sagging and deflated, as if it were possible for painted walls, crisp white sheets, and beeping machines to take on a pessimistic view of the universe. I do this a lot: feel sad for inanimate objects.

I say, "What was that about?"

Jaron says, "That's what he does when the going gets rough. Goes to get ice."

I think for a moment that I should follow him, talk to him, but the thought of leaving Jaron here with Aiden isn't something I'm ready to do. Not for any particular reason, but I have always known that the kind of family you make for yourself reveals more about your character than you ever do alone. And I have a short pang of tightness and anxiety that says what Jaron will expose about me (though I have no idea specifically what) is something I'm not ready for Aiden to see. But here is something I also know to be true: The people who love you the most also help you become the purest, most real person that you always were.

The news guy says, looking more concerned than ever, "No doubt this will be addressed at tomorrow's rally."

I say, "What rally?"

Jaron says, "Some fags have organized a Take Back the Night thing, a protest at Bryant Park." He presses the red button at the end of the cord, and it *bings* again. "They never come when you call them."

The pink-suited woman is on the screen again. This time her expression has changed to a soft, empty smile. Okay, we're supposed to say, this story is more pleasant, we like this story, we like this pink-suited woman. "And now for a quick look at tomorrow's weather," she says.

Aiden starts talking the way someone will when they're actually talking about something else. "Why do they always go live when there's nothing to look at? Like it never occurred to them that just because they have the option to beam somebody in from a thousand miles away, perhaps, just maybe, they shouldn't."

I expect Jaron to have some kind of smartass comment, and I straighten up, prepared to defend Aiden. I almost feel as if that's my job. Jaron looks blankly ahead, as if facing a grave future, or prepared to give a sworn deposition. "Yes," he says, "I think you're right."

Farmer returns, without ice. He's drinking a Coke from the can. "So what was the news?" he says, sort of frustrated and sort of relaxed—actually Farmer's standard demeanor.

I say, "There's a rally tomorrow."

Jaron says, trying to fluff his pillow, "You're not actually going, are you?"

I move over to him, pushing the soft stuffing around, trying to resituate the stack. "I might," I say. I shove the pillows into each other, and they condense and then expand again.

Farmer says, "Here, let me do that."

I let him, backing away. Aiden's arms reach around me, like a summer camp pal, like your partner in the three-legged race.

Jaron sighs, snaps off the television and points his finger to the door. "Well, don't feel like you have to stay any longer," he says.

Aiden releases me. He takes Jaron's hand and he says something that I can't make out because out in the hallway a whole gaggle of nurses have started singing "Happy Birthday" and the blur of bodies and flaming cake goes by like a chubby pastel blob. Jaron smiles at Aiden and I hear him say, "Thank you."

Jaron says, "We'll be in touch."

I say, "Yes."

Jaron says, "Tell Louis he's dogshit if he doesn't come down here. Never mind, he's dogshit already."

Farmer returns to the window of glass that faces the hallway nurses' station. He changes the upward angle of the pale beige blinds. Two dozen strips of light fall across the wall, over the tubes and IV drip and over the curved steel arms of the hospital bed, landing on Jaron's torso and thighs. He looks marked off in sections, like slices of bread. Aiden opens the door and the faint echo of "happy birthday dear somebody" wafts into the room.

Chapter Twenty-three

A skinny, spike-haired fag, originally brown haired, but made blond via one of those sun-in sprays, steps up to me, smiling, flipping through his armful of olive and light blue T-shirts hanging in the crook of his elbow. He fiddles with a clipboard in his other hand, trying to juggle everything at once. A walkie-talkie strapped to his hip squawks a fuzzy, annotated dialogue, but he doesn't pay it any attention. Thumpy, droning music.

"Let me see," he says. "What size would you like?"

"Are they free?"

"Of course!" He cocks his head back and forth, trying to adjust the official-looking headset with miniature microphone that surrounds his cranium.

"Medium. No, small."

"Make up your mind, girlfriend!"

"Small," I say. I refuse to be swallowed up by my clothing.

He pulls a shirt off the top of the stack, not really hearing me, and hands it over. "There you go, Mary!"

I hold it in front of me, trying to read the screen-print design: OUT OF THE DARKNESS SHINES A BRIGHT RAINBOW. "Oh, give me a break," I say. Everyone is wearing color, like semigloss springtime paint chips on steroids. But not *like* they're on steroids, they *are* on steroids. I hang the shirt over my shoulder and walk out onto the grass.

Rainbow flags everywhere. Rainbow stickers and jewelry, shoes and backpacks and ball caps and belt buckles. A flotilla of rainbow-shirted muscle boys, all clumped together, practicing the living flag—one flirty-faced red spot in the blue section, some orange mixed in with the green, and an older fag with a megaphone screaming at them to "get in line." A rainbow arch of balloons blowing back and forth above the stage set with microphones, black speakers, and a silver drum kit. As I walk across the lawn, the sun glints off the sparkling sides of the tom-toms, like the reflection of a watch face, like the static blinking of nautical distress.

A man walks up to the podium dressed in a pale pink shirt buttoned up to the throat and casual-looking ivory pants. He dabs a handkerchief across his brow, then folds it, stuffing it into his pocket. He taps on the mike, gives us one of those stupid "testing one, two, three" lines and fiddles with some papers in front of him. The crowd calms down and the megaphone guy motions for the living flag to be seated. Newspeople point their cameramen toward the stage. The music thumps its way to quiet, and through a short burst of feedback he begins: "We are here today to take a stand against violence, and against hatred."

Then I'm thinking: Where are all the women?

"All of humanity, all persons of conscience should be horrified," the speaker says, pounding his fist on the wood, and the crowd cheers. They sound like a television commercial, or a studio audience. "As gays living in these uncertain times, we are here to demand equal protection."

A roar of applause, and the living flag stands up in unison, throwing their arms into the air and filling the park with noise. I turn around, trying to see how many people have filled in behind me. Among the wash of olive and light blue shirts glows a lime-green, pink-beaded head. A pale, bony hand signals.

Mr. Bartlett stands in a hole in the crowd. People give him space the way they do the homeless, or the crazy. I walk over to him, letting the stupid T-shirt fall off my shoulder to the ground. I leave it there, where it's swallowed up by the listeners' tentative feet, the anxious shifting of weight.

"Oh, my goodness," he says, "pleasure seeing you here. Surprising. But wonderful."

"How are you?" I say.

"You haven't returned my calls." I threw my answering machine out with the trash—a dozen or so messages left unheard, to be discovered by a stranger.

"I've been busy."

"I don't believe you."

"I swear. I was out of town for a while."

"You hurt my feelings."

"I'm sorry." Then I'm thinking, why are you defensive? You don't owe him an explanation. You don't owe him anything.

"I invited you to a show and you never returned my call. I had to go all by myself. There was an empty seat next to me."

"I was out of town."

"Tell me, is there anything more sad than an empty seat at a play?"

"I doubt it."

"Oh, don't get bitter."

"I'm sorry everyone saw you sitting by yourself."

"Fuck everyone else." His jaw tightens up. "I couldn't care less who saw me doing what. I *wanted* to go with you. I had *planned* to go with you."

I don't say anything, and he turns back to the stage, folding his arms.

The speaker continues, his voice echoing off the buildings on Sixth Avenue, skipping off the back side of the library. "If we give in to these people, then they win," and he points his finger in the air, gesturing at nothing. "I sure as hell am not going to." He takes the microphone from its stand, letting some of his notes fall off onto the stage. He jerks the long cord out of the middle of the space, and his posture changes, a confident, concerned aura about him— as if he were a preacher about to take up serpents. "They might attack us," he says. "They might maim us." During the pause in his words there is only the muffled hum of the city. "They can break our bones with their baseball bats."

Mr. Bartlett watches the performance, forgetting somehow that he is angry with me. Or maybe he's not angry. Maybe it's an act. "He's good," he says.

"A little overdone, I think."

"Yes," he nods.

The speaker looks out over the tanned, handsome faces. "They can plant bombs at every gay establishment in the city, but we're not going away." And the crowd explodes, waving rainbow flags and screaming.

"Bombs?" I say.

"He's extrapolating. Theatrics."

The speaker dabs his forehead again, shaking the handkerchief loose, unfolded. "We are all one people!"

"It sounds like a cult."

The guy throws his fist in the air. "Forgive us if we took rights for privileges!"

Mr. Bartlett agrees. "Next they'll be telling us to cut all our genitals off and drink the funny Kool-Aid."

"We will again live our lives in peace!" Random agreements from all directions, unclear, mouthy, and angry.

Mr. Bartlett says, "The funny thing about these people is that I often get the feeling that the fight itself is more important than the cause."

"Meaning?"

He turns away from the crowd, starts walking toward the Avenue, and the masses fill in the hole where we stood, fluid and moving like a school of fish. "Meaning that people need something to get behind." We stop at the street corner, facing uptown, watching the taxicabs stop and start their way through intersections, the walk/don't walk flickering at us across the street, urgent but completely ignored—city people walk as soon as the light turns yellow.

"A conviction." He pauses. "Justification, rationale, whatever you choose to call it." Mr. Bartlett and I walk across the street, a hundred people with us, a delicate meshing of opposing directions.

"Maybe they're pissed off," I say.

"Maybe," he says, though I can tell that he hasn't actually considered this.

Two men walk past us, pressing their heads against their big Robocop-looking radio, listening to the rally. Tight, synthetic fabric pulled over muscles, wraparound sunglasses, and two-day beards. Cargo shorts that end just past the knee, cell phones in pockets, boots with heavy laces—Siamese twins, one of them Latino, joined at the everything.

"Where are we walking?" I say.

"We're simply walking. I'm not keeping you, am I?"

"No."

"Of course not *now*." He lets out a huff of breathy laughter, like he's just heard a stupid joke. "I don't care, Simon. I'm only being difficult. I only do it to get a rise out of you. It's just too easy."

We pass a few Korean-owned delis, fruit displays lining the entrances. Everything you'd ever want or need, vegetables I never knew existed.

"Could I ask you to make an appointment with me?"

"I'm not doing that anymore."

"Oh," he says. He stops to look into a store window. One of those jewel globes, where each country has been carved out of a different rock, or mineral, or semiprecious stone. Then they place each one together end to end to make a perfectly smooth, if a little bit stylized, map of our planet. "Simon, they made the ocean out of lapis. I think that's just the perfect stone for the ocean." He touches his finger to the glass, as if pointing through it, touching the tiny countries themselves. "And that wonderful rose-colored stone for the country of Portugal. I always wanted to visit Portugal, and I don't really know why. I imagine it to be a place where mountains end at the sea. It probably has an unpleasant history. Most countries have unpleasant histories." He puts his hand back down at his side.

"I want you to come over next week," he says.

"I told you—"

"Not to fuck me. There's something I want to give you."

"What?"

"I can't tell you now. Not because it's a secret. Because I haven't decided what it is yet. I won't know until the day."

"Okay," I say. I'm a little uncomfortable, but Mr. Bartlett has that effect on me regardless. He exudes a sense of
unease, a slightly tinny taste, and an odd knowledge that
you've somehow been here before.

"How about Thursday? Late afternoon?"

"Okay," I say. "I can be there."

In the next window is a huge landscape painting in a
gold frame, track spots above, highlighting the muted
shades. A ruddy-brown dirt road, the wispy spray, not a
clear representation, merely the idea of wildflowers. An
empty sky, fading from crayon-inspired blue to peri-
winkle.

"Do you like this painting?" he asks.

"No," I say, "I hate it."

"Yes. That's exactly right." He begins walking and I
turn on the ball of my foot, catching up to him. "I'm so
sick and tired of people not saying what they really feel.
Something can be worthless crap and no one even—"

"Me too," I say.

"It's the worst. Especially when it comes to paintings, or
a foreign film. The high arts are susceptible the most, I believe. The *high arts,* well, there's the problem, I suppose."
His energy is at once excited and reserved, like a person
keeping a secret.

We come to the corner, lined with six or eight newspaper boxes, headlines in red and black, stickers and
sharp-lined graffiti covering Plexiglas doors. Some of the
coin slots are plugged with sugared-out wads of pink
chewing gum, or a folded-up ATM receipt. The trash cans
are full of plastic cups and glistening take-away containers,
a few shreds of carrot and crumpled napkins—overpriced
salad bar detritus. Mr. Bartlett balances himself on the
curb, looking down at the oncoming traffic, taxis with and

without passengers, a tourist-trap sightseeing bus, police cars, and a giant delivery truck.

"I'm so sick of the way people are talking these days."

"Who?"

"Everyone." He steps off the curb, not waiting for the light to change, like he's making a stage entrance. I follow him, almost by accident, my brain telling me *we're going to be smashed to bits by a taxi,* and the cars zoom in front of us, swerving and cursing. But we cross without incident, and I'm amazed and scared all at once, like we're some kind of gay Indiana Jones. "Especially the newspeople," he says. "And people in politics." We come to the edge of Central Park, where the wild, strange nature of the city meets the tamed, path-laden softness of the trees and grass. The smell of horseshit and hot dog vendors. "I'm so sick of hearing everyone talk about how they're Sending A Message. It's so passive-aggressive."

We walk along Central Park South, past the apartment buildings and fancy hotels, the ones people live in like apartments, with uniformed doormen in white gloves pushing rich women with shopping bags through the revolving doors. There are men selling cheap I ♥ NY T-shirts, the charcoal portrait people, the sleazy and charming horse-and-buggy drivers.

"Anyway," he says. "Where are you going?"

"I'm going to work after this."

"I see. And how are your friends doing?"

"Good. One of them is in the hospital."

"Oh, that's terrible. Nothing serious, I hope."

"He'll be fine."

"And how are all your clients? Right, you're not doing that sort of work anymore, I seem to have forgotten. Some kind of moral choice, I assume. You were always so moral, I thought. Really too much for your own good."

"I met someone." Did you ever say something out loud that you know you probably shouldn't, and you know that you'd rather not clean up the pieces once you've said it, and you don't really know why you've said it, but somehow, miraculously, it passes across the synapses and comes stumbling—sometimes racing—out of your mouth for no reason? Saying this felt like that.

"Really?" he says, craning and tilting his head away from me.

"Yes."

"Who is he?"

"Just a guy."

"And where does he live?"

"Across the street from me."

"And what is going on between you?"

"We're seeing each other."

"I don't believe you. For how long?"

"I don't know. Off and on."

"What do you do together?"

"He took me to Vermont." And no matter what you're thinking—even if what you're thinking is *shut up shut up shut up*—you keep blabbering on. "He's nice."

"Nice?" Mr. Bartlett says, as if I had said "He's from Jupiter."

"Yes. He doesn't expect anything from me."

"Oh, that's the worst. The one you choose should expect great things from you. No matter what people tell you about how healthy it is to come into a relationship with no expectations—they're wrong."

"I think I can handle it."

"I'd be careful. You're quite easy to fall in love with."

And to this I don't say anything. I keep walking, turning up Fifth Avenue, past the used-book tables and ten-minute massage givers. We walk another long block without talking, stepping over the sidewalk pushed up by tree roots and weeds, the crumbly octagonal tiles sliding, like plate tectonics, out of order. We let the rhythm of the pavement tell us how to move, and I look over at him trying to see what's going on in there, trying to see what he's thinking. He stares ahead blankly, more relaxed than I've ever seen him.

Then we arrive at his door. I let him pass though, standing not quite inside the room. I'm not going up there with him—and I'm sure he won't ask. I watch his reflection pass in the mirror, covered in leggy canes and lily pads.

"So," I say, my tongue fumbling around in my mouth. "Did you enjoy the protest?"

"Not really."

"Me either. Although I'm glad it happened."

"Yeah," I say.

He picks at the paint with his fingernail. "But speaking of sending a message, they're certainly doing that, aren't they?"

"Who?"

"The people trying to exterminate us," he says, gazing up at the cracked egg and dart. "I can't help thinking, what do they want to bring to attention?"

I watched a man in a brown suit sleeping on the train today on my way to the office, which is what I like to call the rows of files sometimes—ha ha, funny, right? I was surprised by it, actually. His mouth was gaping open and his neck was so relaxed that as the train lurched from side to side, along the shiny tracks, his head bobbed back and forth, his sagging jowls vibrating up and down. I was surprised because he seemed to have no sense of the world. Rather than drifting inside the half-eyed sleep that most New Yorkers enjoy (or maybe tolerate) on their commute, he was completely gone. I couldn't see myself in the same situation—performing such a personal act as sleeping way out here in the open. Which I guess could be a particular kind of irony, because I do so many other extremely personal things with people I don't know anything about. But that's different. I'm usually the one in control there, and this man in the brown suit looked so vulnerable. I imagined placing, with a pair of tweezers, a wriggling, spiny insect on his soft pink tongue.

A few files came in today that—in my peonic opinion, at least—shouldn't be here. All of them are medical instances from the fag-bashing around town. My first instinct is that they were put here on purpose, shuffled out of view by a slimy paper-clip pusher in Administration, a conspiracy trickling down from above.

But I also know how things really work around here.

Which is to say that all the energy goes into keeping people alive, healing them from their mysterious ailments, and therefore the rest of the everyday business can get lost—phone calls are forgotten, paper towels run out in the bathrooms, and files go askew for no reason.

There is a random movement to this world. Entropy asserts itself here like no other place I know.

Sure, some people land here because they smoked for forty years and now their organs are rotten and oozing, or, simply, they got tanked on vodka and fell off a curb. Or they got stabbed by their crack-addict cousins. But the majority of people arrive for no reason whatsoever—at least no reason that we, mere human beings, have been able to articulate just yet.

Like Louis said: Sometimes things just are.

People come in, they hurt, some get better, some die. Those that pass on, all around them is bright swirling energy—from the doctors, the nurses, the frizzled-out families—some people even claim to be able to see it. It's in the objects, too. The silverware is beat up, hinges here go quickly—on bed railings and cabinet doors. And the doctors scratch their impossible handwriting into the files, and that energy, that kinetic movement, moves into the paper and then, if the file is sent to me, into my wire baskets and eventually it carves out red lines in my fingers.

The parts of us that are susceptible to sickness and disease—that is to say the parts that are susceptible to chance—are right there under the surface waiting to be culled out. You win the metaphysical lottery, as it were—for good or bad—and you choose your fate like a bingo number.

Or, in the case of all these gay men getting attacked: People can choose it for you.

Chapter Twenty-four

"When were you going to tell me about this?"

I recognize it immediately. The sound of it flopping onto the stacks of mail was enough—I really do not need to look at it. And so I don't, passing through the kitchen and into the bedroom, where I throw my coat on the bed, rip off my shoes, pull off my shirt.

Already the rumbling in my veins, already the hair on my neck is alert, and far away, in the bleak, gray distance, I can feel the flat place start to bloom into view. No smell yet—but I know it's coming, creeping into my head like a virus.

"You'll lose your job if they catch you," Louis says. The radiator clinks and hisses, hanging an invisible fog in the room. "Maybe even go to jail." He opens and closes the cabinets. He picks up an ice cream scoop and starts clicking the button back and forth, over and over.

I step back into the room, and Louis tosses the manila folder on the table, the worn edge covered in green and orange stickers. Green for first-time emergency visit, orange for same-day dismissal. His name isn't on the outside, but it's all over the forms on the inside, complete with a record of what happened that night—what I told the nurses, or rather, what they wrote down. Not that I need the yellow carbon copy to remind me. I remember it quite clearly.

The police came first, before the ambulance. They chased the guys off, holding their flashlights high above their shoulders like they're taught. There were two of them, one tall and burly, like a lumberjack or a porn star. The other was short and wiry, Puerto Rican maybe, could have been something else—hard to tell, really. They didn't run after the guys. Both of them stopped to help Louis. I suppose this was a gesture of compassion, maybe the urgency of a wounded man, maybe just procedure. They stepped over the puddles and said something to him, something I couldn't hear. And I suppose Louis answered, or maybe didn't, because their reaction didn't seem to be one thing or another. The tall one talked to me, asked me what happened. I don't remember the words. Only the weight of everything, the metallic clanging in my ears. Only the shining, shimmering pavement.

Louis's file came into my box early, only about three months after he was attacked. It shouldn't have appeared so soon, and really shouldn't have appeared at all—presumably there was a police investigation, and those files generally never go dead. But I reached into the basket, past a few inches of slipped discs and minor heart attacks and there it was—a bureaucratic misfire. I hid it away, convincing myself that I could forget it. We play these games with ourselves. I've never been very good at them. I always lose.

Once I made the decision to take it home with me, it

was quite easy. I stuffed it under my arm, slung my coat over my shoulders, and headed out the door into the biting, moist wind. I had the file stuck randomly under the mattress. Teenage boys hide their dirty magazines under there, their Victoria's Secret catalogs, their less-than-stellar report cards, their hand-scrawled lists of who they'd like to fuck on the cheerleading squad. Then when they get older they hide porn videos, or their crumbling stash of weed. It's a stupid and predictable hiding place. It's where our mothers look first, to see what we're up to.

"Why did you do it?" he says.

"I don't know. I wanted it. I wanted to protect it."

"It's goddamn living proof, Simon."

"I'm sorry," I say, sitting down in the armchair. "I'll take it back." I pull half-opened mail out from between the cushions, catalogs and magazines. And more credit card applications, promising me that I can have now what I can't afford. Endless out-of-town banks asking me, "Is Your Future Secure?"

"It was supposed to be investigated."

"It was one of a thousand I was handed that afternoon alone. I don't choose what they give me."

"Why did you take it?" Louis is yelling. I'm glad the table is between us.

"I'm sorry."

"That's *my* history. That's the reason I'm stuck in this apartment. That's why my career is lost. Do you think I wanted to happen across your version of what happened to me?"

"It's not my version. It's just what they wrote—"

"I'm so pissed off," he says, slamming his fist on the table, shoving aside the cigarette cartons. I lean forward in the chair, ready to move fast if I have to. The noise of the flat place continues, the rumbling, the rushing of wind and light.

The phone rings. We both look at it as if it might explode, itching to lunge for it. It rings again, and Louis picks it up.

"Hello." He listens, and I wonder who it is. But nobody calls us except Jaron and Farmer and sometimes, apparently, Mr. Bartlett.

"Who is it?" I say.

"Jaron. He's at home. Is Farmer with you?" He starts clicking the ice cream scoop again.

"Wait," Louis says, "where are they? Simon, turn on the TV."

I step over the piles, click it on with the remote. "What channel?" I say.

"All of them."

On the screen is a mob of people, smashing store windows on Sixth Avenue, climbing lampposts and rolling garbage cans into the street. People are trying to shout into the camera. But you can't understand what they're saying.

"I have to call you back," Louis says, placing the phone back on the cradle. I stand there, watching, trying to make some sense out of what's happening. It's a live shot, panning down the street. More broken windows, shattered glass on the sidewalk, a magazine stand ripped open. The sound of crumpling metal, then the camera spins around, three men marring the hood of a taxicab with bricks and sledgehammers.

"Why aren't they telling us what happened?" Louis says. "Why aren't they telling us anything?"

Then I'm thinking: Where did they get sledgehammers?

There is no running commentary under the feed, no one

telling us how to feel about what's happening. And for a second I start to think *I don't know what to do.*

Then the smell begins, marshmallow and honeysuckle, glowing like embers, crushed into ashes and set aloft on the wind. The sweetness is dizzying, like acres of wildflowers burst into flames.

Louis goes quickly into the bedroom as I watch the chaos break open in Manhattan. "What the fuck is going on?" he says, shouting at me from the other room, louder than he needs to be, hyped up by the energy coming off the screen.

"They're rioting."

"Who is?"

"Everyone from the rally earlier."

Drawers in the bedroom are opened and slammed. Louis comes back into the room wearing what he was wearing when I brought him here: long-sleeved T-shirt and designer jeans bought already ruined.

"What are you doing?" I say.

He takes a pack of cigarettes out of a torn-open carton, slides it down in his back pocket. Then a book of white-tipped matches from a swanky SoHo whiskey bar where we once had drinks with a gorgeous German banker before I trotted off to do something that now I don't remember.

"This is our history, Simon." And the phone rings. Rings again.

He doesn't go to answer it; it keeps ringing, twice more as we watch the TV.

"Where are you going?" I stand there frozen, looking at him, watching his breathing begin to race, the urgent adrenaline flushed out through his veins.

"I don't want to see that file again."

"I'll get rid of it."

He's clutching the doorknob in his fist. "I'm sorry to have acted this way," he says. And the phone finally gives up.

"What way?" I say. "Louis, what way?"

He looks around. "This way. Everything."

In the flat place, the rip in the air opens, and the fleshy hand comes reaching through, desperate, shiny with sticky fluid. The fingers graze my wrist, and then it reaches across my chest, crawling up to my neck, and over my face, like an alien creature, a disgusting parasite. The hand covers my mouth, holding my jaw shut. I can't move, I can't speak. And that sweet smell, that burning marshmallow stink that's followed me around forever is the sticky juice that drips into my mouth, stinging, like gobs of white sugar in my teeth.

Scenarios cloud my brain—all this before and after that's impossible to sort through. Like playing a game of Memory, frantically flipping over card after card and nothing turns up a match, and suddenly an incredible sense of grief. Dumb loss.

Louis bursts out of the apartment, leaving the door hanging open behind him, as if expecting me to follow, as if expecting me to understand.

Part Three

Part Three

Chapter Twenty-five

I ring the buzzer, snapping my fingers out of nervousness, shifting my weight from one leg to another, like a creature in captivity. Mr. Bartlett has scratched his name out on the yellowed piece of paper beside the button marked 6F. Maybe he's planning a move.

He answers the door dressed in white coveralls, some kind of billowy feathered wig on his head. "Come in, Simon." He pulls the door to his chest, standing back out of the way. "Fancy a drink from the cooler?"

"Who are you supposed to be?" I say. "Queen of the Bird People?"

"Always the comedian."

"What's with all the white?" I say, stepping inside.

"I'm purifying myself."

"What for?"

"I don't really know. Because." He doesn't blink, he doesn't smirk, or anything. He stands there looking at me. The freezer switches on, droning away.

"That's a crap answer."

"I know. Isn't that queer?"

"Yes, actually." He's taken the clock down off the wall. There are some boxes stacked in the kitchen, the bathroom is spotless and gleaming. "Mr. Bartlett, are you moving?"

"No."

"What's with all the boxes?"

"I'm taking an inventory."

I sit down on the couch, pick up a ceramic figurine off the side table, a little elephant with the trunk raised. It looks '50s-ish, like those accessories that were at one time fashionable and perhaps indicated some status. I used to see that stuff in my great-grandmother's house—a delicate feminine hand holding a pinkish, glossy conch shell, turned up, its open end to the ceiling. She kept rose-colored emery boards in it. Then, in her bedroom on the makeup table, she had a strange box, one green and one red light bulb in the base, directed up to three tiger-striped clam shells. The center shell held a crucifixion, the bleeding Jesus, near naked and tiny. I'm not sure what forces this memory to surface— maybe the stillness of this room. Could be anything, really.

"Would you like to keep that?" he says, meaning the elephant. "You can have it."

"No thanks," I say, and place it back on the table, trunk facing out to the room.

"Suit yourself." On the table beside him is a padded manila envelope sealed with staples and packing tape. "Simon, I need you to promise me something."

"What?"

"I want to give you this." He runs his fingers through the feathery wig, an absent, luxurious gesture. He pushes the envelope over to me. "But you have to promise me that you won't open it until you get home."

"Okay."

"You have to promise."

"Okay, I promise." I take it, give it a shake, the way silly people do at Christmastime. Mr. Bartlett stands up.

"All right," he says, breathing loudly. "You can go now." So I stand up, tuck the package under my arm, and walk to the door, confused and addled and feeling a bit out of control. "And you have to promise me that you won't call me anymore."

"I didn't call you. You ran into me." I want to ask him what's really going on—there is something missing from this exchange, something he's not telling me.

"I want you to know that what's in that envelope I don't want back. You've been so important to me." He folds his hands across his chest. "From now on pretend that we've never met."

"Done."

"Well," he says, huffing the air out of his chest, "that was easy enough."

I stand there at the door, waiting for some kind of signal, some script.

"Good-bye, Simon," he says.

People enter your life and then leave it. Simple as that.

He closes the door. As I walk down the hallway, before I turn the corner, I hear the clicking of latches and bolts—Mr. Bartlett locking himself inside.

Chapter Twenty-six

I sleep at Aiden's house, curled away from him, my foot barely hanging off the edge of the bed. He pretends to be asleep but is not—his breathing is too controlled, he is too perfectly still. I let my eyes wander across the room, landing first on the sad, over-worn armchair with decorative claw feet, where Aiden pulls on his shoes before he goes out, where he sits when he brushes the dirt out of Caleb's short, tight fur. Then the huge Rothko print that leans against the side wall, framed in dull matte black. The drawer-filled chest that looks like it once belonged to a dentist, or a serious, if eccentric cartographer. Then to the closet, bursting with clothes piled around the opening. I try to imagine myself in the future, try imagining some natural progression; perhaps I could wake up here every morning. We could make address labels with both our names. I wonder how our things might mesh in this tiny room in Queens, where the downstairs neighbor is a funeral home/florist/real estate agency. I wonder if we'd quibble about what thing to hang where. Who would buy the groceries? And who would take Caleb when it's seven-thirty in the morning and he has to go out right now or he'll piss all over the floor and the nice Turkish rug?

I know that Aiden has a sister—there are pictures of them together on a shelf in the bathroom. If I met her, she might say I was nice and smart, or quiet but probably nervous. Aiden would pat my thigh under the table. Tell me, is it foolish to want something impossible?

Some people are fortunate. They know who they are.

I am one of those people.

And the truth is: No. I will never have this kind of life.

Aiden rolls over and rubs my stomach. "Good morning," he says, his mouth slid out of shape by the pillow.

"Do you want breakfast?" I say.

He sits halfway up when I say this, supporting himself on his elbows. "Yeah. Are you okay?"

"Yes," I say.

"What are you doing up?"

"I'm just awake."

Caleb waddles over to the bed, thumping his enormous hard head against my knee. His eyes are clear and deep, like prize antique marbles. "Hey, dog," I say, "what do you want?"

Aiden cracks his neck back and forth. "Come here," he says, kind of flirty.

"No," I say.

"Okay," he says, like a combination question mark and exclamation point. He pulls himself out of bed and takes a white undershirt from the back of the desk chair, tugging it on facing away from me. His bare feet shuffle over the wood, lazy like soft sandpaper, to the kitchen.

"Everyone is coming to the house tonight," I say. "Louis is cooking. He'd love to meet you."

He stops, hangs his hands at his hips. "Everyone?"

"Plus Farmer and Jaron. Five of us total."

"I could do that," he says. "What do I bring?"

"Just yourself."

He walks over to me, cradling my head like he always does, holding me. I lean into him, pushing his shirt up with my palm, pushing my face into his belly, kissing the line of soft hair that reaches into his underwear. I run my finger along the elastic waistband, lean back on the bed. Then he pulls off his shirt and throws it on the floor.

Chapter Twenty-seven

Louis is unpacking groceries, setting things out for tonight's dinner. A whole chicken, some lemons, vegetables, fresh herbs I can't identify. Most of it goes into the fridge, replacing forgotten leftovers that he tosses into the garbage as he talks to me.

"How's the new apartment?" I say.

"Coming along." A jar of mustard thumps into the bottom of the trash can. He holds up a saggy bag of greens. "This lettuce has turned to mush."

"I know. I don't even know why I have it." He tosses it away. "Did you talk to the Calvin Klein people?"

"They said to go fuck myself. Basically."

Louis moved into a small apartment (that he pays for himself) across from the supermarket on Thirty-first Avenue, a few blocks from here. He's gained some weight back, lifting again and doing some torturous cardio thing they offer at the gym down the road—sprawling or wringing, or whatever they call it. He lives above his landlord, a small Greek woman who cares for her ailing parents. He has four whole rooms, and pays only thirty dollars more than I do, but two of the rooms are carpeted, and I swore when I moved from the last place that I would never again live in a carpeted apartment—to me it never feels clean. And sharing a private home sounds nicer when the realtor points it out, and people will tell you that it's better than the big, superintendent-style complexes, but they're lying.

"Look, I meant what I said when I ran out of here like that."

"You don't have to say anything," I say.

"I know I don't." He pulls a big block of wood from the bottom cabinet and unwraps the chicken, laying it on the cutting board. He begins to prepare it in a detailed way that looks at once intricate, elaborate, and casual. I wonder if surgeons acquire this ho-hum kind of dexterity when it comes to procedures they perform daily, twice-daily even.

"But I meant it," he says. "I'm sorry to have acted that way. You didn't deserve that encroachment." A large stockpot emerges from the cabinet above the fridge. Where did that thing come from?

"It's done. We don't have to talk about it anymore."

"Okay. I know."

He pulls a bottle of red wine out of a paper sack. He opens it, with minor difficulty, and tosses the cork over to me.

"Since when do we drink wine?"

"Since right now," he says. "I got a red and a white."

"What do you serve with chicken? Isn't there a rule?"

"The rule is you serve what you like." He pours a glass for himself, and then one for me. "Do you want some?"

I think for a moment. "Why not?"

"It's a beautiful night. I thought we could all go up on

the roof after dessert. Something has bloomed in that little garden. I think marigolds. Farmer will know."

"That sounds nice," I say.

"Aiden eats chicken, right?"

"Aiden eats anything." I set Mr. Bartlett's envelope on the table, shoving it alongside the billowy empty grocery bags. One falls to the floor, making a small, near-noiseless crinkle.

"What's that?" he says.

"Something Mr. Bartlett gave me."

He stares at me. "Aren't you going to open it?"

"Hand me those scissors," I say.

I cut the tape off, pulling it back as I go. I stick my hand down in the envelope. The texture is unmistakable.

"What is it?" Louis says, pulling the stems off some spinach leaves, running them under water and shaking them off.

"It's money."

"It's what?"

"Money."

"How much?"

I pull out five stacks of bills, still tied and counted, bound with light orange bank wrappers.

"How much is it?"

"Five thousand dollars."

"It smells amazing," Farmer says. "Can I open this? I'd rather have the white."

Louis hands him the corkscrew. Farmer peels back the foil on the top of the bottle and twists the sharp end down into the cork. "Originally, I was going to cook at my place. But Simon has the large pot. And I think whoever cooked in my kitchen last must have cooked a giant rat, because it smells like death when you open the oven door."

Farmer struggles with the cork, pulling hard. Finally, it pops cleanly out of the bottle. "Hooray!" he says.

I say, "Where's Jaron?"

Louis says, "On his way. He's late because of his support group."

I say, "He told you that?"

Louis says, "Yes, he did."

Farmer says, "That sounds promising."

I say, "Some of the people are real nutcases."

"Set these out," Louis says, stirring a pot of bubbling corn mush and handing a stack of dishes to Farmer.

The buzzer rings. Farmer, plates in hand, goes over to answer it. "Hello?" he says.

Aiden, sounding occupied and distracted, yells, "It's me!" through the speaker and Farmer lets him in. You can hear the door squeak open downstairs.

I pick up the padded envelope, which was hovering on the edge of the table, tuck it under my arm, and head down the stairs. Farmer and Louis begin talking, the sound of their voices blurring to nothing as I walk down.

"Wait, I'm coming," I say, yelling down, probably annoying the neighbors.

"I've got it," he says.

"Here." I take a sack of groceries out of his arms, leaving him with a white box tied up with red-striped string, some kind of dessert from the Italian bakery. We reach over the stuff; our lips touch. He starts to hand me a bunch of flowers. "You weren't supposed to bring anything."

"These are yours. As soon as I put this down." He kisses me again. We walk up the stairs.

"What's that?" He points to the package under my arm.

"Nothing. Some mail."

Farmer stands at the open door. "No making out in the common area," he says.

Aiden says, "I couldn't help myself."

"It's good to see you again." Farmer takes the sack from me, and Aiden hands me the flowers. "Under better circumstances, I'm happy to say."

Aiden says, "Me too. How have you been?"

Farmer says, "I'm well, thank you."

I take the box from Aiden's arms, place it on the end of the table, on top of one of the place settings. "This is Louis," I say.

"Finally, I have the pleasure," Aiden says, reaching his hand out.

Louis is still tending to dinner. "I'd kiss you, but I have to keep stirring."

Aiden steps over, hugs him. "How are you?"

"I'm doing fine." Louis kisses Aiden on the cheek. They seem relaxed and familiar.

Farmer says, "What did you bring us?"

Aiden says, "Italian cream cake."

Louis pours the polenta into a glass baking dish, smoothing the top with a spatula. He scatters some kind of chopped green herb over the top, cilantro, maybe parsley.

Farmer says, "I knew this woman who made the most amazing Italian cream cake. She wasn't even Italian. Southern Baptist actually."

I fill a tall pitcher halfway with water, and the flowers fit nicely into it, practically arranging themselves. Jaron opens the apartment door.

"Hello," he says. "Someone let me in."

Jaron runs his hand down Louis's back and rests it on

the place where his butt meets his thigh, squeezing him. Louis squirms away, laughs. "Get off me, you creep."

Jaron turns to Aiden. "I'm glad to see you in a room that's not so . . . sterile." They shake hands. Aiden isn't sure exactly what he's supposed to do. Kiss, hug, or handshake, the greeting is slightly awkward.

Farmer steps into the bedroom, and I follow him. He throws his bag on the bed, runs his hand through his hair, messing it up. "I'm glad we're all here together."

I hide Mr. Bartlett's package on the bookshelf.

I decide not to tell anyone about the money—and Louis won't say anything. It is too fresh a reality; I will let it simmer around inside of me for a while. The stacks of bills— a pitiful amount of money, in a way—are now situated between two books: a history of twentieth-century India and a biography of Cole Porter. They don't glow like uranium, or scream out at me from a distance, in my head, I mean, like you would think they might. They're like a prayer—sitting quietly, resting. Like letters never sent, like the name of an old lover, one that you no longer say aloud.

Objects can contain people. Things they purposefully leave behind, things they give you (out of guilt, out of love, out of fear), or things you discover left rotting in their refrigerators after they've left suddenly, maybe never to return. Vanished. I miss him, Mr. Bartlett. Somehow. Not knowing where he is, even geographically, is a little unsettling. And now all I have is this money. And I have this torn envelope, which I suppose will have to do.

"Soup's on!" Louis yells at us from the kitchen.

We ravage the chicken, tearing into the steaming parts. Even Jaron eats—granted, small portions, but it's a start. The cake follows, crumbs pressed into fork tines. Louis produces a bottle of anise liqueur and everybody throws back a few shots—even me. It goes down smooth and soft, like drinking silk, and my stomach warms. Aiden and Louis have another one after that. I can feel the alcohol slip into my veins, bathe my brain in a loose veil. Some kind of happiness washes over me, sitting around the table with all these drunk or almost-drunk people, smiling and flirting. It could be the booze, but I like the way you can confuse the two—happiness and drunkenness—both take hold of you and spread out to your skin from the inside.

Aiden and Farmer stack the dishes in the sink, running water through them and leaving the chicken pot to soak.

We manage to get out the door and up the stairs, stepping out to the roof, walking out over the silvery surface. The air is cool. Jaron and Farmer sit on a couple of lawn chairs, which are bleached almost white from the sun. Louis, Aiden, and I walk carefully to the edge, looking out toward Manhattan at the pale bubble of city light that fades to nothing where the sky eventually turns black. Manhattan twinkles with an algae of halogen and tungsten and burning sodium lights—trucks on bridges, taxis on the FDR, the pulsing red glow of the smokestacks near the water. A car alarm goes off in the distance, like a strange futuristic bird.

Louis says, "Farmer, are these marigolds?"

"Yes," he says, "and there's some basil here. You should pick some."

I say, "Isn't that stealing?"

Farmer says, "They won't miss it, whoever it is. Garden people are generous people."

Jaron shouts at us from the chairs, "Hey, you guys, look at the moon." The moon is full and splendid, a gleaming dinner plate in the sky.

I stand behind Aiden, stuff my hands down in his front pockets. Keys and loose change. He stretches his arm over his shoulder and his hand tousles my hair.

I yell at Farmer, "Get your camera."

Farmer puts down his anise, carried up from the kitchen, in a lazy swagger—slightly drunk he looks even sexier. "It won't work," he says.

Aiden says, "What do you mean, it won't work?"

Farmer says, "It won't work. It's psychology, mankind's fascination with celestial bodies. They always appear larger to the eye than they do in photographs. It's a scientific mystery."

Aiden says, "So what happens when you take the picture?"

Farmer says, "The moon will be small in the picture." He moves a few steps away from the edge. "There is a way to correct the sizing. Not in the picture, but in your head." He plants his feet, shoulder width apart, facing away from the moon. "You have to do this," he says, and bends over, grabbing his ankles and looking back through his legs. "Do this."

Louis steps over beside him, stretches his arms above his head, and bends over as instructed. "It works!" he shouts, his words muffled by the cars cruising Broadway and people walking below. "Simon!"

I walk over to them, repeat their movements, and voilà—tiny, normal-sized moon. Farmer stands up straight again, turns his head around. "See, it works."

I say, "Aiden, come here."

Aiden leans over, slightly creaky. "Wow," he says.

Farmer bends over again, and Jaron steps out toward him.

Jaron says, "You are insane."

Louis says, "Get over here and do this."

Jaron places his wineglass on the edge and bends over. "Oh, my," he says.

Farmer says, "I told you."

I say, "How long are we supposed to stay like this?"

Jaron says, "People pay money to hang upside down like this in fancy spas."

Louis says, "I'm turning into a beet." He stands up, holds his hands squarely on his hips. Farmer and Aiden stand up. Jaron rights himself, sips his wine. I flip up too fast, and for a second everything looks blurry and warm. The wind weaves through the marigolds—quiet like water, and edgeless.

Chapter Twenty-eight

The attacks end.

Not because of the rally, not because of the riot—which we later found out was relatively small, disassembling only a small part of midtown Sixth Avenue, and consisting mostly of straight people who enjoyed the pandemonium without knowing exactly what it was about. The attacks end because whoever it was got bored, or felt like their point had been made. The evening news went on to other subjects. Another Trial of the Century involving a low-grade celebrity. The Summer of the Shark, or the Summer of the Pretty Little White Girl Kidnappings. Pick any invisible menace.

I don't get a job at an ice cream place. I work longer hours at the hospital—so I can pay the rent, but also to keep my mind at a comfortable distance. My life becomes again infected with the endless stack of numerically encrypted names, constantly replenished, marking my fingers with their histories, replacing their pain with mine. I had forgotten how soothing it can be to lose yourself. As long as I stay underground, moving quietly from one side of the basement to the other, I can remain perfectly invisible.

The hospital has taken on a new project. They are converting the huge drawers full of ancient records into digital images, all the stuff that hasn't seen the light in fifty years. Sometimes I sit all alone at a desk, in the office of someone I've never met, loading stacks of documents into a scanner. The papers shoot through the rollers, each one pausing over the glass, and after a quick flash of alien-green light, the image appears on a screen in front of me. The idea is that you will be able to type in anyone's patient number and the computer will then present you with every shred of the paper trail they left behind. It's a sad project, really. Moving these people from thin, brittle papers, illegible and obsolete, to something stranger, even more intangible.

Also—I don't look in the files as much as I used to.

There's been weeks of strange, indecisive weather, where you're hot and cold at the same time. And some mornings, when it's warm enough not to wear the peacoats and leather jackets, New Yorkers wear them anyway, perhaps out of habit. Eventually, they give up and replace the clothes in their drawers with the thinner, brighter ones stored away the year before. The change, once made, is remarkable. Central Park fills with smiling people, Rollerbladers, picnics, and not-so-clandestine beer drinkers. Sidewalk cafés burst out of corner buildings, daffodils bloom along Park Avenue, and in my neighborhood, street fairs every weekend on every block—bad musicians, Spanish and Thai and Moroccan and Greek food, row after row of booths selling all the crap they sell at street fairs: buckwheat pillows, knockoff perfume, Chinatown junk.

Today after work, after nearly twelve overnight hours

of badly circulated air and fourteen cartons of dead files—
a personal best if I'm remembering correctly—I return,
pupils tiny, to the surface and start walking uptown, trying
to shed the personalities, hoping that the walking will
shake the filing out of my system.

I walk past Twenty-third Street, and the strange, whole-
sale-only clothing stores full of men in low-buttoned shirts
wearing chunky gold rings. Through the madness of Her-
ald Square, awash in shopping bags and obnoxious
tourists, then up Broadway past the glittering Times
Square, where every day new sponsorship invades the air-
space. After the vague nothingness of Broadway in the
West Fifties—a strip club, all-night diners, and office towers—I arrive at Columbus Circle, which I decide is my des-
tination. I find a spot under the florid bronze figures of the
Maine Monument. I close my eyes and lie back. The
morning light shines down, warming my skin.

Earlier I came across something interesting. One of the
files was turned backward in the stack. Anything out of
order like that is generally cause for minor alarm, or at the
very least a moment of further investigation. The file belonged to a man named Simon B. Sullivan, which is similar
enough to my own name to give me a weird jolt of recog-
nition, followed immediately by a flash of anxiety and of
course the inability to put it down. Sullivan was just
twenty-four when he was treated for third-degree burns
and lacerations on his hands.

I'm unsure of what exactly happened because there's
not a lot of history in these older files. In this case, just the
note from the intake where someone wrote down that his
hands were "burned and cut" by "the machine he works
on." (People felt less compelled to explain the coinci-
dences, to mark the colliding trajectories that landed them

here in those days. I mean the '40s. The bureaucracy was not intact. Maybe people had more trust in paper.)

Think about those moments when you find yourself alone, wondering if you've spent far too much time in the company of the wrong friends, in the wrong town. Have you been living entirely the wrong life? These moments come upon me sporadically—like dentist appointments, jury duty, or catastrophic weather—plucked out of the cosmos and delivered to my lap.

Foolishly, or perhaps because I did not have anything better to believe, I thought that if I could just hold on a little tighter, claim everything as my own—the men, the files, the cracking sidewalk—if I could hold on to those ghostly pink strings, if I protected the tiny golden kernel inside me, then somehow I would never be alone.

Resisting those moments can rattle you to pieces. That specific refusal can transform you into a shell, a bottomless pit that takes on everything you come into contact with, like plunging a bowl into water until it sinks. But when you loosen your grip on yourself, what you're capable of changes. New doors appear in the distance, sometimes impossible to reach, but still doors nonetheless.

Lying on the cool concrete in the orange morning light in this blistering crushing city, fading in and out of shallow sleep, this is what I dream about:

Summers that are hot and slow. And we're inside his 1986 Chevrolet Celebrity, white with bruise-black interior, the kind of air conditioning that doesn't even *think* about getting cool until we've been driving an hour, and everywhere we go is twenty minutes away. He fiddles with the buttons, tries redirecting the vents, then he looks back at me and says, "Must need Freon." We go to the pool hall, and home from school together. We're standing at the edge of the waterfall, watching the mist rise from below, the birds swooping through the space, the rustling of leaves and branches. And then we're in his kitchen, sneaking quiet kisses in the dark.

And then I dream about friendship and love and sex and violence—and my brain pushes them all together, and I can't tell one from the other.

The gray landscape spreads out underneath me, flat empty earth for miles in all directions, ringed with light at the crumbling edges. And again, the tiny rip in the air opens, sliced like a scalpel on skin, and the glistening pink hand comes sliding through. But this time it's different. The wind is quiet, the charred sugar smell is gone. The hand seems healthy, even tender. The fingers curl up into a fist, and the hand gives me—I'm not even fucking kidding—a solid, unmistakable thumbs-up.

I watch the hand, floating there in the air before it disappears quietly, slipping back into the invisible world on the other side of the sky.

Now I'm awake, aware of my body changing from one state to another. I open my eyes, and I'm lying here among a massive flutter of pigeons. A subway train rumbles below me. And suddenly, like a magician jerking a tablecloth out from under all that fine china, the birds lift off the ground. They cover the sun with the beating of wings.

YIELD

Lee Houck

ABOUT THIS GUIDE

The following discussion questions, author interview,
and additional material are included to
enhance your group's reading of *Yield*.

DISCUSSION QUESTIONS

1. How do you interpret the title *Yield*? What exactly do you think is being yielded to, or what is yielding?

2. With which character do you most identify?

3. At the beginning of the novel, Simon talks about his filing job at the hospital, and how it "shows itself on your body." Later, he admits that he doesn't know "where the sex work goes." How does the body reveal the inner life of a person?

4. Early on, Simon claims to not find his filing job to be boring and that he never says, "Wow, I'd rather be getting fucked right now by a dude on his lunch break." Do you think Simon is bored by sex? If so, why does he hustle?

5. How does Simon use sexual encounters to learn something about himself? Or does Simon use sex to avoid looking inward?

6. Simon's childhood memories often surface when he finds himself unable to cope, even if those memories are complicated or dysfunctional. How do you think Simon feels about his past?

7. One of Simon's memories is of a friend's sister with Down syndrome standing behind the door on Hal-

loween, with him being afraid she would open it. What is the significance of this fear?

8. If you had been in Simon's position when Louis was being attacked, would you have reacted in the same way? Would you have fought back to help your friend at the risk of being killed, or would you have stood by and done nothing out of self-preservation?

9. Why do you think Louis reacts in such a way to being attacked? What does his obsessive behavior say about his sense of self after the incident?

10. Discuss Simon's relationship with Louis. They met doing sex work together, but do you think there was ever a romantic interest between them? Do you think they still had a sexual relationship while Louis stayed at Simon's apartment? Do you believe that gay men can be friends after having sex?

11. Discuss Simon's relationships with Jaron and Farmer as well.

12. How is Simon changed after being drugged at the end of Part One? He claims it wasn't that incident that caused him to quit hustling, that it was gradual. Do you believe him? Do you think it scared him straight, so to speak?

13. What would Simon have to give up in order to pursue a relationship with Aiden? How would his relationship with his friends have to change?

14. Why does Simon continue to see Mr. Bartlett even though he finds the encounters so uncomfortable? Is there something about their relationship that he needs or enjoys?

15. Is the time Simon spends in Vermont a turning point? How do his feelings for Aiden change? And for his friends back home?

16. Simon writes that "pain and pleasure are interchangeable." How is this idea evident in his life? In the others' lives? Do you agree with his statement?

17. Why do you think Simon fought with Jaron in the subway station? At whom was he really angry, and about what? Do you feel his was a natural response to stressful circumstances between friends that could be easily forgiven and forgotten? Or was it something more deep-seated?

18. Think about some of the imagery in the story: Louis's dwindling modeling career, Simon's sexual behavior, the animals at the Museum of Natural History, Mr. Bartlett's desire to disappear. What does all this say about each character's world?

19. The word "condom" is not used once in the entire novel. Did you assume that Simon was having safe sex or that he was barebacking? Consider the opposite choice. Does that change your perception of Simon's character? What does your assumption say about your own views on sex?

20. What does the ending say about Simon's future? And about the future of the characters' lives together? Where do you think Simon and Aiden are in their relationship now?

A Conversation with Lee Houck

What was the genesis of this story? What about Simon's character made you have to write about him? Were you at all worried that Simon might become a clichéd gay hustler?

Simon's voice came barreling out of the void one evening while I was sitting at my desk. Whatever I did to try and get him out of my head—and I did try—he insisted on telling his story, and that's how *Yield* came about. At the time I started writing the book, this would be 1999 or so, I was living in my first New York apartment, with three roommates. (We even had two bathrooms and a dishwasher; it was luxury!) I was trying to find my way into the queer community, or I think I was learning, in a very practical way, what it feels like to have a new family made of queer people, and how they are different from your biological family. I was also figuring out what it meant to have intimate, meaningful, and sometimes difficult or exhausting relationships with friends—the kind of friends who know you better than you know yourself. Simon's voice is not my own, per se, but it is the voice of someone like me at that time, when the newness is so great and vast that it can be overwhelming, but also exhilarating.

I never thought that Simon would be perceived as a clichéd character. At the time, I was simply concerned with getting him down on paper correctly. I felt strongly about his distinctive point of view, his very real observations and

choices—I knew him as a person, fully formed and origi-
nal. That said, although characters often initially emerge
from nothing, the writer eventually has to finish making
them. So, of course, I worked during the crafting of the
novel to make Simon real to the reader, as real and complicated as he was in my imagination. And in those terms,
in general, I work completely on instinct, trusting my
writer's brain to make the best choice for the character,
and ultimately the story.

**Louis, Jaron, and Farmer play no small role in *Yield*. Why
did you decide to tell the story of these four friends
through only Simon's eyes? Do you think you could have
explored some issues—such as Jaron's cutting and the
emotional impact of the beating on Louis—more deeply if
you had gone into their heads as well?**

A lot of what *Yield* says about friendship is that you sur-
round yourself with clever, loving, complex people who
support you through the shifts that life can take, but you
ultimately have to make your own choices. They ignore
Jaron's cutting because Jaron prefers it that way—and
whatever the outcome, his friends respect that choice.
Louis reacts to being attacked in a way that feels right for
him, or rather the only way that feels possible, for good
or bad, and ultimately it strains his relationship with
Simon.

From the very beginning, Simon had such a strong, clear
voice that I couldn't figure out any way to get around him.
I worked on several sections over the years in other voices,
from the perspective of the other characters, even from a
third-person narrator, but none of it had the ring that I

wanted. None of it had the kind of immediate intimacy that I was interested in exploring—I wanted the reader to be looking out through Simon's eyes, to have that kind of concentration. The novel I'm working on now is in third-person, and it's very refreshing to have the openness of that perspective, and the distance that a wavelength like Simon's does not provide.

How much of the interaction between Simon, Louis, Farmer, and Jaron is based on the relationships you have with your own friends?

Some of the lines, like when Jaron says, "I'm so hungry I could eat the ass out of a rag doll"—that is from my friend Foster, verbatim. But really, it's all invented. I drew from my queer family for a kind of basic inspiration, sort of understanding how gay men talk to each other, and how love can sometimes look like meanness if you aren't listening close enough. But, of course, gay men can also be extremely cruel to each other, even crueler than straight people, I think. So I wanted to have lots of scenes with the boys just living their lives, being themselves, and loving each other. It might look like a dysfunctional family, but they really are everything to each other.

What was the first scene you wrote? What was the most satisfying for you to write? Which gave you the hardest time?

The first scene that was really finished, and that still reads basically the same as I originally wrote it, is the Central Park scene, where they are watching the opera. I had written much of the dialogue for a play—back when I was sort of, almost, barely working in theater. And I was digging through old material, looking for starting points for scenes that I knew needed to happen in *Yield*. So I started to build the prose around the dialogue. A few of the early scenes in the novel happened that way—they are reworkings of older material.

The scene that was the most satisfying to write was the last chapter in Part One, when Simon is being drugged and shifting his consciousness back and forth between the now and his childhood. I say that because I don't actually remember struggling with it. That's not to say that the writing was just flowing out of me—it still went through countless revisions, but I always knew exactly what tone and weight that chapter needed, so it never felt problematic. It was always about listening carefully to the words, and letting the scene become as big and lost and illusory as it could be. Many of those childhood memories really are my own—the bike riding, the driving through Mississippi, burning pine needles in the road—so, in that way, I was surrounded by those comforting ideas during the rather terrifying present I was inventing for Simon.

One of the last scenes I wrote is the first chapter in Part Two, in which Simon explains his journey moving to New York, and the difficulty dealing with his parents. I knew this background needed to be addressed, but I was resistant to having to, you know, go there. I think you really feel the melancholy of Simon's life in that chapter—as much as he is in love with New York City, you can feel the sadness of having to leave his home, even though that place is really a lonely existence as well. I had to force myself to write that one, absolutely. I avoided it for a long time.

Simon has a very flat, jaded, affectless voice. Can you talk about that some? Is it something he developed to deal with his profession, much like the flat place, or is it a quality he's always had that makes it easier for him to do his job?

I actually think that Simon is very emotional, although he does cut through all that to the most basic of feelings, and I think, yes, he's been desensitized to a large degree. But then again, Simon has good instincts when it comes to the emotional life of his friends, even though he might say that he doesn't—take the scene with Jaron at Rockefeller Center, for example. Also, people tell him things, deep, difficult things, so I think that even though he seems away from so much of life, people trust that he understands a lot.

The beginnings of Simon's voice began somewhere in his childhood—with the mother who spoke only in notes left on the counter, and the father who was mostly absent. That ability to compartmentalize certainly allows him to hustle and not become totally destroyed by the experiences. And, I think, conversely, his tendency toward empathy probably makes him a good hustler. With the distance comes few judgments.

You wrote *Yield* a few years ago, yet it seems so relevant today, especially with the fight for marriage equality shining a spotlight on the gay community, as well as the backlash and continuing antigay violence around the world. We're also seeing more and more spontaneous rallies like the one at the end of *Yield*. What is your reaction to these parallels?

I consider myself a part of a community of artists who are also activists. The frank truth is that in this country it's still okay to have a public hatred of queer people, in a way that other racist or classist prejudices have to be more hidden—which, of course, is its own kind of insidious hatred. You can see it in the votes against marriage equality in New York, New Jersey, California, especially the votes coming from senators. Maybe unconsciously at first, I was drawn to telling a story, at least in an emotional way, that would force the reader to empathize with a radical-ish, queer hustler who did things with his body that might scare you to death. Maybe I was, indeed, looking outward to readers who aren't like me, who might not know anyone like Simon or Louis, but who understand their otherness and can see some part of that in themselves, even when the character's circumstances are so extreme.

At one point in Chapter Four, Simon recites his menu, yet there's no mention of bareback sex. In fact, there's no mention of condoms throughout the book. What was your intention in doing that?

I realized early on what kind of sex scenes the story required—fluid, powerful, ethereal, seamless—and I made a choice not to mention condoms. My characters are not representations for how real people should behave in real life—I think people should be having safe sex. Period. Have safe sex. But I'm not really concerned about whether Simon's sex life is safe or unsafe, I'm just thinking about what he's feeling in those moments, where his own brain takes him, and what he chooses to tell us, the audience. And whatever feelings readers might have about Simon's choices, I think novels that lack ambiguity, or that suggest a tidy morality aren't very interesting.

Farmer seems to be the only character without a flaw or debilitating weakness. What was your reasoning for not giving him a downfall? Or does he have one that wasn't as obvious as the others'?

Farmer originally appeared because I kept thinking, "Someone has to be the voice of reason." Then he eventually became a real person with complicated motivations. He's more put together than the other boys, yes, and in some ways he has the biggest heart. He gets trampled every now and then, but he's stronger than he appears. Farmer is also the most like me, or rather the most positive-thinking version of myself distilled into a character. He has big ideas, but a realistic vision. I like him.

What's the significance of the dream at the end of Chapter Seven, the one with the chomping typewriters?

That's not a dream that I had, although it sounds like something a writer would find nightmarish. The sound of typewriters falls somewhere between productive and menacing, doesn't it? They have teeth, after all. And I wanted imagery that combined Simon's past—in this case, a country road with a wooden fence, something you'd never find in New York—and something more industrial, but maybe also antiquated, something your unconsciousness would pull from nowhere, like the typewriters. I wanted the reader to feel real vulnerability in that moment, a real uncertainty about the future, and I think Simon's dream does that.

Ultimately, *Yield* is a romance between Simon and Aiden just as much as it's about friendship, and introducing a new boyfriend into any group is significant. So where do you envision Simon and Aiden after the novel ends? Now?

I always thought that Aiden was the boyfriend who sort of prepared you for your next boyfriend—you know, the guy who somehow shows you yourself in a new way, and ultimately that new you, the more real you, isn't the kind of person who can be in a relationship with that person. But I don't have a clear idea for what happens to Simon and Aiden. The uncertainty is interesting to me, the striving. I like that the readers aren't left with any neat endings. There is only a little hope. And lots of love.

Talk about Mr. Bartlett. He's an interesting character, at times a little creepy (I was sure the freezer was straight out of a murderer's supply catalog), but he seems to truly care about Simon and want to protect him. Is he based on anyone you've come in contact with? Are his intentions pure? When he gives Simon the money toward the end, I sensed he might have planned to end his life; is that what you meant to imply?

Mr. Bartlett is a combination of lots of people that I know and don't know—including a lady who lived down the street from me when I was a kid. She dressed all in white on Halloween and answered the door to trick-or-treaters in this bright feather wig that scared us all to death, for some reason—and that image is in the book. He is also a kind of aristocracy gone bad, or gone lazy, maybe British, maybe just old school Connecticut blue blood. And there is a dash of Quentin Crisp thrown in for the kind of leisurely pace I wanted him to have. When I hear Mr. Bartlett talking, I sort of hear Quentin Crisp's one-man show from the '70s, which you can find on CD somewhere.

Yes, his intentions are pure. I think he really cares about Simon, he's just a strange person. He's old enough to not care what other people think of him. At all. He's probably been through it, everything, over and over, and he really knows himself, probably more than any of the other characters. Mr. Bartlett is probably the most at ease, the most at peace person in the book. It's possible, yes, that Mr. Bartlett decides to kill himself. He either does kill himself, or he wants Simon to think that he's going to kill himself. I don't think it would be out of character for Mr. Bartlett. But, at the same time, Mr. Bartlett could very well turn up on the Silver Star line to Miami, cooking himself to a crisp in the summer sun until he shrivels and disperses with the wind.

Why did you choose to title the book *Yield*? What does it mean to you?

For me, the entire story gets distilled into one idea at the end of the book. Simon says: "When you loosen your grip on yourself, what you're capable of changes. New doors appear in the distance, sometimes impossible to reach, but still doors nonetheless."

The yielding is growing up, taking responsibility for your life, for your emotional well-being, and for the well-being of your relationships. I think the early twenties is a difficult time to get through, especially if you don't have a very clear sense of your direction. You can spend a lot of time defining yourself in opposition to things, because, really, you're trying to figure out who you are. If you allow yourself to relax, to bend a little bit, I think you'll discover that everything you need is already there. You just have to slough off all the shit left over from the confines of being a child, being a teenager, and the effects of high school, maybe college. The growing up is really in learning how to let all that out. Those doors that Simon talks about, they are always there. You just have to be able to see them.

Dear Reader,

When I started working on *Yield* there were only these impulses and these images. For a while the characters didn't have names. The short section that follows is a scene I intended to be the opening of the novel. Eventually, it felt like something I needed to write in order to write the actual story, and I removed it. These peripheral narratives often crop up when you are writing, and sometimes it is difficult to see what is the novel and what are the DVD extras.

I was having a lot of these rooftop conversations when I first moved to New York from Tennessee—sometimes we moved the mattresses out there when it was too hot to sleep inside. The lawn mower story is a real story from my childhood. I admit that I don't know if it was something that actually happened, or if the neighborhood kids invented it. It's certainly true that we never went to that house on Halloween. At the end of this piece, Simon says, "But the line blurs, bleeds, bends to suit new circumstances. Your limits can dissolve." This is, I see now, a raw version of what I later learned to be the crux of the novel—allowing yourself to yield.

Lee

The Lost Opening to *Yield*

This isn't about violence. It isn't about fear, or obsession, or sex, or digression. It's really about progress. You can't always see where things are headed, but you can easily look back and see what has been so far. I wonder about our capacity for violence, and our capacity for pain. Now, looking back, I see the limit lies far beyond the line you might draw for yourself and say: I refuse to go that far. Still, in the early morning hours, so still that even the birds are still sleeping, when I'm slipping out of his apartment, out of the fancy walk-in closet, out of the CEO's office, I can smell the blood and I can smell the sweaty underwear. I can smell the fear seething out from the hollows of my body. In the movies (I think) they say don't look back.

Mostly I don't.

The bricks jerk in a fast line, one row after another, like running your thumb down venetian blinds. The insides collapse first, pulling the walls toward the center, which fall like a curtain of heavy fabric. We sit, waiting, until the smoke drifts downwind and away, and the rubble finally relaxes into chunky dead piles. Yellow machines arrive, beetling in from the edges. Strong, bearded men sit encased in tiny glass booths, moving levers with their hands, with their feet. People have come to watch the old building go, maybe to say good-bye, maybe just to see what people are looking at. There's a small crowd gathered around the block marked SAFE AREA to the north. Lately, there is no such thing as a "safe area."

Was there ever?

Louis sits down beside me and lights a cigarette. Louis is a model from the untouchably sexy era, before chic meant ugly-but-interesting. Before skinny, impish freaks became so popular. Seeing the enormous construction machines plow through the rubble from such a distance is quite pleasing, and as the promotional posters promise, the air really does smell like progress. I brush the toe of my boot around in the square of dark, loamy dirt, the previous tenant's attempt at a roof garden. A few abandoned pots and a plastic watering can are thrown around by the wind.

"I wish there was some way we could live a moment over and over again." I look away as Louis pauses to take drags off the cigarette—I can't stand cigarette smoke. "I want to see that building demolished about ten more times." He pulls the cigarette to his lips and turns to look at me. The bulldozers push the piles of bricks from one place to another, not really changing anything. Louis jerks his head, turning to face the other direction.

"Do me a favor," I say. "Tell that story."

"What story?"

I lean my body against his. "About the woman and the lawn mower."

"Why do you want to hear that?" he says.

"Just because," I tell him.

Louis begins: "When I was little, there was this house in this other part of the neighborhood where this woman was killed. She was in the shower and this guy broke into her garage, you know, trying to steal her lawn mower. She heard him, or something, so she got her towel and went out to the garage to see what it was.

"He strangled her with the telephone cord. It was late at night, and he put her body in the middle of the driveway and covered her with the car. There was blood all over the pavement."

"Keep going," I say. I like stories about suburbia, even awful ones. They remind me of home.

"The real estate people tried to clean some of it off with bleach and it made a big white spot that glared more than the places where her blood was. Nobody went trick-or-treating at that house." My head is leaning on his shoulder now, and he lights another cigarette, takes a drag. Then he says, "Where the hell are we, Simon?"

An enormous billboard is going up in Times Square—a photo of Louis in white boxer briefs. You can see the head of his penis in the picture.

"When is that billboard going up?" I say.

Louis says, "Tomorrow." He sits up and pushes me off. I look past him, look at the blank open space in front of us. The wind catches his hair again. We sit unmoving and quiet for a minute—inert. In our stillness the bulldozers carry most of the bricks away.

I say, "You're going to be forty feet high."

Louis says, "It hardly seems real." He stamps the cigarette out in the dirt. "Nothing seems real."

But he's wrong.

Then, like a pair of stereo speakers spinning in circles, I hear Sandra Bernhard ranting in my head—*Open up, baby, you're going to fade away.* Here's what I know: You can draw a line for yourself. You can say, I am only willing to go that far. But the line blurs, bleeds, bends to suit new circumstances. Your limits can dissolve.